'A wild ride. Imagine the film *Desperado* scripted by Hunter S. Thompson'   Ian Rankin

'A tough and uncompromising debut – you'll be glad you read it'   Lee Child

'A hilarious, gripping, poetic off-the-wall crime story set in a delirious Mexican underworld that William Burroughs, Sam Peckinpah & Hunter S. Thompson would have recognised. I loved it'   Adrian McKinty, author of *The Chain*

'Intoxicating and chilling'   *Observer*

'Feverish, lyrical and gripping from beginning to end . . . a searing indictment of corruption and murder in Mexico and a darkly moving gay love story'   *Independent*

'Pacy and exciting . . . The novel is written lyrically, with an offbeat humour, which helps defamiliarise a situation to which Western readers have become inured, and communicate its horrors afresh'   *Daily Telegraph*

'Strong stuff . . . MacGabhann's blend of violent action and vivid, even lyrical description is laced with dark humour and is very readable'   *Guardian*

D1189964

'Arresting: it spins a tale of murder and murky deeds, but really excels in how it seems to capture something essential at the heart of his adopted country . . . an extraordinarily vivid picture of Mexico, in all its seething, sweltering madness and beauty'
Irish Independent

'Intense, inventive and gritty'
Attitude

'Both a harrowing thriller set in the horrific wilderness of the Mexican drug wars and a moving, gay love story, this striking debut by a new Irish author hits many buttons and deserves to be singled out for acclaim . . . this is a memorable book that has arrived out of the blue, and is all the more welcome for it'
Crime Time

'Impressive'
The Herald

'A superb, realistic rollercoaster of a read from an incredible new talent'
Irish Examiner

'Compelling and bold'
Irish Times

'A must-read for those who were glued to *Narcos* and *Sicario*'
Dead Good

'Terrifying, riveting, emotionally wrenching . . . this is the most beautiful writing about Mexico in an English-language novel since Malcolm Lowry's *Under the Volcano*'
Francisco Goldman, author of *Say Her Name*

CALL·HIM·MINE

Tim MacGabhann was born in Kilkenny, Ireland, and began his writing career as a music journalist while studying English Literature and French at Trinity College, Dublin. Since 2013, he has reported from all over Latin America for outlets including *Esquire*, *Thomson Reuters*, *Al Jazeera*, and the *Washington Post*. His fiction, non-fiction, and poetry has appeared in *gorse*, *The Stinging Fly*, and *Washington Square*, and he holds an M.A. in Creative Writing from the University of East Anglia. In 2017 he was awarded the Arts Council of Ireland's Literature Bursary.

Call Him Mine is his first novel.

CALL*HIM*MINE

TIM*MACGABHANN

WEIDENFELD & NICOLSON

CITY OF KAWARTHA LAKES

First published in Great Britain in 2019 by Weidenfeld & Nicolson
This paperback edition published in 2020 by Weidenfeld & Nicolson
an imprint of The Orion Publishing Group Ltd
Carmelite House, 50 Victoria Embankment
London EC4Y ODZ

An Hachette UK Company

1 3 5 7 9 10 8 6 4 2

Copyright © Tim MacGabhann 2019

The moral right of Tim MacGabhann to be identified as
the author of this work has been asserted in accordance
with the Copyright, Designs and Patents Act of 1988.

All rights reserved. No part of this publication may be
reproduced, stored in a retrieval system, or transmitted
in any form or by any means, electronic, mechanical,
photocopying, recording, or otherwise, without the
prior permission of both the copyright owner and the
above publisher of this book.

All the characters in this book are fictitious, and any resemblance
to actual persons, living or dead, is purely coincidental.

A CIP catalogue record for this book is
available from the British Library.

ISBN (Mass Market Paperback) 978 1 4746 1046 9
ISBN (eBook) 978 1 4746 1047 6

Typeset by Input Data Services Ltd, Somerset

Printed and bound in Great Britain by Clays Ltd, Elcograf S.p.A.

www.orionbooks.co.uk
www.weidenfeldandnicolson.co.uk

I

Nobody asked us to look. Every day, ever since, I still wish we hadn't.

'Just a second,' Carlos said from behind me, crouched above the body we'd found. His camera clicked so fast it could have been the crickets shirring in the humid pre-dawn gloom.

'C'mon, man, your seconds last about ten minutes,' I said through a yawn, wiping my glasses on my shirt, my voice a rasp because four days of jeep and hotel-room air-conditioning had given me a throat like a sock full of broken glass.

Carlos laughed and said, 'Yup.'

Until we found the body, I didn't expect to remember a thing about Poza Rica. Just another story, we'd thought. '*Waiting for the Black Gold Rush*' was the provisional headline – a profile of Poza Rica, the crumbling oil city in Veracruz, eastern Mexico, '*a place caught,*' I'd written, '*as though in suspended animation, waiting for foreign investment to capitalise on the region's fifteen billion barrels of oil – and raise the city to its former height.*'

Just four days' worth of interviews, we'd figured, and we'd

be back home to file text and photos for the kind of dull, well-paid gig all freelancers dream of until they actually have to do one.

Yeah, well, you know. After eight years of living in Mexico, I should have known there's no such thing as just another story.

Call it Iguala or Reynosa, call it Manzanillo or Apatzingán, it's the same poor-town generica of pulled-down shutters and bad-luck motor shops, the same blue Alcoholics Anonymous triangles, the lurid blood cursive of gang tags.

It's the same taxi-rank shrines to Saint Jude and the Virgin of Guadalupe, the same faded Revolution murals, plaza, bandstand, and busts of the illustrious dead.

It's the same 'missing' posters on every lamppost and shop front, the same blood-and-sulphur odour of wrecked drains.

After we found the body, though, nothing would ever look the same again.

Ten minutes into our drive home to Mexico City, the AM radio playing bolero songs, we would stop now and again for photos of wellheads for the story: at the centre circle of a balding football field, in the yard of a pay-by-the-hour parking lot, at the bottom of an alley between the Best Western Hotel and the Banco Azteca.

So there we were, coasting down the main boulevard, closing in on five a.m., nobody heading out to work, nobody coming home from the late shift, the shadows under the big overpass holding only trash from the previous day's market, when we passed a small oil-derrick swinging back and forth at the bottom of an alley between a shuttered bar and a gleaming

Oxxo convenience store, and Carlos said, 'Oh, shit. Stop the jeep, *vato*.'

'What?' I'd said, parking at the top of the alley, but Carlos was already legging it towards someone lying on the ground.

For a second I wanted to tell him it was just a drunk, but then I got out of the jeep and saw the guy, his limbs splayed at angles no drunk sleeper would ever choose, and I stood there, winded, at the top of the alley, my heartbeat shaking my throat, my knuckles white where I gripped the jeep's doorframe, as a light, clammy rain petered down over me.

Bodies, I was OK around. They tell you the same amount of nothing, whether they sit calcified in a burned-out car, lie hog-tied and dumped on beaches, or rise greenish and soapy-looking from mass graves. But the poor guy lying by the oil derrick under the streetlight, his wasn't like any body I'd ever seen before. His counterfeit Levi's and white briefs had been pulled down to show a nest of pubic hair around a bloody hole, his cock and balls, peeled like grapes, left resting on his broken hands. His cheap pleather jacket was open over a polo shirt whose red wasn't dye, a red whose sugary butcher's-shop cloy drew the 7/11 coffee I'd been drinking in the jeep almost all the way back into my mouth.

'Don't get sick, *vato*,' said Carlos, laughing when he heard me spit. 'You'll wreck my shot.'

'Yes, because it's just gorgeous right now,' I said, lighting a cigarette to kill that dead kid's smell while the oil derrick just kept right on clanking.

People who tell you death has a smell, they're wrong: it's got dozens, and I only know some. After the Acapulco jet-ski drive-by me and Carlos had covered a couple years before, you couldn't tell the blood-smell from the bladderwrack parching on the shore. After the big warehouse massacre we'd reported on in Tlatlaya, in mid-2014, the main stink had come from the wheaten note of bullet-holed guts. At the mass graves uncovered in Taxco, the stench had been deep, fungal, butanoic, enough to put me off Roquefort forever.

Even from there, I could see what they'd done to the kid. The blood on his shirt wasn't from a bullet-wound: his neck was a collar of bruises where he'd had the life choked out of him, and there were no punctures in his chest or face. Matter of fact, he had no face. That's where all the blood had come from: his face had been taken, his eyes thumbed out, leaving a wet red mask specked with dust and grit, his teeth climbed black. A Stanley knife, I figured: criss-crossed incisions edged the wound above his right jaw, and, from the ragged edge of skin under his left, I could tell they'd stopped cutting once they'd worked up enough of a loose end to tear the rest of his face off with their hands.

An ant picked over the ridge of bone and cartilage where his nose had been. My stomach gurgled like a volcano. Carlos stooped to blow away the ant, then unlidded his camera.

'Watch the street,' said Carlos gently, his back turned to me.

What I wanted to say was, *If you don't hurry, I'll be sick everywhere.*

What I said was, 'Ugh, fine,' and swallowed back the sour taste in my mouth.

'You're OK, *vato*,' Carlos said to the body as he knelt with his hand above the kid's mussed and bloody hair, murmuring so quietly he could have been praying. 'It's over now.'

Carlos used to say ghosts lingered at murder scenes for a little while after the victim died. Used to say it was something the Jesuits taught him at the high school back in Juárez. Used to say that because of how furiously the soul was expelled from its body, the soul was too scared, too shocked to fray out into nowhere.

'Don't be scared,' he said to the faceless kid, taking a long drag of cigarette smoke to breathe over the body like funeral incense. 'Don't let us keep you.' He raised the camera lens to start taking his photos. The flash was the white of candlelight. 'We won't take a minute.'

'It was "I won't take a second" a minute ago,' I said.

'Take it easy,' said Carlos, and I couldn't tell if it was me or the kid he was talking to.

'We were headed home,' I said. 'I can't believe you.'

'Relax,' said Carlos. 'We're having fun, aren't we?'

The street beyond the alleyway was dead as a moon. There weren't even the usual sharp-faced teenagers in brand-new baseball caps and space-boot-looking trainers guarding corners, their smartphones and pistols hidden in their kangaroo-pouch bags. They'd been everywhere the whole four days we'd been in Poza Rica: hanging around alleys, lingering by market stalls, even tipping off cops outside houses in poor neighbourhoods.

But now? Nobody. Just the boulevard's matte and tarnished buildings, just streetlamps mottled with old petrol fumes.

'C'mon, man,' I said, watching a wounded dog clitter past on its three good legs. 'How many pictures do you need?'

'Just keep an eye out, yeah?' His boots gritted as he shifted for the right angle.

You can spend a lifetime watching over people. All through secondary school, back in Ireland, I'd been the guy who'd keep an eye out for teachers during lunchtime scuffles, or hidden the booze nicked from the drinks cabinets of other lads' parents, or stowed my mates' weed and ecstasy stashes in my flat, and now here I was keeping sketch while someone else took a picture he really shouldn't.

'Is your back turned?' said Carlos behind me. 'I'm almost done.'

From the red hills of Michoacán to the flicker-lit Zeta nightclubs in Coatzacoalcos; from the mass graves in the stiff-grassed hills of Cocula to the Huejutla warehouses where rats and damp gnawed the Gulf cartel's unlaundered bales of money; from the Kodachrome skies and parched dirt roads of the Tarahumara Mountains – to here, to now, to this alley of broken glass and drying blood in Poza Rica, Veracruz – in every one of those places, I'd watched over Carlos while he got his photos, and I hadn't fucked up, not even once.

'Bro,' I said, turning over my shoulder to see Carlos' face lowered to a face that wasn't a face any more.

Carlos' hand was inside the dead kid's jacket, reaching for the inside pocket.

'You'll get your prints everywhere,' I said.

'Oh, yeah, because forensics are, like, super-diligent round here,' Carlos said, the kid's wallet already flipped open in his hand.

'I can't believe this,' I said, even though I could.

Carlos opened the kid's wallet and slid a Universidad Vera-cruzana student card out from behind the Cinepolis and KFC discount cards, then took a photo of the ID. Name: Julián Gallardo. Date of Birth: October 1996.

'*Mire, güey*,' said Carlos, sliding the card back into the wallet and the wallet back into Julián's pocket. 'No harm, no foul.'

Tyres squalled beyond where I'd seen the dog jogging out of sight.

'You weren't keeping an eye out.' Carlos laid his camera on the ground.

Gravel crunched. A siren cut through my skull. Then police-car lights washed over us, red and blue and halogen white, and doors slammed as two shadows climbed from the big white Guardia Civil pickup, while a third aimed a mounted AR-15 assault rifle down at us.

'Get down,' said one cop, in a frightened whisper.

'Can't believe you fucked this up,' Carlos said.

'All right, man, whatever you say,' I said to Carlos, and got to my knees, hands behind my head, my press laminate held high and its lanyard around my wrist.

The first cop moved forward, the second one covering him from behind, light gleaming along the telephone-wire coils of his gun's security cord.

So we knelt there in the white glare, hands behind our heads, broken glass pricking through the knees of our jeans, the cops' shadows looming bigger, their footsteps closing in.

2

The two cops stepped out of the light and into our faces. The first to reach us took the laminate from my hand, while the cop standing in the back of the pickup swivelled his mounted rifle back and forth along the avenue. You could still hear the clunk of the derrick and my jeep radio petering sad melodies into the dark.

'This is a crime scene,' said the first cop.

My skin wasn't skin any more: just a hot prickling shiver all over.

'We thought he was alive,' I said.

The cop looked over at Julián, then back at me.

A wad of shit pressed hot against my asshole.

'Until we got close,' I said.

The cop didn't say anything, just gave Carlos a chin-jut.

'You took pictures?' he said.

'Was about to,' said Carlos. 'Sorry.'

The first cop smashed Carlos across the jaw with the stock of his pistol and said, 'You stupid bastard. You'll get us all killed.'

The word *Help* hit the roof of my mouth and bounced back into silence, but Carlos didn't even cry out, just went down, docile as a felled cow. The second cop kept the muzzle of his gun trained on him.

'Get his ID,' the first cop told the second one.

Moments like that, nothing matters to you. Your head's got the clean emptiness of a spilled-out goldfish bowl. Nothing you thought mattered means a thing, not your coffee-breath or your headache, not the shit-wad about to hit your thighs, not even your memories of the people you won't see again. All you are is the tarmac smell in your nose and the grit and broken glass under your hands.

The cop loomed over me, and said: 'You want to end up like this kid?'

'No,' I said. My breath skittered loose grit.

'Me neither,' said Carlos.

The cop crouched beside me. 'You know who this town belongs to?'

'We're doing a story about oil,' I said. 'Just numbers. Nothing about crime. Heading home, we saw a body, stopped to see what was up.' I sucked in air that tasted of road. 'That's all.'

The first cop pressed his fingers to his forehead. 'Look, I'll repeat myself. Do you *know* who this town belongs to?'

'I don't think they know,' said the second cop. This guy, his voice was high, nasal, a newbie's. 'They wouldn't be here if they did.'

The first cop looked at me, then at Carlos, then at the newbie cop.

'Let's get out of here, seriously,' said the newbie cop, a plea in his voice now.

The first cop dropped his eyes to the ground, nodded, then holstered his gun.

'You've been lucky tonight,' he said, his hands on his hips. He shook his head.

Carlos slipped me a wink from further along the alley floor. His jaw was red, darkening to cinnamon, and his lip trailed a string of dark blood. The salt taste welling up under his tongue; I tasted that under mine as well.

The second cop said, 'I'm sorry about your jaw.'

The first cop jerked his head towards our jeep and said, 'What are you waiting for? Go, *go.*'

Carlos dusted off the knees of his jeans, patted my shoulder. 'Come on, yeah?'

The second cop coughed and the air was instantly the smell of puke.

'Where are they getting these new guys?' said Carlos, his arm around me.

'Ten years of this drug-war shite.' I held my press laminate up at the third cop in the back of the pickup. 'Not many tough lads left.'

'Must be that,' said Carlos, and looked back over his shoulder at the body in the white-lit alley. 'Poor guy, though. Wonder where they're taking him.'

The cop who'd hit Carlos dragged Julián Gallardo by his shoulders towards the pickup. The one who'd talked to me was muttering into a radio now. With one hand he held one of Julián's feet. The other foot dragged.

'Same place they all go,' I said, and turned the key in the ignition.

The cops slung Julián into the back of the pickup, and he thunked against the metal, his limbs awry, and the cop on the radio kicked away the lines his heels had dragged through the dirt and grit.

'Yeah,' said Carlos. 'Nowhere.'

3

Driving out of town, Carlos smoked a cigarette in literally four five-second drags without even coughing, while my fingers drummed a non-rhythm on the steering wheel. Even though the sky was fading from ink to cobalt, every shadow that passed over the jeep – the buildings, the streetlights, the big mall with its Cinépolis and KFC – seemed darker than the one before it.

We pulled in at a petrol station on a fog-drenched curve of highway above the valley, the tyres' drone across the forecourt numbing my adrenaline-crash headache, and then bought breakfast: doughnuts and over-sugared coffee for me, cigarettes and pre-mixed tequila-and-soda in a can for Carlos. He lingered inside, having struck up a conversation with some hefty biker guys who were heading for the El Tajín pyramid.

'How are you not terrified right now?' I asked when he got back.

Carlos looked at me, lifted my hand to his throat. 'Feel that?'

'Fuck. Like a cartoon mouse.'

'That's it slowed down, *vato*,' said Carlos. 'Thought my heart was going to burst out of my chest back there.' He spun his Fidel Castro key ring around and around on his finger. 'Full John Hurt style.' The USB stick clipped to his keys whipped in circles. 'So glad they didn't get my camera,' he said.

'Yeah, but they got your face,' I said. 'Your name.'

Carlos waved a hand. 'Oh, whatever, so I shave before I go back there. Buy some fake glasses.'

'You already wear glasses.'

'Oh. Oh yeah.'

'Those scratched?' I leaned in to check his lenses for dings, but they were too smeared for me to tell.

He put up his hands, patted my shoulders away. 'Nah, *vato*, chill, yeah?' He stretched out along the mosquito-flecked bonnet, his hands behind his head, and uttered a long ragged groan that turned into a cackle. 'That was amazing. We totally have to come back.'

The valley was a slow ocean of fog. All you could see beyond the highway siding was a sheet of pure white, wet air that pearled on my boots and darkened a hanging strand of my hair.

'I don't know,' I said. 'Even those cops looked scared.'

'Cops are people too.' Carlos gave a one-shoulder shrug. 'Kind of.'

'At best.' I scratched under my chin, looking into the road at lights shaped like dark number '7's against the fog, at road-lines broken like dashes along the slick asphalt. 'But why would they be getting rid of a body someone else left? And why would that scare them?'

Carlos slung an arm around my shoulder and wagged a finger under my chin, then said, 'Well, that's why we're turning around, right?' He let me go and sat back again, tapping the top of his can of tequila and whatever. 'You don't mind?' he said, the ring pull raised.

'You don't have to ask every time.'

The can clicked open. 'Stressful times, though, *vato*.'

'Aren't they all.'

Even so, when Carlos popped the can and swigged the whole thing I had to turn my back on him and light up again.

Carlos took out his phone, started texting.

'You telling your mother?' I said.

'Nah. Just chit-chat,' said Carlos. 'You OK?' He didn't look up from his phone.

'*I'm* fine. You're the one who got hit.' I lifted his chin. The bruise on his jaw had now darkened from cinnamon to aubergine.

He jerked his head away. 'It's cool, honestly.'

'All right.' The doughnut I bit into was so stale that it powdered in my mouth. 'It's weird, though,' I said. 'Leaving that body out there.'

'Yeah,' said Carlos, and I shut up, dunking the other half of my doughnut until it didn't taste like chipboard.

At some of the graves we'd been to in Cocula, all that the locals had found were nubs of bone and yellowish gelatine traces in the dirt, because the bodies had gone into vats of caustic soda. At the burial pits in Taxco, we'd seen mould eating tattoos of saints, of kids' names, of gang affiliation.

'If it's so easy to make a body vanish,' I said out loud, 'why dump one in public?' I kicked the dirt.

Carlos puffed out a long breath, his eyes shut. 'You know, you *could* keep asking questions.' He opened another can. 'Or, you know, we could just – *drive back and ask*. Like reporters, or something.'

I ignored him. 'You see a single lookout on the street back there?'

Carlos shrugged.

'Yeah,' I said. 'So, whoever dumped that body, they wanted it found.' The second chunk of doughnut went down about as smoothly as a bite of highway. 'Why?'

Carlos clicked his tongue. '*Ni puta idea, güey.*' He pointed at the jeep. 'This magic thing, we should get in it, and go ask people who the kid was.'

'No mention of Julián Gallardo on the missing persons site.' I flipped through the tabs on my iPad. 'Nothing in local news. Nothing on Twitter.'

'Check his Facebook.'

I scrolled down. 'Couple pictures of him at a protest. Some hashtags about pollution.'

Carlos tapped one of the hashtags, which read 'AJENJO ASESINO' – 'Ajenjo are murderers' – and said, 'That's a lead.'

'Not when every oil company gets called "murderer" round here,' I said, and locked the iPad screen.

Carlos' hands were deep in his pockets. Another wave of

fog rose and broke. He bit his lip, scuffing his heels against the concrete and said, 'Bit of a waste to find a body and do nothing about it.'

'Our day-rate's not high enough to do something about it,' I said.

'Maybe,' said Carlos. His eyes moved from the screen of his camera, still showing the picture of Julián Gallardo's ID card, over to the bikers unwrapping their breakfasts.

'Let's just see if his name shows up in the papers over the next few days,' I said. 'If it links to what we're working on, I'll ask Dominic if we can do a follow-up.'

Carlos didn't say anything.

'It's a compromise,' I said, cuffing him on the shoulder. 'I feel for him too. But, well.' It was my turn to shrug. 'You know how it is here.'

'*I* do,' he said, peering at Julián Gallardo's thin, serious face, then up at me through falling strands of his brown hair. 'But you?' He wavered his hand in the air.

'I'm tired,' I said, opening the door of the jeep. 'Come on.'

From the jeep's speakers rose another old bolero song, all lorn tenor harmonies and guitar notes the colour of almonds.

Carlos was looking at the bikers again. 'You know what, you just keep going.' His fingers drummed the roof. 'I'm going back.'

Pure close tenor harmonies sang about the madness of trying to change a lover's fate, and I could almost see the beaten smiles on the singers' faces, see the lyrics printed on the air, feel each word sticking deep in my belly.

Carlos tapped a cigarette against the pack. 'Unless you want to come too. Keep me warm.' He winked at me. 'You and me, cosy inside that foreign correspondent ring of fire.'

'You know how much it costs to ship a body from Mexico to Ireland?' I said.

Carlos exhaled a long coiling gust of smoke and flexed his tattooed fists: praying hands, a watching eye, an anchor marked *NEC SPE NEC METU* – no hope, no fear. 'C'mon, man, you have some making up to do. Weren't for you being so *tired* and wanting to get *home*, maybe the cops wouldn't have caught us.'

'*So hard of heart*,' sang those voices on the radio.

'No?' Carlos doused his cigarette in one of the coffee cups littering his side of the jeep.

The radio voices sang about lying on the floor of a motel room, peering up at a lover who was seated on a crescent moon.

'Stop,' I said.

'Ah, but where's the lie, bro?' Carlos' fish-hook smile deepened to a leer.

My fingers pressed against my forehead. 'What do you want?'

'I want you to do your job,' he said. 'I want the story.'

'*These brown tiles under my cheek*,' sang the radio, '*colder than the heart in your chest.*'

'This guy's story.' Carlos held up the iPad screen to show me Julián Gallardo's mute eyeless scream. 'Right here.' He leaned into the car, his breath's heat reaching me across the gearstick. 'Be a real journalist, *vato*,' he said. 'For once.'

17

'*Drunken madness,*' sang the radio, '*to think I had anything good to offer you.*'

A truck roared out of the fog, threw fantails of rain over the windscreen, and shook the jeep on its suspension.

'OK.' I turned the key in the ignition so hard I thought it'd snap. 'We're done.'

'*Drunken madness,*' sang the radio, louder than the engine roar, '*to think you might ever be mine.*'

'Pussy.' Carlos jerked his camera bag from the foot well and it thunked against the door. 'I'm off. I'll text you.'

'What, hitch-hiking?' I snorted.

'Eh, yeah?' Carlos jutted his chin toward the bikers outside the Pemex, then slammed the door, and started walking back across the forecourt, face lowered against the thin rain, already waving hello to the bikers.

In my rear-view mirror Carlos shook hands with each of the bikers in turn, borrowed a helmet from one, and slung his skinny leg over the saddle of a BMW.

'Ever the charmer,' I told nobody, lighting another cigarette.

As the motorcycles blatted into life, Carlos raised one hand above his shoulders, the middle finger aimed backwards at me. The praying hands tattooed on the back of that hand looked like they were begging me not to be mad at him.

'Good fucking luck, then.' I took off the handbrake, put the jeep back into first gear. Gravel rasped under the tyres like a record needle jerked from its groove as I punched off the radio. Before merging onto the freeway I watched him disappear.

Carlos flipping the bird like that as he vanished in the rear view, I thought maybe that was him saying this was just another fight, that he wasn't about to get himself killed in Poza Rica, that he'd be right back.

Yeah, well, you know – turns out I was almost right.

4

My phone pinged just the one time as I was driving back to Mexico City, and it was when Carlos sent the photo of Julián Gallardo's dead face. When I called him to yell at him, he sent me straight to voicemail.

My heart ticked in my mouth. All the way home, mile after mile along that freeway, under the blazing white sky, I kept calling, and Carlos kept hitting 'Reject'. By the time I passed the pyramids at Teotihuacán, an hour from home, I figured I'd tried past hope and earned his time, but he didn't pick up. So I left messages instead.

'Carlos, if you get this, you're being a dickhead.'

Joining the traffic on Avenida Insurgentes, I messaged him again.

'Carlos, if you get this, you're a drama queen.'

At a red light on the corner of Xola and Dr Vertíz I called him a poser, a wanker, a glory hound.

The streets of my neighbourhood were busy already: hip, tattooed graphic designers or wait-staff or hairdressers, street-sweepers in orange overalls, stressed-out nine-to-fivers in cheapish suits, all half-jogging along the pavements, in that baroque show of trying to be on time in a city where *on time* just doesn't exist.

The *tianguis* market was already in full swing by the time I pulled in outside my house, food-stall workers scrubbing detergent into the pavement. Pickups from Estado de México and Morelos and Tulancingo stood parked by the curb, laden with strings of chorizo and big wheels of white cheese, stacked egg-boxes, whole forests of cilantro. Just another day, I decided, and all that normality around me stacked the odds in Carlos' favour, because he couldn't vanish on a day like that.

When I opened my apartment door, the venetian blinds were slicing the light into grapefruit-orange lines. Newsreader voices burbled from the speakers of a laptop. I'd asked my friend, Maya, a staff writer at a big local paper, to do some house- and cat-sitting for me while I was in Poza Rica because she hated her new apartment. She sat by the table on a red leather Gio Ponti knock-off that I'd picked up at the Mercado Lagunilla, while my cat, Motita, eyed her from the chair, her tail swishing.

'How'd you two get on?' I hung my jacket on a coat stand that stood beside a Guatemalan deity that my friend Luis had covered in Hello Kitty stationery. The deity had a rather distraught plaster Jesus half-down his throat.

'This cat, yeah?' said Maya. 'She's a misogynist.' She didn't look up from her laptop. 'Three days. Three nights. She yowls, I feed her. She yowls, I clean up. And still –' she swatted the air beside Motita with the back of her hand '– this resting bitch-face.'

Motita could tell I was there but she didn't look up. Cross-eyed, obese, and almost nine, she could no longer miaow: she just uttered this weird yowl-cough instead.

'She's ignoring me, too, if that helps,' I said, dropping my backpack and crossing the room to the fish tank. 'And how're my fish?'

Maya's fingers thrummed on her laptop keys. 'They have snails.'

Curled amber shells pocked the glass, the pebbles, the thin green weeds.

'Fuck's sake.' I took a butterfly net and a tin bucket from the shelf. 'An algal bloom.' I started scouring the depths. Motita thought it was the fish I was after and coiled herself around my feet, so I flicked water at her until she coughed and waddled across the room, body checking a cupboard on her way to her food bowl.

'Fucking snails,' I said.

In the tank, clouds of tetras billowed around a male and female betta couple who twitched their lilac fins and glided between the ferns and sword-plants.

'The cannibal snails just didn't cut it.' I tapped where a tiger-striped shell inched along the glass. 'They eat a couple of small ones then go into a food coma.'

'Never lead with desperation,' said Maya. 'Especially not in pet shops.'

More snails tinked into the bucket.

'They'll screw you, man,' said Maya. 'Matter of fact, they already have.'

'The bait, those chunks of calabaza I left, they didn't work either?'

'Fish ate them.' Maya flicked through a book she'd found on my shelves – a retrospective on the Semefo collective, '90s artists who put on black-metal raves, flayed horses, stole body-parts from morgues. She flipped to a diamond-studded tongue on a pedestal and stuck her own tongue out. 'Should I get one of these?'

Julián Gallardo's face flashed in my head.

'What, a piercing?' I said.

'Yeah,' said Maya. 'Looks good on this guy.'

'That's just the tongue. How can you tell?' I shook the bucket, studied the clacking wet load. 'Look at this. A disgrace.'

'I was house-sitting,' said Maya. 'Not paying the mortgage.' She flicked the page so hard it nearly tore. 'You flushing all those at once?'

'Eh, yeah?'

'You sure that's wise?' said Maya. 'There's all sorts of mutant crap down in those sewers. You want killer snails to murder you in the night?'

'Then don't put trash down my sink.'

Maya slammed the book shut. 'I did not.'

The toilet emptied, sucking the snails out of sight.

'An algal bloom,' I said again, shaking my head as I stowed the bucket under the tank.

'Blame the pollution,' said Maya through a yawn. 'Not me.'

She wasn't wrong. Every day on its website the city government published an air-quality map: green dots for clean air, yellow for not-so-clean, then down through grey and red all the way to black. On my way home, I'd checked the map, seen how the city's stomach-shape was rashed all over with grey, yellow, red.

Mexico's worst pollution since 1983, the papers said, but you didn't need the papers to know. Mornings, your throat hurt from the bad air you'd been breathing all night. Afternoons, your eyes turned bloodshot and stung. Nights, mosquitos and flies collected on the cold ceramic of your toilet cistern like a galaxy in negative.

You could taste it in the ozone sting of the air even going up the stairwell of your apartment building. You could see it in the sepia colour of your windows even an hour after you'd cleaned off the airborne crud.

Times like that, the pipes burst in the heat. The sewage dried, the dust rose. Got so bad you'd sometimes wind up writing news stories about nineteenth-century diseases in the poor areas of the city: typhoid, dysentery, cholera.

As I washed my hands, I heard Maya ask, 'And so, how was the trip?' through the open bathroom door.

Julián Gallardo's wet peeled face in close-up, the ant picking slowly across the gouged bridge of his nose.

'Ah, yeah,' I said. 'Fine.' Back in the room, I saw my phone still hadn't buzzed. 'Long drive, though.'

'You want coffee?'

'Ah, savage, yeah, cheers.'

'Well, you know where it is.'

'Fuck's sake.' I went to the kitchen to make some breakfast. Three mangoes lay at the bottom of the crisper. 'Nice one on the mangoes.' I took a bag of Café Garat from the freezer and dumped a thick dark layer into the cafetière, then put water on to boil.

'Got one for Carlos, too,' said Maya. 'You drop him home, or?'

'Um.' I scooped out the mangoes' wet pith. 'He's, you know. Still down there.'

Maya's fingers stopped typing. 'What?'

Water bubbled on the hob. With the gas off, and the bubbles settled, I poured out water and watched the grounds churn.

'Is he crazy?' Maya said.

'Well, yeah,' I said, bringing out a brimming cafetière and the mangoes.

'You know what's happening down there, right?'

Shaking my head, I slid her the plate of mango.

Maya turned the computer towards me. 'A protest, man. A big one.'

On the screen, choppy GoPro footage showed students and workers, mothers and kids holding up pictures of a young man's face, above the words 'WHERE IS HE?'

The face on their signs was Julián Gallardo's.

Coffee grounds spun in my cup. The lines of my hands were rivers of salt water.

Carlos, if you get this, get the fuck out of there.

'You knew this was on?' Maya said over the protest video.

'Not at all.' I scratched my neck. From the wall, between the cocktail-glasses on my shelf, a Jesús Malverde icon gave me a pained look.

Maya watched me through a spreading web of cigarette smoke. 'Something happened down there, didn't it?'

'*México no se vende!*' shouted the crowd on the screen. *Mexico's not for sale.*

'Kind of.' With my teeth I tugged a loose dry edge of skin on my lip until the pain zipped red through my skull.

Maya never let me get much past her: she was the first student I'd had, back when I was still teaching English. Being raised on the same teenage diet of Radiohead lyrics and quotes from *Daria*, and, given that all she'd needed from the school was a certificate saying she was bilingual to get a promotion at her paper, our classes had consisted of shit-talking, drinking coffee, and occasionally proofreading her articles.

'Well?' she asked me.

'See that kid on the signs?' I pointed at the laptop screen. 'We found him.'

Her eyes widened. 'What? And you didn't tell anyone?'

'No.' I kneaded my eyes. 'Police found him – Guardia Civil. They found us, too. But they seemed scared, to be honest. Just gave us a warning. Let us go.'

Maya sat down hard on the chair. 'And you let Carlos stay there. After that.'

My back teeth sounded like someone moving furniture, I was grinding them so hard. Two years, six months, twenty days since my last drink or line, and I couldn't feel that resolution any more – just the coffee-warmed William Howard Taft mug bought for me by Maya after I'd tried and failed to grow a walrus moustache.

Swallowing coffee to kill the sting of pollution, I shook my head and said, 'Honestly? When have we ever stopped Carlos doing, like, literally anything?'

Maya sucked air through her teeth. 'You're not wrong.'

On the laptop, the crowd was snaking through a gap in the wall of police riot-shields. Their chants beat the air.

'Big crowd,' I said.

'They're saying the kid was important,' Maya said. 'Some sort of activist leader. Pretty well known.'

'Still a lot of people to get out that fast,' I said.

She shook her head. 'Nah. I mean, the amount of people pissed off at the cops and the companies down there? All it takes is a few Facebook posts and people will be jumping on it.'

'Huh. Well, I'd better add to the story, then, I guess,' I said, draining my cup. 'Speaking of which – time to file, I think.' Maya and the thought of work were all that kept me from buying a bag of coke, speed up the time until Carlos was back to me. 'Want to hang out here? See if Carlos calls, or whatever.'

'Sure, yeah,' said Maya, pouring herself another cup of coffee and holding her hand out for my mug.

Motita slammed herself against the cupboard, knocking the door open.

Maya pointed. 'But you're feeding her this time. She and I are done.'

5

Maya took her laptop down the hall while I fed Motita and took a shower, the tiredness seeping from between my back's bones like the silt-heavy waste water pumped out of Poza Rica's drill sites. The bathroom mirror made me wrinkle my nose. Thirty-one, I was then, but the deep insomnia caves around my eyes meant I didn't look a day under forty.

If I looked bad, I felt even worse. The curdled, sour grogginess of being up since dawn sloshed in my blood, and my belly was knotted with worry for Carlos. Behind my eyes, with every blink, Julián Gallardo's empty red eye-sockets loomed up at me.

Outside, the sky loured with brassy storm light and boiled with smog-brown clouds. Days like that, the hallway was the coolest place in the house, and so that's where I kept my desk, in a cave of taped-up pages, printouts, maps, scraps of transcript.

Maya was lying down on the red and gold scroll-backed chaise-longue in the corridor with the Semefo book when I came out of the bathroom and sat down to work at my big metal desk.

'Is that a picture of Díaz Ordáz on your noticeboard?' she asked.

'This?' I unpinned the sheet and handed it to her. 'Oh, it's just an acid blotter.'

She ran her fingers over the cut-out squares. 'Weird choice of picture.'

'Carlos bought it for me. Said the picture fit, since human history's such a bad trip. It's like a joke.'

Maya looked at me the way I'd looked at my snails. 'Díaz Ordáz did the Tlatelolco massacre,' said Maya. 'It's a bad joke.' She handed back the blotter. 'Anyway, didn't you . . . like, quit? Like, everything?'

'Yeah, I mean, it's not like I'm going to take any.' I pinned the A4-size sheet back in place. 'It's just funny is all.'

Maya recoiled a little. 'There's nothing funny about Díaz Ordáz.'

The arms of my office chair clunked against the desk as I pushed aside the snowdrift of printouts and sat down to work. Huge and rust-flecked, the desk had belonged to some Mexican Communist Party guy. Its drawers were why I'd bought the thing: their locks were as close to uncrackable as you could get, and so that's where I kept the only stuff it would kill me to have stolen – the tapes and notebooks built up over my years with Carlos.

A floral altar stood beside my iMac, a skeletal Santa Muerte wrapped in a blue boa and a starred black cowl that hid her bone grin. After lighting a couple of candles for Carlos and a cigarette for myself, I cracked into the story for Dominic, Maya napping while I typed, until the chugging of the printer woke her.

'Anything from Carlos?' she said through a yawn.

On WhatsApp, his *Last Online* status read ten forty-five in the morning.

'Not a peep.' I collected the pages from the printer and walked up and down the hall checking over them. My sternum itched with sweat. The story in my hands, I wanted to feed it to the snails. The hook was buckled, the body in tatters, the tail measly, wizened, tapering. Before the paragraphs had dried on the page I could see Dominic's red editorial biro slashing through every line.

Maya batted the air. 'Jesus, how many cigarettes do you need?'

'Have to get in character.'

'As?'

'A Pemex refinery.'

She pulled a face. 'All this smoke hurts to look at.'

I flicked the pages. 'So does this draft.'

A legacy of pollution and violence in Mexico's former oil capital looks likely to deter future investors in the ailing industrial city of Poza Rica, eastern Mexico, I read. Despite sitting on a treasure trove equal to around fifteen billion barrels of crude, the people of Mexico's former oil capital remain cynical as investors circle those areas of the country which have been earmarked for privatisation and resale.

'It's a corrupt deal,' said former wrestler and restaurant owner Gilberto Herrera, 52, at the fonda which he runs with his wife and son in the city's gritty centre. 'The companies build shiny new

headquarters, the hotels get a bunch of new extensions, and then the investments fall through and we all wind up unemployed.'

As in so many areas of Mexico — locked in a decade-plus war against its major organised crime groups — unemployment in Poza Rica is linked with a spiking crime rate. The elite Guardia Civil police unit has been active in the city since 2014, but they continue to struggle against the notoriously brutal Zetas cartel.

'All that brought us was bloodshed — not safety,' said local opposition leader Janiel Vizcaya, 57, at his home on the city's leafy outskirts. 'We're years and years on from that operation and still people are shot on the main boulevard.'

'This is awful,' I said. My eyes felt baked in their sockets.

'What, Carlos or the story?'

'Both.'

'Carlos'll be OK,' said Maya. The brightness in her voice was fake. 'He's resourceful.' She sat up and stretched. 'Anyway, look, I better go. Date tonight. I look like deep-fried shit.'

I squinted at her. 'It's more of a light sauté.'

She glared at me and slung the strap of her bag over her shoulder.

'Hope it goes well.' I stooped over the draft, crossing out a line about how even the police looked scared. 'Good you're getting back out there, after — well, you know. That whole thing.'

Maya made a fist and pulled a heroic face. 'Thank you, yes, I am a brave motherfucker.' She hitched up the strap of her bag. 'But yeah, so, text me if you hear from Carlos, OK?'

'Shall do.' I pushed back my hair, sat down with the pages spread out and my red pen stabbing at the words.

★

Mexico City's pollution content is measured in something called *imecas* – an acronym for *índice metropolitano de la calidad del aire*.

Imecas are a parts-per-million measure of all the carbon monoxide and ozone and sulphides hovering in the air on a given day.

At fifty, you can't taste them. Up at a hundred, though, you'll get a dry throat, blood in your snot. Past a hundred and twenty-five, the air smells like a swimming pool, your snot goes black, and your eyes weep and tack at the corners.

That night, the levels tipped a hundred and fifty, the sky was dirty yellow cotton wool, and my headache was louder than the bass-drum of the hip-hop blasting from the apartment behind mine.

The taste in my mouth, and the noise, and the heat, and the headache all made me crave a rain big enough to chase the parties in from the terraces, to dissolve the smog, to douse my windows in a cold roar that cancelled all thought, all worry, all fear of what might have happened to Carlos.

My red drapes were shut, and my windows, too, but that didn't make much of a difference against the noise and bad air. On the altar, the candles I'd lit for Carlos' safety guttered out in blue pools.

I'd gone all out trying to bribe my saints' statues. On top of the bookcase, the Santa Barbara shrine I'd bought in Cuba was uplit by flickering black candles that bathed her pleading ceramic face in a feverish pallor. On a baby-blue shelf, between the old cocktail glasses I collected, stood Saint Jude with his quiff of fire, his hand resting on the large medallion of Jesus in profile that hung around his neck, a spray of bird-of-paradise flowers at his feet. The Jesús Malverde icon peered out, unimpressed, while I cooked something nobody would flatter with the word *dinner*.

After wedging that down, I went over to my indoor garden, knelt on the pallet loaded with giraffe orchids, and *pata de elefante*, begonias and ferns, wetting their leaves with a damp cloth. Then I fixed the corners of the cowhide draping the chair – my favourite one, late-'60s, steel-framed leather, made in Frankfurt – and sat down, headache-friendly light pulsing from four orb-bulbs behind the screen of leaves.

None of that calmed me down, though, and I knew it wouldn't.

Me and Carlos, we'd done stories about missing people. That's a story you never stop having to do in Mexico. Feels like every lamppost on every street wears a peeled lagging of 'Missing' posters. You see photocopied hair banded with white lines. You read the name, the sex, the age, the stature. You read the complexion, the hair type, the nose type, the jaw-shape. All that scattered data, it's debris flung by the blast of a vanishing, all of it jumbled, all of it lost.

My cupped hands held faces I'd known. My breath became their voices.

In my hands I saw Mario, the pool-hall owner in Cocula, with his pencil moustache and his wide-brimmed canvas hat, toting a metal rod whose end he'd drive down into the red earth, pulling it out to check for the molasses-black stain of human rot that might be the brother of his, kidnapped eight years before.

'One person is missing for you,' he'd said, leaning on the pole, his eyes aimed up at the hot blue sky, 'and that's your whole world empty.'

There was Guadalupe, the bank teller in Ecatepec, with her prim lilac suit, and her Princess Diana hair, and her photos of the caved-in skull and two thigh-bones that had belonged to her daughter and had been dredged from the Río de los Remedios by the police.

'That's all they found, they said,' she'd scoffed, refilling her camomile tea, rolling up her sleeves. 'After three weeks in the river? Sure, it's polluted. But to dissolve a body that quickly? Nonsense.'

Next came Priscilla, the beekeeper from El Salvador whose son had been kidnapped by immigration agents two nights before she and I had spoken at the refugee shelter in Ixtepec.

'Usually when we slept, we belted ourselves to the upper branches of trees,' she'd told me, showing me pictures of her son on her cracked smartphone. 'Marvin went down to go to the toilet. He didn't come back. Soon after, I saw the migra coming through the woods with their torches. They have to have him. Who else could it be?'

A psychoanalyst I interviewed once, she told me how a disappearance hurts worse than death.

'Freud says that mourning is a loss of hope,' she'd said. 'In mourning, you accept that the hope for permanence is false. But when you can't accept that somebody's dead – when you have no body, no confirmation – that hope can't burn out. You can't let go. You can't mourn.'

The hope burned in Mario's eyes, in Guadalupe's voice, under the mask-like calm of Priscilla trying to keep it together at the migrant shelter in Ixtepec.

'There's a chance she's still out there.'

'One of these days, we'll find my brother's body.'

'The cops said they were my daughter's bones, but they're too long to be hers.'

'Any day now, my father will call to say Marvin's home.'

That clenched-gut dread, that burn in my veins, that feeling was how their stories had all begun. Like Mario's brother, like Guadalupe's daughter, like Priscilla's son, Carlos had gone from a solid body to a message that wouldn't come, a door that wouldn't open, a phone set to 'Loud' that never rang.

How long I stayed there gripping the arms of my chair, smoke clouding around me, the rain seething down, I couldn't tell you. From my window the other apartments around me looked like the dark wood cabins of a huge ship, while my own was a raft lost in a black nowhere. It was just like the nights when he'd stay out doing whatever, except also totally not.

At some point I shut my eyes, so lost in the storm's lull that I full-on fell asleep, dreamed of me and Carlos on a cinder beach in Uruguay, Carlos dipping kelp into mercury-coloured water, mopping a dark red headache from my skull while Julián Gallardo's body rocked in the near-shore waves. Until the dream thinned to an unease with pictures, cops in ski-masks chasing me and Carlos through a forest of my lungs' blackened inner tubes, Gallardo's body toted on our shoulders.

When my phone buzzed, the clock on screen read six a.m., and I lurched up, alert, from the sheepskin rug on the floor to see four messages, all from Carlos.

'I'll text,' he'd said.

That thing where they say *My heart leapt*, they're not wrong: it really does feel like something of you has upped and ripped free of your chest.

Then I saw his first message, and my heart slammed flat against my ribcage.

Delete this number.

My chest was an empty lift-shaft.

Don't go to the house.

My heart kept dropping.

You're not safe.

My gut was a dusty basement.

Andrew.

That's when my heart stopped its freefall, hit the dirt and grit, and I grabbed my jacket and keys and went running for the jeep.

6

No sirens when I got to Carlos' apartment: just blue lights and silence.

Meaning me, and the ambulance, and the forensics technician – still wearing her loose white Hazmat – we'd all arrived too late.

Mineria 45 was all heavy coral-pink brick and barred windows. Whenever you went through the front door, it'd slam behind you like a bank safe.

The paramedics pulled the door back, way back, so the trolley's belts didn't snag on the handle. The body on the stretcher was covered by a red blanket patched with darker red, brown hair overhanging its edge, each curl stiff with blood.

A dizzy whirl lurched me against the fender of my jeep as the stretcher rattled through the door.

Back when I was a teenager, playing football, I broke my toe so far out of shape that it had curved from my foot like a crab's leg. A red bell of pain had clanged in my skull all the way to the hospital, where a nurse stuck in an anaesthetic needle and yanked my toe into line, my bones jerking back into place, but in a way I could hear rather than feel.

Seeing Carlos come down the stairs was the same. You knew what was happening. You just couldn't feel it.

A cigarette that I didn't remember lighting stung my lips, and a cop watched me from the curb, smiling at me, his hair thinning and chestnut, the silver caps on his front teeth winking all the way over to where I knelt beside Carlos' body, as it shunted into the ambulance. He looked away when the forensics technician cuffed him in the back to get him to turn around, but he just leered at her.

'No photos,' said the paramedic when he saw my press lanyard.

My back teeth bit a notch in the wall of my cheek.

'What happened?' I said around a salt upwell of blood, getting to my feet.

'We're not authorised to say.' The paramedic slammed the ambulance doors, the engine roared, and Carlos was gone.

The dawn was loud with birds. Two street-sweepers across the road kept their eyes to the curb, and a tamal seller studied the fire starting to lick the base of her battered steel olla. The commuters hurrying toward Metro Patriotismo kept their eyes averted from the blue flicker of lights outside Carlos' apartment.

'Who was the first responder?' the forensics technician said to the cop, her hand chopping the air.

The cop with the teeth just shrugged.

'Show me your badge number.' She grabbed his shoulder.

'That's a Veracruz State number – you're not supposed to be here.'

He shouldered her away and looked toward me.

'Go home, *gringuito*,' said the cop with the teeth, and threw out his hands, let them clap by his sides, backward-walking towards his squad car, laughing, his eyes on me, like two drill-bits boring through my navel.

'What are you doing here?' The forensics technician's hands rose like she wanted to strangle the air, but the cop ignored her.

'We won't tell you again,' he said to me, then slammed the door and revved out of sight, heading along Avenida José Martí.

Once he was out of sight, the technician stood at her car and picked up her phone again. I headed around the corner to an abarrotes to buy a Coke through the grille. The fifty-peso note I'd handed through wagged back at me and the owner said, 'I don't have change.'

'Keep it.' My voice was a winded croak, and it could have been the white clouds of smog turning in the air, but it probably wasn't.

The forensics technician walked towards a white Toyota Camry with the Mexico City prosecutor's logo on the side of it.

'Actually, give me two,' I said, and took the cans and ran towards the technician before she could get into her car.

Carlos' *portero*, Don Jesús, stood at the door, his paunch straining against his blue plaid shirt and twisting his faded

Chivas baseball cap in his hands, a poor Edomex *campesino* adrift in the big concrete roar of Mexico City, eking out an income, watching Futból Azteca repeats, seeing nothing, staying out of trouble.

Yeah, well, you know.

Trouble moves.

When he saw me, he put his cap on, then crept back to the security booth's smoky den of escape and TV. In front of him the football commentary rose in volume, became a yell, became the long delighted vowel of the word '*Goooool!*'

The technician was sitting half-in, half-out of the car, still on the phone, saying, 'A Veracruz State cop at a Mexico City crime scene. You believe that?' Her black hair was tied back in a bun, and the ventilator mask around her neck hung under a weary lined face. I put her at about forty, but tired like she was older. She ground a cigarette out with the toe of her shoe and gave me the pinched-finger gesture that means '*Hold on a second*' in Mexico.

'Alejandro, you know that's not the point,' she snapped. 'This is our jurisdiction.' She put another cigarette in her mouth, but her lighter didn't work: she kept flicking the wheel too hard, so I stooped in with mine and lit it for her.

'Right. Well, see you at the precinct.' She hung up, breathed out a long plume of smoke. 'Can I help you?' she said to me.

'Yeah,' I said, and held up my press lanyard again.

Her face shut. 'I can't tell you anything,' she said.

'Off the record.' I reached out the Coke can.

She looked at the can with mistrust. 'You people always say that.'

'But this definitely is.' I gave a backward nod at the apartment. 'This guy. The victim? I knew him.' The road blurred so much that I had to press myself against the wall to keep from hitting the curb.

The technician took the can. 'OK. But I won't say much.' She leaned against the ash-streaked bonnet of her car. 'That scene – worst this year.' She breathed out smoke. 'Animals.' She shook her head. 'I don't know what's happening to this country. I say that every time. But I really don't.'

'Yeah,' I said, and sipped my Coke, and tasted nothing. 'How'd he look?'

She cracked open the Coke and took a long swig, then said, 'Tortured, you know? Broken fingers. Shot through the hands.'

His tattooed fists: the praying hands, the anchor and the motto.

'Shot through the wrists.'

In my head I saw a burn hole the octopus tentacles inked on his skin.

She paused. 'Broke a chair off in him. His rectum.' She shut her eyes, breathed out hard. 'Look, I'm really sorry.'

The street wavered. 'He bled out?'

She shook her head. 'Petechial haemorrhaging around the eyes. Hyoid bone snapped.' Her voice had gone flat, like a printer spitting pages. 'Not much blood from the chest wounds. Less from the forehead.' She swallowed. 'I'm guessing strangulation. Reverse chokehold.'

My eyes shut on pictures of Carlos spraying aftershave on his throat, of my fingers winding in the hair that hung to his shoulders.

'Shot in the chest,' I said.

The technician nodded. 'Twice. Impact spread suggests hollow-point bullets.'

'Gang-issue?' I said, even though I already knew what she'd say.

She shook her head. 'Six impact cuts around a central wound.' Then she nodded in the direction the cop car had gone, then shook drops of Coke into her mouth. 'Police issue.'

A cold weight shunted down my gullet.

'Veracruz State Police,' I said. 'At a Mexico City crime scene.'

She nodded. 'And he wrecked the scene, too – so much fingerprint dust that I couldn't see the blood patterns. Samples are destroyed.'

'On purpose?'

She gave me a withering look. 'I couldn't possibly speculate.'

My belly squirmed. So crass to have blood, to breathe air, to hear my stomach groan even though I wasn't hungry, never wanted to be hungry again.

She checked her watch. 'Look, I have to go. Here's my number.' She took a pen from her pocket and unlidded it with her teeth, before scribbling on a Superama receipt that she handed to me. 'You need more, you call. I'm Teresa.'

'You sure?' I turned the card in my fingers. 'That cop gave me the creeps.'

42

She swatted the air. 'I'm nobody to these state cops. They make shit for me, my boss makes shit for their bosses.' She climbed into the car. 'Thanks for the Coke.'

The door slammed, and her car threw dust onto my jeans as she drove off towards Eje Cuatro, and for the first time in four years I found myself alone.

7

Back home, I lay down on the chaise-longue, the heels of my hands pressed to my eyes until I couldn't see Carlos' body on the stretcher for all the white stars. For a while my head was nothing but the noise of my fish-tank filters. Then Maya called, and brought everything back.

'Oh, thank God. You're OK.' She sounded out of breath. 'You heard?'

'I saw.'

Above my head hung framed encyclopaedia cut-outs about rural Mexico, the pictures taken back in the '60s and '70s. The looted pyramid at El Tajín stared back, a pile of empty eyes.

'You *went*?' Maya sat back so hard that I heard her chair roll backwards to thunk against the table. 'How are you not terrified?'

Julián Gallardo's face watched me from the noticeboard.

'Oh, I am,' I said.

Air pollution can do a lot of damage over time. Post-mortem studies of teenagers in Mexico City showed that the stuff in our air kinks your genes, makes your heart tougher over the short-term, but claps it out faster overall.

Meaning you needed a mutant heart to live there, I guess.

Me and Carlos, our hearts had gone mutant a long time ago. Meaning it hadn't felt wrong to print out Julián Gallardo's peeled face and hang it above the desk. Because if he hadn't been our story before, he sure as shit was now.

Maya's breath went in hard. 'You call Carlos' mother?'

'Hah.' My voice was a torn wet tissue. 'Yeah.'

'What'd she say?'

Behind me, the wall-size photo of a half-nude American footballer in Captain America body-paint looked from the wall, his creased-mouth smile mournful.

The thought of his mother's silence on the line when I'd called her, the blame in her voice, they shook me harder than that cop's metal grin.

'As little as possible,' I said.

You could practically hear Maya grimacing on the other end of the line.

'It'll be OK,' she said, even though we both knew it wouldn't. 'But, well – this is going to sound crazy,' Maya said in my ear. 'But after this? You need to protect yourself, yeah?'

'How?' I rubbed my temple and got up from the chair, unpinning the blotter of Díaz Ordáz from the wall, running my finger over the tabs that me and Carlos would never take together.

Maya paused. 'Well,' she said. 'How do the bad guys do it?'

She wasn't bluffing. One of the first news stories Maya had showed me of hers – back during the English teaching days – was about how she'd bought a gun in Tepito for three thousand pesos.

'You're right. That is crazy,' I'd said to her then, in that basement classroom on Calle Alfonso Reyes, and I said it to her again now.

'True,' Maya said. 'But after this, yeah? You're kind of crazy if you don't.'

I stopped at the giraffe orchids, ran my fingers over their petals, their black centres neat as zeros.

Hollow-point bullets, Teresa had said. *Six impact cuts ringed each wound.*

My hand was damp against my forehead. 'I can't believe this is real.'

At the clay *garrafón* in the kitchen I filled my dinged metal water flask to just below the neck, tore off a strip of tabs, halved them and tamped them in, then put on the lid before shaking until the dissolved tabs slopped against the metal.

'What are you doing?' said Maya.

'Uh,' I said. 'Making a smoothie.'

'Good,' said Maya. 'Get something down you, yeah? Even if you don't want to.'

'Oh, I will.' Cold gulps rocked my throat, washing away the rust-taste leaking from my bitten cheek.

Microdosing, it's called, when you dissolve acid tabs in water and top up your high over a period of hours, and it spreads your thoughts out in a gauzy web, makes your attention into a spider-pick along ideas as clear and bright as metal struts.

Yeah, well, what I was doing now, call it megadosing.

'So, tomorrow?' I wiped my mouth with the back of my hand, half-dissolved chunks of blotter clogged in my teeth.

'Yeah, he says eight a.m.,' said Maya. 'Meet me at the Salto del Agua church.'

Acid takes an hour to metabolise, usually, but I was so strafed with grief that the serotonin had already rushed my brain, thick and white as steam, meaning I had about a minute to get things set up before my medulla was drowned and I was more acid than man.

'You don't want me to pick you up?' I asked, unlocking my desk's bottom drawer and pulling out a tape marked '*CARLOS // EL PASO // 30 / 12 / 2012*'.

'Nah, you just eat something and go sleep, yeah?'

The cassette clicked into my tape recorder, the one I'd stolen from the school where I'd taught, and I flicked the switch marked '*PLAYBACK*'.

'You're so calm,' I said.

I heard her swallow, take a deep breath and say, 'Well, someone has to be, right?' She coughed, sniffling, and said, 'Here, I'm gonna go mop my face off, yeah? I'll check on you later.'

When she hung up I turned my phone off and lay down on the chaise-longue, my Sennheisers snug on my ears. On the recording the mic stopped crackling and mine and Carlos' voices rose through my headphones, turning my cigarette smoke to snow over El Paso on the morning I met him, while the river noise of my fish tanks washed me back into four years before.

8

The plane to Ciudad Juárez that December morning left me the same greenish tinge as the snow clouds above. None of what I was doing made any sense to me. It was all too sudden, too new. But I told myself that this feeling was what I wanted, and kept walking to the taxi rank.

A week earlier, at the end of class, Maya had been zipping shut her bag when she'd asked if I'd wanted to make some extra money over Christmas.

'Obviously,' I'd said, lifting my tie to show her the frayed end.

'Well, if you want, right?' She'd taken her phone out. 'I got asked to go up to El Paso. A story. This journalist who can't go back to Juárez. Some death thing.'

'"Death thing"?'

She'd pulled a face. 'Well, OK, so some death-threat thing. But Juárez is fine now.' She'd wavered her hand. 'Ish.'

'I don't know, Maya,' I'd said, tidying a sheaf of papers. 'I get nervous in the colonia Juárez – and they're gentrifying the shit out of that place.'

'C'mon, please? I don't want to do the story.' She'd pouted like a toddler.

'Because it's dangerous.'

'No, because I want to go back to Durango and lie on my back at my mother's house, eating my own fucking weight in *bacalao*.' She'd handed me a slim business card with the name '*CARLOS ARANA // FOTÓGRAFO*' on one side and a picture of a cage fighter whose inner-lip tattoo read *JARDCORE*.

'Consider this,' Maya had said, bowing, 'my Christmas gift to you.'

The cage fighter's lip shone livid pink on the card.

'Well, thanks,' I'd said. 'I think.'

In the backseat of the taxi I turned the card in my hands, driving through the smoky winter morning, as far as the International Bridge. On the pavements either side went revellers headed for home and labourers headed for work, their breath smoking in the air, their chuckles and gags breaking through the window. Army trucks roared past under switched-off Christmas lights that looked as sad as dead coral. From the newsstands the morning papers said '72 HOURS WITHOUT A MURDER', like that was a good thing. 'Missing' posters hung from the post boxes – 'Help find Marisela, Carmen, Estefanía' – under a flitter of snowflakes as pale as moths.

Getting out at the border crossing I stepped into an explosion of laughter from a gang of twenty-something girls off to work the El Paso malls' Sunday-morning shift, turned my collar up against the wind's big gusts, and walked through customs and into the U.S.

Carlos' hotel on the El Paso side was a rain-faded shade of orange, between a shuttered Walgreens and a bail-bondsman's sign that read 1-888-GET-U-OFF.

When I texted Maya to say I'd arrived OK she replied with a picture of an extremely tall sandwich beside a box-set of *The Wire*, so I leaned against the wall, smoking, checking my notes on Carlos, and burning all over with envy, because, back when I was driving my dad's 1991 Toyota Corolla through the fields and taking pot-shots at rabbits, Carlos had been working the crime pages and avoiding pot-shots from gang members. His bylines hurt to read: *The Times*, the *New York Times*, the *Financial Times* – and that was just the papers with *Times* in the name.

And then there he was, a stooped shape in a black coat, held at the crux of the glass and steel buildings at the end of the street. In one hand he held a battered guitar case. From the other swung a twelve-pack of Dos Equis.

Through a curtain of cigarette smoke and wavy brown hair, he raked a look over me and said, 'You the interviewer guy?'

I pointed at the guitar-case. 'You definitely the photographer guy?'

He coughed out a one-syllable laugh.

'Sometimes your side gig's your main gig, you know?' He had that smooth, sidling NAFTA English, all wide vowels and clipped consonants. When he shook my hand I saw a black-and-grey tattoo of octopus tentacles reach up over the back of his hand, tapering right up to his bitten nails.

'You eat breakfast?'

'No.' I held out my hand and took the beers from his hand. 'You?'

'You're carrying it.'

His room smelled of hash-smoke, adrenal sweat, stale beer. Books by Mallarmé, Nicanor Parra, and Michael Herr were stacked on his locker.

'Take a seat.' Both the room's twin beds had been slept in, or at least passed out in, littered with rumpled Levi's and cigarette-boxes. '*Mi rúm es tu rúm, güey.* Shove over whatever, the whole place is chaos anyway.' He shook a bottle at me. 'Grab what you want. They're not dead cold, but hey.'

'Bit early for me,' I said. 'Thanks, though.'

'Don't let me drink alone, *cabrón.* Sign of alcoholism.'

'So's drinking before noon.'

He cocked the base of his bottle at me. 'So's timetabling your drinking.'

'Fine.' I cracked a bottle open with my lighter.

Carlos shucked off his coat and slung it on the back of his chair. His white shirt was crossed by the thin leather harness of a shoulder holster.

'Jesus,' I said.

'Don't worry, *vato.*' He unbuckled the harness. 'I can barely shoot a camera.'

'No bullet-proof vest?'

'No,' he said. 'Too heavy to run with.' He slid a stout grey Colt .45 from the holster. 'And the *mamónes* know how to make sure anyway.' He stowed the gun under his pillow.

'Wearing a vest is like saying your life's worth more than the people you're reporting on.' He flung himself down on the bed.

'What's the gun say?'

'That my life's worth more than a cop's.' He gave me a hard look. 'You want to argue that one?'

'Not with that lying there.'

The grimy windows were a balcony on Juárez. Grey fog coiled under the arches of the faux-colonial international bridge, while Yaqui vendors toted their wares in and out of the traffic stalled on the Avenida de las Américas, the whole scene shadowed by a grey ruck of mountains.

Carlos took a drag of smoke and a long pull on his beer, his chest heaving as he suppressed a belch. 'And so, these questions?'

'Sure.' I unsnapped the elastic band that held my notebook shut. 'How does it feel to be Mexico's best young photojournalist, but not to be able to work in Mexico?'

Carlos' eyes narrowed. 'Fuck called me that?'

'Maya.'

'What else she tell you?'

'That you're not as much of a try hard as your business card.'

He cackled and rubbed his jaw. 'Fucken ouch, man. Nah, but not working? That shit's hard, *vato*.' He gestured out the window. 'The things going down back home, we're talking pictures enough to make a career, *cabrón*.' His voice was warm with awe, envy, bloodlust. 'And I'm missing it.'

'You feel safe here?' I said, then clicked my tongue: I was

snapping into my questions too fast, and I'd probably spook him if I kept it up.

But Carlos just shook his head and said, 'Not after this morning, man.' He took a swig of beer. 'You know why I left, right?'

As I shook my head, he took a cigarette from my pack, lit up, and, after three drags, started talking.

'So this is nine months ago. And I'm driving home from work at Diario de Juárez. And where I lived at that time, me and my mother, yeah? This place, our place, it was way out. You can hear nothing out there.' Cigarette smoke traced the wave of his hand in the air. 'Like, for example, as a kid, I'd be staying up, late nights, just watching the trucks come speeding through the dark, from Hermosillo, Chihuahua, Ciudad Cuauhtémoc, from all these places.' He rapped the air with the edge of his hand. 'Like, that's how boring we're talking. Those trucks passing by all lit up was, like, an event, or whatever.' He flicked ash. 'And so, you know, there I am, driving home. Desert road, black all round, lights on green signs, shadows of cactuses, nothing else. And then this fucking cop car, blue and white, out of nowhere.' He took another drag. 'Three cops. Federales. Big units, yeah? One waves me over. Has this sort of wrestler beard.'

'Wrestler beard?'

He mimed a circle around his mouth. 'That fucken goatee thing.' He shrugged. 'Metal fans, wrestlers, perverts, they all have this beard. What it's called, I don't know.' He cackled again and took a long drink, scratching his neck. 'Anyway, these guys, right. They give me the usual: "Can we see your

53

licence, get down from the vehicle, please," all that, yeah? And, when I do, one of them kicks out the backs of my knees, drops me to the ground, while this wrestler beard one, he puts his gun right here.' Carlos screwed his finger against the skin between his eyes.

The tape recorder whirred in the silence. 'But why?'

He sat up. 'My job, *cabrón*. Crime reporting. And if the cops are doing the crimes, the cops get pissed off.' He took the pack of cigarettes from the bed I sat on, then took the gun from under his pillow. 'These cigarette right here, yeah? That's the street gangs. You have your Barrio Azteca, your Artistas Asesinos, your small local sets with, like, eighteen soldiers, max. Harmful in numbers but –' he shook the packet '– you know, lightweight. And this, yeah? –' he held up the gun '– this is the main guys, Chapo's boys, the cops, the local politicians, a couple businessmen, all the big cheeses sticking together. And so when the army comes into Juárez, what are you going to do?' Carlos held up the cigarettes. 'You go after a numbnuts coalition of goons?' He held up the gun. 'Or a bunch of guys protected by the government since the year dot?'

'You go after the small-timers,' I said. 'You see can you work your way in with the big shots. You see can you get a cut.' I was quoting stories Maya had told me. 'Same as everywhere.'

'You may collect your free burger,' said Carlos, and stole a cigarette from the packet before tossing it back to me. 'And so, yeah, the cops, the soldiers, they turn the blind eye on the gangs they'd prefer to see win. Massacres, drive-bys, suddenly

they're all copasetic, long as it's the right gangs doing them.'
He curled his lip. 'And me, I think that's bullshit, man. And
so I just take pictures of everything, everyone, the shit the
army pulls, the shit the locals pull, no matter who I piss
off.' He blew out smoke. 'Which is why I wind up on my
knees, begging, and pleading, and offering those Federales
my sister's ass.' He shook his head. 'And I don't even have
a sister.' He shrugged, looking embarrassed. 'And I mean,
OK, so I didn't shit myself. Well. Not much. But I think I
must have –' he cackled '– *shamed* them into letting me go,
you know?' He drank some beer. 'And so they accepted my
offer.'

I let my jaw hang slack. 'Your poor imaginary *sister*.'

Carlos laughed. 'Nah, man, just my cameras. Wallet, jeep.
Computer. They did this other fucked-up thing, too, right,
drove me to the nearest ATM, parked their cars right up by
the cameras, not a care in the world, and had me take out my
daily limit, then drove me around till after midnight so's I
could fetch them *that* day's limit.' He shook his head. 'Dump
me, then, after, in some shithole *barrio*. Walk myself to my
friend's house. How I didn't get mugged was a bigger miracle
than the first thing. Friend drops me at this here hotel, and –'
he spread his hands '– voilà.'

He took a long, slow pull on his beer and looked out the
window, a view of the footbridge, the mountains, and the
border's stark wire lines reflected in his glasses. 'Nine months,'
he said, 'watching the debt fatten on my credit card while my
city burns two hundred metres away.'

My pen tapped my notebook. 'And this morning?'

TIM MACGABHANN

He laughed. 'Shit, you're worse than me. Can't let a thing go.' He took another of my cigarettes. 'Nah, so, this is, like, two nights ago. Source calls me. Gang member. Nice guy.' The bottle sloshed. 'And so this guy, he asks me how I've been. *Where* I've been, too. And so I just spill, right?'

'Oh, shit.' My voice sounded hollow.

Carlos did his one-shoulder shrug, but it looked like an electric shock. He said, 'My guy, he tells me to get my guitar. Come back across the border. Make it look like I got rehears-als. Go walk past the first Starbucks I see.'

'Which is what you did.'

Carlos nodded slowly, his eyes aimed at nowhere.

'And boom. There they are,' he said. 'The Federales who jumped me.' He took out his phone and held up a picture of a police-car windscreen frosted with bullet holes. Just below, on the bonnet, lay two Federales, shot to mince.

Carlos circled one of the faces. 'See? Wrestler beard.' He swiped shut his phone. 'My guy shot them. Favour for all the stories I did, I guess.'

'Nice guy,' I said, my breath hot in my chest. What I was feeling, you couldn't call it fear, or want – envy, maybe, or whatever word there is for that feeling when you're not sure if you want somebody or just want to *be* them.

'So now you can go back?'

Carlos huffed out a laugh. 'Nah, nah, my mother'd be scraping up hot chunks of son from the fucken Avenida de las Américas within, like, ten minutes.' Carlos stared out at the sky's frozen orange slush and shook his head. 'If I could go anywhere? I'd go south. Uruguay. This hotel there, me

56

and my mother, we stayed there when I was a kid. Some fellowship deal she got to Buenos Aires – art thing. She's into all that, painting, sculpting, video, the whole bit. But the Porteños were all assholes, so we got ourselves a ferry across the bay. Country life, you know? Cycling. Forest walks. The beach. Yeah, that's where I'd go. Take all my pictures. Print 'em all out, shred 'em, and file them into the surf.'

'What's stopping you?' I leaned over and cracked my second beer.

He scratched his jaw. 'Doing the photos thing too long, I guess. I'd miss it.'

My arms tensed. 'You could work from Mexico City. Far from here. Who'd care? I mean, you know, I'm just starting out, articles-wise,' I said. 'But we could do some work or whatever, like, together.'

He frowned. 'But this is for a big paper, though, right?'

'Uh, yeah. Maya slung me the gig. It's. Well. It's my first article.'

Carlos leaned forward for another cigarette. 'You got others planned?'

'Oh, yeah,' I said, and cringed at the new-kid shine in my voice. 'Tons.'

Carlos poked a loose thread with his toe. 'And so, Mexico City. You think you could find me a place there?'

'Think so. A friend and her boyfriend, they're looking for somewhere new.' I had electric eels swimming laps in and out between my ribs. 'Want me to call them?'

He walked to the window. The cigarette between his fingers had burned past the writing. He didn't notice.

57

'Do you want to?' he said, looking at me.

'Well, yeah.' I didn't even think. I just started tapping on my phone. 'I'll say you're a friend.'

'Yeah.' I could feel his eyes on me. 'Yeah, you tell them that.'

9

The morning after that acid memory, red early, I stood in the cool brown perma-dark of the Capilla de la Inmaculada Concepción, breathing in lilies and busted plumbing.

The only sound was from a man in a cheap suit, shuffling on his knees from one altar to the next, the straps of an old Wilson rucksack hanging slack and frayed from his shoulders. When he arrived at a chapel off the nave, he stopped in front of a statue of Jesus swaddled in purple, bleach-white dust stuck to his bloodied face, a distant look on his face that you might translate as '*This has gotten out of hand*'. Then the guy in the suit crossed his hands across his face like he couldn't bear to look, murmured a prayer of thanks for his family, his safety, his home.

State I was in, shivering in the post-acid throes, that made me blink back tear-sting and look over to where an older nun whispered prayers as she relaid candles on a brass tray in front of a Pietà. Mary's upcast tearless eyes and outstretched arms morphed to become Carlos' mother, Veronica, carrying his body in her arms.

'Quit shaking,' I hissed at my hands, 'people are watching.'

Four pews in front of me knelt a hefty shaven-headed *cholo* type, a Tupac blackletter chest-piece showing through the scoop of his vest, his shut eyes aimed towards the risen Christ on his wire above the altar, his face a warm gone dream of peace. When the security guy's shuffling made him sit up they exchanged smiles before lapsing back into their devotions.

Elbows on the pew, my face in my hands, I counted breaths through my fingers until Maya slid in beside me and slung an arm around me.

'There she is,' I said, returning the hug.

A shaft of moted light cut through a gap in the church doors.

'I keep thinking,' she said, breaking the hug, 'that he's going to walk through that door, any second now, giving us both the finger.' She dabbed a Kleenex at the corners of her eyes and offered me one.

'Nah, I'm good.' I stood up on legs whose tendons felt frayed. 'Shall we?'

Maya adjusted the pristine strap of her JanSport and looked up at me for a second. When she saw that I wasn't going to stop, she slid out of the pew and followed me to the door.

Outside, the hot draught of a bus hit me full in the face. Even at this hour on a Saturday, the street was busy with mothers toting loads up from the Mercado San Juan, shoe-shine boys jogging for change, teenage beggars whose eyes were a stun of paint-thinner.

'You sleep at all?' Maya said, as we crossed to where I'd parked outside a tall hotel built of blood-colour tezontle stone.

'Last time I slept, Carlos was still —' I swallowed '— well, you know.' My reflection in the bonnet had burned-out zeros for eyes.

'I should have brought coffee.' Maya sat into the passenger's side.

'Oh, there's plenty here.' I swiped a couple of styrofoam cups out of her way.

She tucked her elbows close to her sides. 'God. How did it end up like this?' She kicked a cup from under her feet and a brown dribble snaked onto the carpet. 'I mean, like, I *breathe*, yeah? And I hear something spill.'

'Just drink some of it, honestly,' I said. 'It's mostly fresh.'

The jeep's tyres sizzled through last night's drench. You could feel the Centro's collective hangover seeping down out of the soaked grey air.

'Am I OK to park this up where we're going?' I asked.

'On your own? No,' said Maya. 'With me? Yeah.'

Couples from the gay bars and punk clubs and mariachi cantinas off Plaza Garibaldi huddled in around the tamal sellers' steaming buckets, the bags under their eyes deep enough to carry the whole neighbourhood's empties.

'And so this gun guy,' I said. 'How come you're so tight?'

'He liked the story,' she said. 'Said I made him sound like Scarface crossed with Juan Gabriel.'

My tyres crunched over a Bacardi bottle. Mopeds zipped ahead of us, quick as hornets. Orchids nodded before a Saint Jude shrine. Vendors hollered prices from every stall, kids' bikes, life-size teddy bears, four-foot bongs. Through my open window a voice asked me in rapid English if I wanted weed, coke, ice, whatever. The frantic slam of reggaeton rose from the pink-walled *vivienda* across the road, mixed in with yells and laughs from the *tianguis* market workers roping tarps into place. Sudsy water slapped out of buckets. Brushes rasped. Our bumper nudged a couple of slow walkers.

Maya leaned toward the window in her seat. 'Third fruit shop on the left.'

Beside a lamppost stood a six-foot shrine to Santa Muerte; roses dried to rust in the tequila and cognac bottles at her feet, a worshipper in a dirty vest standing before her, his eyes shut, clasped hands dappled pink from a crack-cook gone awry, lips moving as he put flame to what smelled like White Widow mixed with good tobacco, drawing a chestful of smoke and exhaling his prayer.

Maya cuffed me on the shoulder. 'Buck up, love. It's the weekend.'

Hip-hop rippled from a taco-stall where a big cheery kid chopped out *carnitas* for a couple of worse-for-wear bank-clerk types, his big cleaver thocking out a staccato cross-beat against his stereo's frantic slam, tipping out halved lemons onto the two guys' plastic plates with a gag about *panochas* that made all three of them roar. Under the taco-stand vitrine stood rows of glossy pigs' ears, steamed brains, thick cables of fried entrails. My stomach flipped fully over.

'Park here,' said Maya. 'This fruit shop here, with the nice sign.'

With the acid still firing my synapses, the sign's halved pineapples, split mangoes, and bad grin of watermelons all blurred into Julián Gallardo's lipless face.

Maya checked her phone. 'He says he'll be a minute. Let's go eat, yeah?'

'Cool.' The handbrake jerked back with a breaking-neck sound. *Fractured hyoid bone*, said Teresa's voice again in my head.

Maya found us a quesadilla stall around the corner from the fruit shop. This side of the street was easier on my head, mellow with chatter, cooking-smoke, the rich gold odour of vegetable oil.

'They make the Metro free, to keep the traffic down, and the pollution down,' said the old woman who owned the stall, spooning *tinga de pollo* onto ovals of dough that she slid into a pan of oil so hot that little drops pinged against the tin. 'Makes the Metro too full to get on board. And how can I feed my boys if I can't get on board?'

'You should go on strike, *señora*,' said one of the kids, taking his cap off to adjust his hair.

The TV news above her stall showed a body found in a canal. A girl on a gurney dragged across the screen, her forehead bulged and sallow from the water.

The kids' quesadillas were ready. They watched, ate, said nothing.

Maya leaned forward, spooned salsa verde onto her plate then dipped the fried end of her quesadilla. 'You want one?'

The news ticker read '*Between twenty and thirty bodies have been hauled from the canal.*'

'Nah, I'm good.' I watched the kids watching us.

'Couldn't eat all yesterday,' she said, frowning at the

63

quesadilla before taking a small bite. 'Like there was a ball in my stomach.'

'It's all right,' I said, rubbing her shoulder. 'What's it you said to me yesterday? Even if you don't want to, just eat something.'

'I guess,' she said.

'Here,' I gestured to the vendor. 'I'll eat one if you do.'

On the corner, at a red-striped DVD stall, a vendor sat in a blue haze of smoke, his mouth cat-arsed around a joint. One of the leaflets caught the light: three sleek bald athlete types plugging a tiny blonde girl. Apart from the wares, that stall and its red-and-white striped tarp could have been the one where me and Carlos used to buy European arthouse bootlegs to watch on the old brown couch at his apartment. My thoughts were nearly fully back in those days – cigarette smoke knitting in the light through his blinds, drinks in our hand – when Maya held out a can of Coke bought from the vendor.

'You OK there?' she said.

'Just thinking,' I said, cracking the can open. 'About this guy Carlos found. Over around those dodgy stalls. What he was doing there, I'll never know. But he found, like, snuff porno, you know?'

Maya shook her head. 'He had such lovely friends.'

'Yeah. But the stall guy, right? He told Carlos that one time, this customer turned up. Stocked up by the fistful. Couldn't believe his luck. The sickest, most repugnant crap he could ever dream of, all in one place. Takes the DVDs home. Pops the first one on. Unzips, or whatever, I don't know.' I swirled the can and took a sip. 'And what pops up?'

64

Maya grimaced. 'Do I want to know?'

I shook my head. 'Some Adam Sandler shite. Stall guy sold him an armful of duds.'

'And he didn't ask for his money back?'

'What, would you?' I said. '"Excuse me, sir, I paid for DVDs of sex murders, but was not given the DVDs of said sex murders"?'

'That is exactly what I'd say,' Maya said. 'Yes.' A door opened in the shuttering of the fruit shop and a man wearing a black vest leaned out to give Maya a friendly wave, cords of muscle rippling his arms. With his wizened face and his blond-speedboat hair, he could have been a John Lydon puppet made out of leather.

'That's him,' said Maya, handing our plates to the vendor with a fifty-peso note.

'Maya, what a miracle,' said the guy in the vest as we reached the shutter. His voice was cotton-soft. He patted her cheek. 'Gosh, you look so thin. Is everything all right?'

'More or less.' She wavered her hand back and forth in the air. 'Hey, so, Osito, here's the guy I told you about, yeah?'

'Andrew.' I shook his hand. 'Thanks for this.'

Osito ran his eyes down me. 'Where'd you get this one?' He cuffed me on the shoulder. It was only a tap, but the play-punch knocked me off-balance. 'Come on in.'

'Look at these.' I hefted an avocado that I took from one of the creosote-darkened wood shelves. 'Absolute units.'

'Stop by whenever you like.' Osito lifted a box of apples to the counter. 'Give me a hand?' He held an egg box out to me. 'Put this on the shelf behind you, please.'

When I turned back around, Osito was unwrapping newspaper from a snub-nosed black .38.

'That's not the one you sold me,' Maya said.

'No, that was a Five-Seven,' he said. 'This is a Smith & Wesson Bodyguard. Five shots, light as a feather. Little laser-sight. Switch is on top of the stock.' A red line caught motes from the dark air.

'Looks like a water-pistol,' I said, watching the targeting dot come to rest on a papaya's fat hip. 'Is that plastic?'

Osito's fingernail tinked against the frame. 'Aluminium. I'll show you the basics, OK?' He pressed a switch behind the cylinder and it dropped out, then handed me the pistol by the stock, the barrel barely clearing my thumb. 'Double-action, no hammer, so it won't snag in your pocket.' An oily smell tacked to my fingers, same as I'd get from the machines in my grandad's carpentry workshop.

'Clean, too,' said Osito. 'You get caught, serial number leads as far as a Walmart in Texas, six years ago, so you won't be done for anything but an illegal firearm.'

'And the penalty for that?'

Osito's laugh was bright, clear. 'Let the cop keep the gun.'

The grooved plastic guard was snug in my hand. 'Lighter than my phone.'

'Probably more durable, too,' said Osito. 'A fourteen-year-old could use it.'

'I'm sure they do.' I aimed the laser sight at a photo of the Club América 2010 line-up that hung on the wall. 'This is so new to me. I only know rifles. Shotguns. For rabbits, pheasants. Things like that.'

'Same principle,' said Maya. 'Point and shoot.'

'Well. Kind of,' I said. I'd only seen one person shot in front of me, outside Ensenada, where fishermen were often pressed into service as smugglers. While I was interviewing one of them, a guy sitting at the bar got into an argument with someone else, pulled out his gun, and dropped it right into the lap of the man he was shouting at, then got himself popped in the top of his skull, the blast tipping his eyes from their sockets like two poached eggs.

Osito walked back behind the counter, collected two resealable kilo bags of Café Garat, and opened them. 'Forty-grain, full metal jacket, you even graze somebody with this, and you'll break his arm.'

'Lead-free, too,' said Maya. 'For your health.'

'I don't want to know how you know that,' I said. With a flick of my wrist I flipped shut the cylinder of the gun and slid it into my bag with the coffee-bags of bullets. 'Time to pay you, I think.' I reached for my wallet.

Osito thumbed through the notes. 'Grab some avocados, too, if you like.'

'Ah, seriously?' I picked out six. 'I'm definitely coming back here.'

'Anytime.' Osito wrapped the avocados for me, then pulled me in for a hug, gave me a kiss on the cheek. 'Take care of yourself, now, won't you? Maya says you've had a tough bit of news. If you need us to sort something out, you know where to come. Here is your house.'

What I wanted to say was, 'As soon as I get those names, I will be right here.'

But Maya cut across me. 'Andrew's not going to need that. See you soon.'

'Well, OK.' He gave her a hug and a kiss, and then we stepped back out into the street, where the teenagers from the quesadilla stand were waiting by our jeep.

One gave us a wary nod and said, 'We watched your car for you, man.' He tugged the brim of his cap forward.

'Ah, thanks, buddy.' I held out ten pesos. 'Much appreciated.'

'Nah, friends of Osito's, man?' he said, waving away the coin. 'They're always welcome round here.'

Getting into the car, I dropped the avocados in Maya's lap.

'Late Christmas present,' I said, like that weak line might set off the kind of banter we'd already be locked in if nothing was the matter, if Carlos was still here, if I hadn't just bought a fucking gun.

But Maya just opened the bag, looked inside, frowning a little, and said, 'This is a lot.'

Passing through the *colonia* Obrera, down a street of lilac- and turquoise-walled hip-hop clubs shuttered for the day, a mural across one that showed an old-style mariachi serenading a skeleton girl under tapering gold cursive that read *AL SON QUE ME TOCAN BAILO*, Maya asked, 'What time you going to the funeral?'

The question went through me like a pin. 'Wait, what?'

Maya pulled a face like she'd seen a nasty football tackle. 'Oh. So his mother didn't say.'

'My God,' I said. 'Like, OK, so she and I, we don't get on, or whatever –' I flipped the indicator so hard that it waggled '– but *this*?'

Maya squirmed in the seat, and said, 'Yeah, well, don't tell her I told you, but tomorrow at noon, in that big cemetery on Constituyentes.'

'Huh.' I cut past a pesero bus that shuddered with a cumbia bassline.

'She's upset, yeah? People get strange when they're upset.'

The purple lights of a European off-licence broke over the windscreen. For the first time in a long time they looked warm to me, inviting.

'I'll say,' I said.

Slowing onto the concourse outside her apartment, Maya patted the bag of avocados, and said, 'You want to take these?'

'You don't want them?' I said. 'I thought we could make something.'

Last night's acid intake was a crack in my sobriety, sure, but it was like the ding gone out of my Aviators – only a big deal if I thought about it. Cracking and hitting the off-licence, though, that'd be like smushing those Aviators underfoot. Staying at Maya's would have kept me away from that, I knew, but she was ashen tired.

'Ah, never mind,' I said. 'We could both do with a rest.'

'I don't think I could eat even one of these,' she said, looking into the bag. 'Feels so weird, you know? Moving on with stuff. While Carlos is in a fridge somewhere.'

My hand found her shoulder again. Hers was less bony than his, but I gave her the same squeeze as I'd have given him. 'Sorry for today. Dragging you out. Last thing you needed.'

Maya lingered with her legs half-in, half-out of the car, rolling a Starbucks cup with her foot. She shrugged. 'Well, I don't want to lose both of you, do I?' She leaned in to hug me goodbye, and said, 'Yeah, you need that sleep, right enough. I could shoot pool-balls down those pupils. What you *do* last night?'

'Reminisced,' I said. 'Heavily.'

'Right,' she said, with a doubtful look. 'Well, don't *reminisce* too hard then tonight, yeah? Big day tomorrow.'

'Yeah, I promise,' I said, then left, my arm around the back of Carlos' seat same as when he used to sit there, driving home under a towering grey sky.

10

The handful of breakfasts I'd had with Carlos' mother over the years had been tense, memories that made me shiver as hard as anything I'd seen that week. Needing bodies between me and her, I got to the funeral as late as I could, and arrived to a packed chapel. In the cool marble dimness of the crematorium, down the back, watching other reporters' cameras flicker over Carlos' coffin, I basked in the mammal warmth of the crowd. Beside the lectern stood an A2 photo of Carlos framed in orange and purple crêpe paper flowers. The picture was his byline photo: dark sunglasses, black leather jacket, his hair wavy and shoulder-length, and his trademark fish-hook grin.

Carlos' mother stood before the mic. 'I had to ask the agency for this picture, you know. Two photographers, and we took hardly any pictures together – probably we were too busy just *being* together, mother and son.'

You could hear people sobbing in the gaps between Veronica's words.

Veronica shook her head. 'My son, the photographer, and

71

this is the only one I have of him. And I had to get it from the papers.' She laughed gently. 'This is my lesson from all this. Take pictures of your loved ones while you still can. You never know when there'll be no more pictures.' She shifted her posture and blew out a sigh. 'Mothering Carlos was the best job I ever had – and the toughest, too. He had his beliefs. I had mine. And we spent thirty years of dinners arguing about them. Breakfasts, too, if there was a stone left unturned on his side. Plus, sometimes, he'd duck home at lunchtime to finish a dispute begun earlier.'

A laugh rippled the congregation, fading as her face grew serious.

'My son brought me so much pride. His daring, his courage, his willingness to take a stand where others fell to their knees,' she said, her Vermont accent poking holes in the Spanish words.

My eyes moved across the congregation to where a Mater Dolorosa stood in the corner, her face pleading through her black lace veil.

'I can't separate my pride from the pain I feel today. Not just because his pain was my pain. Not just because the wounds to his dignity hurt me as much as his loss. No – it's because the very thing that makes me proud of him – that daring, that tenacity, that courage – has led him no further than here.'

Maya turned in her chair and caught my eye, gave me crease-mouthed smile.

'My son's murder,' said Carlos' mother, 'is a case of power learning the mistakes of history with the aim of repeating them.'

That drew applause further up the chapel from a couple of journalists I knew, rising towards the maple rafters, catching echo from the marble, all the way to where I leaned against the wood-panelled back walls.

As the applause faded, Veronica set her jaw and glared at me through the red frames of her glasses.

'We don't know who killed my son yet,' she said. 'We may never know.'

The air was thick with cloying smells: lilies, mid-range aftershave, shoe-polish, fresh dry-cleaning.

Veronica pointed at the photograph. The smile was back on her face now. 'But we know what has to happen when the state, or a cartel, or whoever, tries to silence their critics. The people have to pick up the noise where their dead left off.'

The applause started again now, a sound of waves rushing. From the speakers came the green wash of organ chords – some generic sad classical thing. When I took a last quick look over my shoulder the coffin was rolling up along a short conveyor-belt towards the elevator that would take it down to the oven, and I slipped out of there, dodging past a guy in a shirt, tie and bike-shorts, standing on the steps, squinting into the noon glare and the red light of a BBC video-camera.

The tombstones wore black stains like tear-run mascara. I headed for the shade of yew and cypress, because, from there, I'd be able to see all of the chimney from which Carlos' smoke would be appearing any second now. At my feet stood a San Judas Tadeo statue, serene in his green robes, a flame quiff above his head, his eyes aimed up at the clouded-out heavens.

'Easy for you to be chill,' I told the statue.

The saint eyed my cigarette like he fancied a drag.

Then Carlos' thread of smoke frayed up from the crematorium, and I slid down the tombstone, knocked over the candles and dry dead roses, and sat in a mess of bird-of-paradise flowers, the base of my skull pressed against the headstone while I waited for a crying jag that wouldn't come, not even when Carlos' smoke rose and scattered.

Maybe it was that whole mutant heart thing he and I had shared, the same trait that had made him talk to the bodies he'd photograph, the same trait that had made me pin Julián Gallardo's face to my noticeboard, and drop acid instead of properly remembering him, and go buy a pistol instead of going home.

Maybe that's why my eyes stayed dry as his smoke petered down to a pale grey line that the wind erased. Part of me wanted to tell him that I was going to get whoever it was who had put him there, but I suspected he knew anyway.

When there was none of him left, I just loosened my tie and got out of the cemetery before anybody could see me, as a gust blew the smoke over the chapel eaves, greying the backs of my shoes.

II

Friday nights, a big scattering of us foreign correspondents would get together at a yellow-lit *cantina* in La Condesa. The older hands, the veterans, the superstars, they sat at the head of the table, pucking war stories back and forth from behind a thickening cluster of shot glasses and beer bottles, while, right at their elbows, sat the new hacks, all anxious attention. My first time coming here was when Maya brought me, to celebrate the Carlos interview and talk me up to editors, meaning my seat was at the middle of the table, where the freelancers swapped contacts and tips and brags across a thinner cluster of cheaper drinks.

When I walked in that night, though, it was like someone had pressed pause on the shop-talk and tipsy hand-gestures. After a beat of silence people raised their glasses, nodded their 'Hello's, went back to talking with the volume down just a notch. Me, I did the handshake rounds of the table, gave the usual stilted questions – 'How are you feeling, are you OK, what's new' – my usual stilted answers – 'I don't know, I don't know, I don't know' – and took my chair beside Maya.

'Evening, Reservoir Dogs,' she said, plucking the sleeve of the suit I'd forgotten to change out of. 'Thought you'd be at home.'

'Yeah, well, I needed some background noise.'

On the TV above the table the news was looping footage of the scene outside Carlos' apartment: UNAM kids laying candles, a couple of local journalists I knew holding up signs that read 'FUE EL ESTADO', the head of the Artículo 19 press freedom NGO talking into the microphone.

'Great choice of background noise,' said Maya.

'Yeah, well,' I said, swirling my glass.

A couple of young kids – boy and a girl, early twenties, American – were whispering and trying not to point at me, so I gave them my darkest scowl.

'More of these every month,' I said, loud enough for them to hear. 'More reporters than English teachers around here, I swear.'

'Andrew,' said Maya.

I ignored her. 'War on drugs, great for the C.V.'

The girl looked furious, the guy looked embarrassed, just like I'd wanted.

'Oh, they'll forgive me,' I said. 'They'll want my contacts.'

Maya shook her head.

'Don't know how you're still on the water,' said Pau from CNN beside me. 'Given the circumstances.' She raised her cognac and Coke. 'To Carlos.'

'To Carlos.' We clinked glasses.

Then everyone was doing that – Bloomberg and the *Financial Times*, the *Daily Mail* and *VICE*, the *Wall Street Journal* and the *Dallas Morning News*, arms raised above the table like the rafters of a building. People clinked glasses as if they were shaking hands at the end of Mass. The kids I'd dissed, they took a second, but then they joined in, too, and I gave their glasses a knock just to be nice.

After the toast ended a brief hush dropped and a couple of people stole glances at where I was sitting, like I might be about to make a speech or something, but I just watched the bubbles pop in my water and asked Maya if she wanted a cigarette.

'If it stops you picking fights, yes.'

When we slipped out a couple of friends of mine were leaned up against the wall: Jon, an Iraq War vet turned photographer, and Sadiq, one of the *New York Times* guys. They offered condolences, cigarettes. I accepted both.

Sadiq clapped me on the back. 'You OK, brother?'

'It's fucked up as fuck,' said Jon. 'One of ours.'

'They're all one of ours,' I said, and turned the cigarette between my fingers.

'Don't know how you're keeping it together,' said Sadiq. 'Man, in Afghanistan, when the journalists' bar got shot up that time? Didn't know what to do.'

'Ah, sure, what can you do.' The wheel of my lighter turned, sparking, under my thumb.

All around, the bloody neon thud of Friday night echoed out of the clubs on Calle Tamaulipas. Cop cars prowled the curb while six-year-olds in faded clothes hawked sweets and single cigarettes all along the bar terraces. Buffets of smoke rose up into the humid night.

'You want another water?' said Jon. 'I'm gonna grab a drink.'

'I'm all right.'

'Well, don't get too hedonistic, anyway.' He cuffed me on the arm as he headed back in the door. 'Hang in there.'

'So weird,' said Maya, 'Never seen him earnest before.'

'I'm glad we all were here for that,' said Sadiq.

Behind us, back inside the *cantina*, the chatter and laughter was back up at the usual volume. The thronged empties gleamed.

My eyes drifted back towards the jeep. Sadiq gave me another meaty slap on the back without breaking eye-contact with Maya, and that was all I needed.

'I'm gonna get rolling,' I said, when I couldn't resist the pull of the flask any longer. 'Head's not really at the races.'

'Bring it in, bro.' Sadiq clapped me in a bear hug. 'See you next week, yeah?' A gale of laughter came buffeting out through the door as he went back inside.

'Background noise get too loud?' said Maya when I went to hug her.

'Ear-bleeding,' I said.

'Well, how about a coffee?' she said, poking at the step to the *cantina* with her toe. 'I don't know. Today was hard.'

'It was.' With my finger I whipped my key ring around in circles. 'But yeah, let's do it. I know a place. Let's do some brainstorming or whatever.'

In the car, driving along Avenida Insurgentes, Maya dropped her window and let her hand ride the buffets of rain-cooled air. Headlights swept past, flaring to white, while an inane house playlist rattled my gun inside the glove compartment.

'Here we go,' I said, and parked across the road from the Ángel de la Independencia monument, its tall pillar lit up purple. Shimmers of chrome light flowed along the windscreen. The tarmac shone like oil.

'What? Where?'

'Right there.' I pointed at the 7/11.

'You sure know how to treat your friends,' she said.

When I'd picked up the coffee and doughnuts Maya was standing with her laptop propped on the bonnet of my car, the draught of cars flicking her hair. She looked up when she heard me unwrap the doughnuts.

'Your diet, man,' she said. 'It's a colonic tumour waiting to happen. Or else an ulcer.'

'I'm trying for twins, actually.' I offered her half a doughnut.

She wrinkled her nose. 'No way. The sugar in those, you know what it is?'

'Aspartame,' I read from the packet. 'And?'

'Aspartame,' Maya said, opening her laptop and leaning it on the jeep bonnet, 'is science for embalming fluid.'

'So I'll have lovely young guts.' I dunked the doughnut. 'How is that bad?' I swiped open my iPad, Julián Gallardo's skinless face appeared on the screen. The crickets pulsing in the trees grew shrill.

'That the kid you found?' said Maya.

'That he is.'

An elderly jogger nodded to us on his lap of the roundabout. Other than that, we were alone: all the action was happening on Calle Genova a few blocks away, gleeful yawps, yellow blats of banda music.

'You find anything else about him, then?' Maya asked.

'Bits and pieces,' I said, reopening a bunch of tabs. 'Like, he's tagged in a whole lot of pictures from protests, but other than that he's just another kid. Second-year student at the engineering school.' I turned the screen to show Maya a picture of Julián with his arm around a man in a cowboy hat and a woman with dyed red hair, the lush stretch of ferns and mandarin trees behind them shadowed by the orange flame of a burner.

'Sad picture,' said Maya. She tapped the caption. '"Two years since we took this photo",' she read '"Missing you every day, Dad".'

'Shit. I didn't see that.'

She gave me a backward nod. 'Anything else?'

'Just bits,' I said, opening a local news portal with photos of students and housewives standing shoulder to shoulder, toting placards that read 'MÉXICO NO SE VENDE', and oil workers carrying banners and yelling.

'Nothing special here,' Maya said, then pinched the screen to zoom in on the placards. 'Wishy-washy. You see it at every oil protest.'

'These guys, though.' I dragged the screen across to the placard that read 'AJENJO ASESINO'. 'They're not popular, from what I could gather.'

'They do OK in the business pages,' Maya said, tapping through an image-search of front pages from the past few months, all of them showing a grey-haired man in a suit with a large, well-trimmed moustache, captioned with the name Roberto Zúñiga. She nicked a doughnut.

'"The architect of Mexico's second oil miracle?"' I read. 'Huh.'

On my iPad I flipped to a picture of someone at the protest holding a sign that showed Julián Gallardo's student-card photo above the words 'WHERE IS HE?'

'Hey, this is something,' said Maya, reading aloud from a quote in the article I'd sent Dominic: '"*Poza Rica went from being a field to an oil capital in thirty years. Most of the region hasn't caught up. It's war out here, and indigenous mandarin growers are the ones losing*". Think about it.' She counted on her fingers. 'A darling of the Mexican oil industry rents fracking gear to multinationals. A bunch of indigenous folks being kicked off their land. A dead kid.' She grabbed her pinkie. 'And now Carlos.'

'Run it by me,' I said, kicking a rat-looted corn-cob from one foot to the other.

Maya shrugged. 'You know how it is here. Wherever there's mineral resources, there's a shit-ton of crime. Guerrero, you have the gold. San Luís, silver.'

'And Veracruz has oil,' I said.

Maya nodded. 'And it's the same shit everywhere, right? Government and companies and gangs terrorise people until they let in the miners or the frackers or whoever.'

In my head I saw Carlos holding up the gun and the cigarettes, telling me how politicians and cops and gangsters had held his entire city to ransom.

'Fuck,' I said.

'Indeed,' said Maya, as she studied the smoke ring she had blown.

My hands were clamped to the side of my head. 'That brings the state in. And foreign companies. Big story. What proof do we need, do you think?' I said.

Maya frowned, tapping her foot. 'Well, like, death squad stuff. Infiltration. Zetas in uniform. Protests. Crackdowns.' She waved a hand. 'All that good stuff.'

The elderly jogger finished his lap of the roundabout and curved back towards Parque Chapultepec.

My next kick sent the corn-cob flying into the road. 'And all that proof died with Carlos.'

Maya tutted. 'You really think so?'

They broke his fingers, Teresa had told me.

I shrugged. 'Probably got it out of him, didn't they?'

Maya narrowed her eyes. 'They can't have gotten *all* of it, no?'

Twisted a chair off in him.

'Else you wouldn't be here,' said Maya.

'Fuck.' I pushed back my hair. 'What they did. He held up under all that.'

Maya nodded. 'He must have loved you or some shit.'

The howl of distant cars reached us. The jogger passed through the pools of yellow cast by the streetlights.

'If he was going to hide something for you,' said Maya, 'where would it be?'

Carlos standing by the foggy highway, twirling his Fidel Castro key ring, his USB stick whipping in circles.

'Not a clue,' I said, and reached into my jacket pocket for the receipt with Teresa's number.

Maya slung her arm around my shoulder. 'Something'll come to mind.'

'Maybe.' I heaved a fake sigh and looked up at the burnished gold angel on its pillar. Bells tolled out there somewhere. 'Want me to drop you home?'

'Nah.' Maya tapped on her phone. 'Like, there's an Uber literally around the corner.' A Prius slowed off the round-about, and she pulled me into a quick hug. 'Sleep tight, yeah?'

Before Maya had even shut the door the phone was at my ear. The dial-tone pulsed once.

'Who's this?' said Teresa, her voice hovering somewhere between tired and suspicious.

'Hey, yeah, it's Andrew,' I said. 'The journalist – we met at Mineria 45.'

'Ah, right.' I heard an office chair sinking backwards. 'Well, can I help?'

'Well, how do I say this?' I swallowed. 'I want to get into the apartment.'

'Shouldn't be a problem. Scene's been declared open. Clean-er's going in tomorrow. The landlord wants a new tenant in before the story sticks to the place.' Her office chair's wheels rumbled on the floor. 'But the cleaner's a good man. I'll tell him you want – what, exactly? Some memento?'

'Yeah,' I said. 'A jacket.'

'That's fine,' she said. 'I mean, Lucio, the cleaner, he just puts things in bags. Doesn't go through people's wardrobes or anything: it all goes in the bag.'

'Yes.' I sucked a breath through my teeth for effect. 'God, I'd just be so worried the jacket might be thrown out.'

'That's understandable,' she said. 'He won't mind. Just be at the scene at –' I heard the chair creak as she craned backwards '– well, let's say eight o'clock tomorrow, OK? And I'll talk to him before that. Arrange something. Take care now.'

'Thanks, Teresa,' I said, but she'd already hung up, leaving me with the smell of rain-wetted tarmac in my lungs and a wind chasing dead jacaranda leaves past my feet.

12

The remains of my nails were long bitten away by the following evening, sitting outside Mineria 45, by a doorstep that was already a shrine: spatters of candle-wax, stiff brown wreaths, photos of Carlos that had already started to warp. Someone had chalked the words 'IT WAS THE STATE' on the pavement. The yelp of kids playing and the tinny sound of workout music travelled from an outdoor gym class happening in the park one block over. The air was mellow with the odour of warm tortillas, their steam rising towards the window that had once been Carlos'. Soon, all that was left of him would be rinsed from the floor, squashed into bags, and wrestled into a dumpster. Then that square of light would belong to somebody else.

Car headlights' halogen cones cut the gloom, and I counted them while ashing into a quarter-empty Oxxo coffee that stood in the passenger door, until finally a black Jetta slowed down to park outside. A tall man got out, wearing a beige raincoat over a black suit and red tie, his black leather shoes shining like his car bonnet didn't.

'Señor Andrew?' His accent's postcode read either north inner-city Mexico City or Estado de México.

'Lucio, how're you doing?' I said. 'Thanks for your help.'

His crew-cut was neat and grey, his shave clean, and he carried his bodyguard's physique like he wanted to be smaller, and his handshake was a bodyguard's too. With a sideways nod towards the building, he took a packet of Montana High-Tars from his pocket, and said, 'First time at a murder scene?'

I scuffed the *FUE EL ESTADO* chalkmarks with the toe of my boot. 'Not even my first time at *this* murder scene.'

His eyes were a timid, steady gleam when I turned towards him. There was something gentle in him, I figured, or perhaps just broken.

'Well, my condolences, then,' he said. He struck a match, nested the flame, and wiped his fingers on a tissue. 'Up there, the killers were professional. Two affected rooms, no carpets, no humidity. A lot of tissue, but it's localised. So, a fast operation.' His voice was cottony with cigarette smoke. 'Two hours to clean, I should say.' His eyes scanned the street, back and forth, again and again, and he took a toothpick from a paper sheath, slid the tip under the pristine half-moons of his nails, chasing dirt-flecks only he could see. He looked at one of the buckled photos on Carlos' makeshift shrine. 'It's a hard thing, grief. But a cleaning can be beautiful. You'll see,' he said. Smoke clouded from his mouth, then he chucked his cigarette and popped open the boot of his car. 'Let me show you what we'll be using.'

Inside the car boot, a ventilator mask lay on top of a

disposable Hazmat suit beside a metal briefcase with a combination lock, which he clicked open to reveal four bottles with sprayer-heads laid in black foam. 'I make them.' He propped a bottle on one end. Petrol-colour liquid sloshed thickly. 'This one's for blood.' He tapped the bottle. 'Blood is dangerous. Even without the stain, you can still find HIV, tuberculosis, hepatitis live at a scene.' Lucio propped a second bottle on its end. 'Different events, different formulas. Where the heart is damaged, you'll find pericardial fluid.'

Teresa's words rang in my head. *Twice in the chest. Six impact points.*

Lucio propped a third bottle on its end. 'Because bullets cut through multiple tissues – blood, bone, viscera – you need to clean up multiple residues.' Now he lifted the fourth bottle. 'Scenes of torture and rape require formulas for semen, faecal matter . . .'

Broke a chair off in him.

When he saw my face, he cut himself off, scratching the back of his neck, then shut the boot and said, 'You still want to go inside?' The ventilator mask hung around his neck, and the Hazmat was balled under his arm.

All I could do was nod.

'OK. Well, let's get ready,' said Lucio, slotting a plastic scraper into one end of the mop handle.

One after the other he handed me a pair of blue cloth covers for my shoes, a pair of see-through polythene gloves, and a surgical mask on an elastic band.

'Don't put these on until you're inside,' Lucio said, sliding off his jacket and raincoat, loosening his tie, and climbing into his Hazmat. He fumbled for the keys. I took them from him and opened the door.

My stomach was a nest of rats as we climbed the stairs to Carlos' door. In the four years he'd lived there, I'd climbed up and down these stairs to greet dealers, to collect pizza, to clasp his light body in my arms when he met me at the door.

A pram rattled down the stairs above us, the mother and father laughing and talking about the restaurant they were off to. Lucio and I stood back as they passed, and the parents went quiet and looked right through us. The baby in the pram kept up its no-word chirping and craned around in the pram to point at Lucio, who smiled at her. Then Carlos' door was in front of us for the last time in my life.

'You can put the protection on now,' said Lucio, setting down his briefcase and shaking out his Hazmat.

By the time I'd pulled on the shoe-covers and gloves, and slung the surgical mask around my neck, Lucio had zipped himself into his Hazmat, his breath a Darth Vader gargle now through the ventilator mask. He turned the key in the lock, pushed open the door, and reached inside to turn on the light.

Like I said, death has dozens of smells, and I only know some. This one was sallow and warmish: the carbon dioxide fug given off by bacteria feeding in a closed space.

You could see where they'd shot him: black dots of coughed-out lung-blood specked the wall and floor, while the head-shot's comet-trail of brain matter streaked the floor, the legs of his two unmatching chairs, the floor by the sofa.

The brown leather sofa Carlos had rescued from the street,

where we'd sit with our films and our pizzas and our smokes, its springs so worn-out they were comfier than a mattress, that sofa was clad in a hide of blood.

Carlos, if you get this, they really went to town on your couch.

A broken-off chair-leg lay in the middle of the stain, its splintered end coated and dark and obscene.

That's what made my stomach jerk, and sent me running to the bathroom.

Only when the vomit came surging up my throat did I remember to get the mask off. Even then, it was just barely in time. For a long time I knelt there, with my forehead against the rim of the toilet. Rinsing my mouth at the sink should have made things better. But Carlos' hairs were caught there on the cracked ceramic, and I couldn't keep from swirling my fingers around them, gathering them up into a little spider-shape that I slid into my pocket. He hadn't replaced the lid of his VO5 hair wax, either, and so for a second I laid my fingers against the scoop-marks left by his fingers before screwing shut the lid.

Carlos, if you get this, you're still a complete slob.

I spent almost a minute huffing the ghost of his Armani Code shower gel and stale cigarette-smoke from his towel, and the remembered warm jumble of him under me was almost real, almost there.

From the sitting-room came a deep sound like a zip being pulled. When I walked back out, Lucio had slit open the sofa with a box-cutter, foam wadding from the cut like subcutaneous fat.

'The worst job I ever had,' he said, peeling away the outer

layer of the couch cushion, 'was in La Del Valle. Eight bodies. Robbery gone wrong. '

The leather covering slapped to the floor.

'Big house.'

On the table stood a stack of the seven-peso action-movie DVDs Carlos would pick up from the Calle Jesús Carranza a handful at a time, beside a bag of Red Dot and his scrolled brass hash-pipe. Pebbled rings left by bottles of Dos Equis criss-crossed on the smudged glass. A credit card had left broken chop-marks through white lines.

'In my head I saw what happened,' said Lucio. 'People running, falling. Throwing up their hands. You could nearly hear the screams just looking at the stains.'

In the kitchen, the microwave door was wide open, the dish pitted and ashy where they'd nuked his camera's memory cards.

Carlos, if you get this, you are gone, man.

'Here, though?' Lucio shook his head. 'Nothing. No self-defence injuries. One blood source. One attempt to escape.' With the scraper he pointed to a long, dragging hand-print beside a greyish scuff. 'Looks like he was smashing his phone.'

Delete this number.

'That's where they grabbed him in the chokehold.'

Blood thrummed in my ears.

Don't reply!

'And then.' Lucio shrugged, pointing to the big slick near the chairs. His face was stone.

Please.

'The stains are so localised,' said Lucio. 'Never seen a victim so calm.'

'Huh,' I said. 'So, you don't mind if I go look for something, then, no?'

Lucio whumped open a yellow plastic biohazard bag, his back turned to me. 'Go ahead,' he said. 'I didn't see anything.'

'That's "Yes" enough for me,' I said, and headed for Carlos' room, where the WiFi router still blinked green in the corner, and the Venetian blinds were all rucked where they'd slammed his head against the window. Even his bins had been turfed out: Hershey's wrappers and Frito packets glinted silver on the floor. One of the wardrobe doors lay in two halves, with his Hawaiian shirts, his jeans, his single grey three-piece suit pooled on top.

Carlos, if you get this, you left mondo ironing to do, man.

No desk, no bed, just a foam mattress and four pillows reefed open by serrated knives, and no laptop, iPad, phone, or cameras, either – not even his Kindle or e-cigarette, just a bunch of cables tapering out of the sockets like eels.

From the sitting room came the brief squizz of Lucio's spray bottle.

My phone buzzed with a low-battery screen so I crouched by an outlet, slotted in my phone charger, and nothing happened.

'Yeah, you've got a dud, right enough.'

Flicking the safety switch back on and off did nothing, so I pulled the charger from the wall. For a second I mooched around looking for another plug, but then my foot caught Carlos' Swiss Army knife lying beside the tangle of cables.

The Swiss Army knife was open.

At the other end of the hall water was rumbling into a plastic bucket.

The Phillips-head screwdriver was popped out.

Lucio glugged a bottle over the floor.

The screws in the wall-mount, they were the Phillips-head kind.

Carlos, if you get this, you're a genius.

My fingers shook when I started unscrewing the wall-mount, so much so that I had to switch hands more than once, but then the third screw dropped free, the lid of the wall-mount swung open part-way, and a black edge of gaffer-tape showed in the gap. When the fourth screw rattled to the floor, I fumbled inside to feel Carlos' Fidel Castro key ring taped to the inside, the USB stick swivelling in its sheath to rap my knuckles.

It's like Lucio said: A cleaning can be a beautiful thing.

With Carlos' leather jacket slung over one shoulder and his key ring in my fist, I made it back out to where Lucio stood gouging his scraper against a crust of blood and hair and shit and fingerprint dust, moisture-lines tracking the dark red, wetted chunks loosening to a brownish goop. Even through my mask the air had that cat-piss taste of ammonia.

'C'mere, Lucio,' I said. 'I think I've got what I need.' Fidel Castro's square metal beard cut into my hand when I shut my fist.

Lucio looked up, his ventilator fogged, his Hazmat suit sweated to a dark grey. The broken chair leg protruded from the yellow biohazard bag.

'I appreciate this.' I slipped off the mask and the shoe covers and the plastic gloves and dumped them in the bag beside the chair leg. 'Genuinely.'

He propped the scraper against the wall and gave me a mute thumbs-up. Our gloves squeaked when we shook hands. Then I left him in the smeared mess, slid on the jacket I'd found, and went back downstairs to the jeep, breathing in Carlos' smell of leather and cigarettes and too much aftershave.

13

Outside, the park had fallen quiet. Maya's *Last Online* WhatsApp status read 8.54 p.m. Now it was after eleven.

'Maya,' I said into a voice-note. 'You up?'

Two blue ticks. No reply.

Mineria 45's heavy brick, barred windows, and bank-safe door all scrolled to the edge of my mirrors and broke off into nowhere.

'Ah, Maya,' I said into the phone. 'Be sound. Call me back.'

Two more blue ticks as I passed the dreary row of blue-lit Chinese restaurants all along Revolución.

'C'mon,' I said into the phone. 'Just because I'm not one of your booty-calls.'

This time she called me back. 'I'm in my pyjamas, man.' Her voice was thick with sleep. 'Watching *las putas Gilmore Girls*.'

'That's OK,' I said. 'I'm overdressed, too.'

Her breath huffed static in my ear. '*No mames*. What's this about?'

'I'm coming from Carlos' place.'

Red-lit drops bled across the windscreen.

'*No chingues*,' said Maya. 'Really?'

'Yeah. I got in,' I told her. 'Found something. Memory stick.'

Maya said nothing. The tyres' drone rose to a whine against the blacktop.

'*Chin*,' she said at last. 'Well, you'd better come over, then, yeah?'

The fastest way to Maya's from here was along the forty-foot-high Segundo Piso highway. With the city lights like a spill of protozoa below me, and nothing but cold skyscraper lights all around, it was like driving through the sky.

'Want anything from the Oxxo?'

'I want to say "cigarettes" but it's healthier if I just steal yours.'

'Absolutely.' I switched to fifth gear and dropped down onto Universidad.

Maya must have let security know I was arriving, because, when I pulled on to the concourse of her building, there was this guard wearing a cheap suit over a quarterback's build, waiting to beckon me past the uplit palms, and onwards to a parking space. When I flashed him a thumbs-up in thanks, he gave me a cheery wave that revealed dental braces and the sleek bulge of a shoulder-holstered pistol. After I parked, he held the door open for me with a warm 'Good evening' and an orthodontic perma-smile. On the tablet in his hand I could see he'd been looking at a bunch of cat pictures on Pinterest, and, seeing that I'd seen, he swiped shut the screen to walk me to the lift.

When the doors pinged open on the fourth floor I stepped through smoke towards Maya's door, where she was waiting for me, outlined black against the light.

'*Que chingados, güey.*' She swatted at the smoke. 'In the lift?' She wore a maroon Adidas zip-up, men's pyjama bottoms, and a deep frown. A ballpoint pen wagged at the corner of her mouth. 'Couldn't wait till you got upstairs?'

The eco-friendly light bulbs in her sitting room were on full blast, a white-edged hum that set my left eyelid twitching.

'Whoa, are you wearing Carlos' jacket?' she said, taking a step back from me.

'You don't have a dimmer-switch, do you?' The hair I pushed back from my forehead was tailed with sweat and grease.

Maya dropped the lights to sepia. 'Better?'

'Little more.'

Shaking her head, she turned the room's sconce-lights down to the mellow red of a darkroom. 'Have a seat, yeah?' Maya handed me a glass of water and crossed to the white L-shaped couch, where she pulled a blue and purple floral Chiapaneco blanket over herself. Floor-to-ceiling windows looked out over the empty avenue.

'I don't know,' I said, running my hand over the butcher's-block kitchen counter. 'This place is all right.'

'Feel like I'm living in a lab.' From the maple coffee-table her laptop cast a clamshell of glow over her face. 'Haven't really unpacked.' She clicked her tongue and lifted her laptop onto her knees. 'Old place was home. This is just a place.'

One month before, Maya had published a story about a narco safe-house operating in a hip neighbourhood full of clubs and Americans. The day after, some guy had broken into her old place, left the shower on for hours, destroyed her ornamental vegan soaps, emptied her Moroccan hair oil down the toilet, and robbed not a thing. The following week, leaving her gym, some guy had pulled a gun on her beside her car. The headlights of a passing car had scared him away. Next day, she'd moved house.

'You cold?' she said.

'Hm?' I'd been hugging my shoulders, pressing myself deeper into Carlos' jacket. 'Oh. Yeah. Wee bit.'

'Your fault for weighing less than your own laptop.' Maya drew back the blanket and dialled down the brightness setting on her screen. 'Get under here.' She shut an open tab showing a pirate streaming site.

'Glad to see I've improved your evening.'

'Dramatically. Plug that USB in, yeah?'

When I did, a folder popped up on the screen: *I WOULD GIVE IT TO ANDY'S MOTHER.*

'Fuck's sake, Carlos,' I said.

'Let's see what dirt he's got on your mother, then,' said Maya, then pushed up her glasses and clicked open a photo of students and oil-workers, beat-down-looking field labourers, women and school kids, all gathered into one protest march, Mexican tricolours waving, their red and green sections dyed black, placards held up that read 'WHERE'S MY MONEY?', 'I CAN'T BREATHE', 'POZA RICA SE ESCRIBE CON "ZETA"', 'AJENJO = ASSASSINS', photographs of Julián Gallardo's I.D. photo. You could almost hear the crackle of loud-hailers, taste the smog on your tongue.

'That's a good one,' said Maya.

Carlos, if you get this, you're still the best.

In the next picture riot cops outnumbered protesters about six to one, their pulled-down visors and the sectioned shoulder plates of their armour throwing back the hot glare. A fleet of black Dodge RAMs stood parked among the police cars. A big guy with a long beard like a heavy-metal bass player leaned against the bonnet of one, his arms folded, wearing a black T-shirt and desert camouflage pants. Next came shots of heavy-set men just in front of the riot shields, with no uniform, no ski-masks: just crew cuts, machetes, the deadest of eyes.

'Oh, shit,' said Maya. 'What was it we said last night? About all the stuff you needed? Death-squad stuff? Infiltration?' She clicked through shots of those men in plainclothes running, the protest line buckling, students running, people falling to kicks, punches, coshes, swinging blades. 'Because Carlos has pretty much got it all here, yeah? You've got your crack-downs,' she said, and flipped from a pool of blood to a photo showing an arm in a policeman's uniform aiming a bloodied machete right at the camera. 'And this here, that machete – that's not police shit. That's narco shit. And the police are just letting him go right ahead and do it, in their clothes.'

The next image was zoomed out to show the guy holding the machete: light-skinned, balding, enormous. Carlos' photo had caught black drips of blood falling from the machete blade. A kid lay at his feet, clutching a dark stain on her jeans, right above her opened leg. His mouth was open in a yell of anger, and you could see silver caps on his incisors.

Maya lifted her hand to her mouth. 'You know who that

is?' She did a couple Google searches and opened a tab: a Veracruz State police mug shot, silver-capped teeth bared in a grin, and a name beneath that read Abel Carranza, '*Dientes de Tiburón*' – 'Sharktooth' in English.

'Huh.' I tapped a cigarette against the packet, said nothing about where I knew the face on the screen from.

Maya watched the cigarette.

'I'm not sure whether to offer or not.'

'*Va, pues, chingue su madre.*' She took a smoke and opened the next photo. Here, Sharktooth was dragging the girl with the opened leg behind the police line and barking an order at the riot police.

Maya shook her head and stooped to the lighter. 'So Carlos snapped one of Mexico's most violent men in a Veracruz State police uniform.'

'And ordering cops around,' I said.

'No wonder they killed him,' Maya said. 'It makes the company look bad, if they've got cops and narcos working together for them.'

My eyes were on the kid's face. Through the long hair fallen across her face you could see she was crying.

'You're shaking again,' said Maya, rubbing my shoulder.

The corner of my left eye jumped. 'You ever really want to sleep, and, like, also not want to ever sleep again?' I said, because I didn't want to tell her that Sharktooth was the guy I'd seen outside Carlos' place.

Maya made a crease of her mouth. 'Every night since moving here.' She spread her hands. 'Get you some camomile tea?'

'OK.' She squeezed my shoulder and crossed the kitchen. 'You go see what else he's got on that stick.'

'Some good stuff in there,' I said, clicking open four pages of news clippings about oil thefts, murders, kidnappings. 'Lots by this Francisco Escárcega guy.'

'He's good.' Maya put the kettle on. 'Email him.'

It always feels like you're imposing, when you contact people out of the blue like that, but whatever, I tapped out a draft, introducing myself as someone who'd been to Poza Rica before and was looking to learn more. As I was pressing 'Send', Maya handed me a cup and slid under the blanket.

'It was really fucked up in the apartment,' I said, my hands wrapped around my cup. 'I mean, we've both seen things. But – well, you know.'

'Never someone who mattered.' She put her sleeve to the corner of one eye. 'Fuck, man. Fuck these people.'

'I know.' I gave her another hug, but a quick one, because the smell in Carlos' apartment wouldn't leave my nose, and I was afraid it was tacking to me all over, that she'd breathe in all the stuff I'd had to see there.

She shook her head, pulling the laptop across. 'And there's so many of those bastards, too.' Her voice sounded clotted. 'That's the worst of it.' She opened a link for the Veracruz Attorney General's most-wanted list, a four-page spider diagram whose top photo showed a slim oval face captioned with the name Evelio Martínez and the nickname 'El Puccini'.

'This is the guy who runs Poza Rica,' she said, 'and these –' she ran her finger down the next row '– are the guys who help him do it. Some police who've switched sides, and some lawyers, accountants, union officials, guys like that.'

The names and photos blurred together as she scrolled down: a beefy, unshaven, black-haired guy, followed by a guy called 'El Mangueras' – pudgy, curly-haired, dark-skinned – and the tall, white guy with the beard who I'd seen leaning against the police car in one of Carlos' pictures. Then, last of all, with his silver grin and thinning hair, the guy I'd seen outside Carlos' apartment – Sharktooth.

Maya zipped all the way back up to El Puccini and tapped the screen. 'But this boss, yeah? He's the worst. Take a look.' She opened an old *Los Angeles Times* article capped by a picture of a soccer stadium, a leaden tropical sky swagging low above row after row of soldiers wearing jungle camo and red berets, lowering rifles to the grass while red flares clouded them with smoke. A slight figure stood on the edge, eyes locked on a weedy guy with a moustache standing on a podium to the left of the shot.

The guy with the moustache was Alfredo Cristiani, former president of El Salvador. The guy watching him was El Puccini.

'Maya.' I raised my hand for a high-five.

'It's just the Internet, man. This article has been around for ages.' She fluffed her bedhead and tapped a photo of the huge portrait hanging from a tall flagpole behind the podium. 'Recognise this guy?'

'Not at all.'

'What about that logo?'

Clustered around that tall flagpole stood smaller poles hung with red banners, each one emblazoned with a skull pierced by a lightning bolt.

'Nope.'

'Jesus. What do they teach you in Europe?' She shook her head. 'This officer, he's the head of the Atlacatl Battalion, a unit trained by the CIA at Fort Bragg. Used to travel the jungle in El Salvador, murdering rebels, poor people, indigenous people, quote-unquote communists.'

Grainy pictures from documentaries flickered in my head: men silhouetted against flaming jungle, kids stumbling over rubble, corpses stacked in army lorries.

'The death squads.' My eyes moved back to El Puccini shrouded in the red smoke of flares. 'Where our man got his start. And now he's working for cops and oil companies in Veracruz.'

Maya nodded. 'This ceremony was after the '92 peace accords, when the unit was disbanded.'

'"*You served a transcendental mission,' said President Cristiani.*"' I read aloud. '"*You fought with mysticism and discipline, courage and valour'.*" Jesus.'

'Best bit's here, though.' She highlighted a chunk of text.

'"*After eight years, it's a little sad,' said Evelio Martínez, 26, shortly before relinquishing his weapon. 'But I'm satisfied to have served my country.'*"' The teacup had gone cool in my grip. 'Fuck. Eight years. He's been at this since he was a teenager.' I read on. '"*Afterwards, I hope to serve my country another way'.*"'

'That's not what happened.' She scrolled down the text.

'Did he join the cops?'

Maya wagged a finger. 'No,' she said. 'He was one of the "good guys".' She added air-quotes.

I snorted.

'No, like, I mean it.' She opened a link to a small local item from a Salvadoran daily. 'People in a unit like that tend to wind up in ministry positions, police chief roles, army roles after that. But this guy?' She shrugged. 'Nothing for years. Next time he pops up, it's 2001. He's working as a bus driver. Gets himself shot by a street gang. After that, nothing until 2008, when he's in Guatemala, and he goes by El Puccini.'

The news item was from *Siglo 21*, about a vigilante group called Sangre Azul, *'responsible for the deaths of thirty suspected members of the Mara Salvatrucha gang over the course of just three months.'*

'Back in the death squads again.'

'But fighting against the baddies,' said Maya. 'Well. Like, if you go by all the right-wing memes on Salvadoran Facebook. He's sort of a Robin Hood figure.' She opened another tab. 'They even have a Twitter site for him. Fake, obviously, but it links to this weird fan site.'

The website was pretty ugly, white script on a jungle-camo background complete with silhouettes of soldiers in fatigues, and Puccini's army photo up top, under tabs that read BIO, AWARDS (MILITARY AND CIVIL), and PHOTOS. A yellow blat of martial trumpets and drums autoplayed in the background when the whole lot had finished loading.

'God,' I said. 'People really fucking suck, you know that?'

'Weird Central American fascists with Web 1.0 skills do, certainly, yeah,' said Maya. 'He killed a lot of addicts and homeless people around that neck of the woods – "social-cleaning" type deal.' She scrolled to a story from *El Faro*. 'Anyway, look, for a couple of years he pops up around Guatemala and Honduras doing the same thing. Name's misspelled sometimes, but it's him: Salvadoran, veteran, vigilante.'

'This is fucking brilliant, Maya.'

'It's just copy-paste, honestly. Most people know this stuff anyway.' She clicked open a photo that showed a muddy square lit by the lights of a small white church. The photo accompanied some text from the Control Risks security analysis consultancy. 'Anyway, here's where he stops pretending to be one of the good guys and joins the narcos.'

Outside the church, right on the step, a severed head rested on a circle of dried blood, the dead mouth hanging open as if in a martyr's ecstasy shiver.

'And so, you know, there's big crossover with the Central American guys and that Gulf side of southern Mexico, yeah?' she said, highlighting text from the Control Risks report. 'Puccini winds up in Huimanguillo, Tabasco, in 2010, working for the kind of people he's been killing for, like, thirty years or whatever. Takes over a section of Highway 180, transporting kids, drugs, organs, you name it.' She tapped the screen. 'And this severed head, yeah? It belonged to some Gulf cartel bigshot.' Maya switched tabs to an article from *La Jornada de Veracruz* from March 2011. 'And so that was like his audition, or whatever. Zetas liked what they saw and brought him in.'

I read aloud from the next article she'd brought up: ' *"Late last night, a fleet of black Dodge RAMs roared through the streets of Poza Rica. A nightclub in the Zona Rosa was shot at, injuring four. Seven bodies were recovered outside an auto-repair shop on the outskirts of the city, bearing signs of torture, and accompanied by a narcomanta announcing an alliance between Los Cocodrilos and Los Zetas"*.'

Maya scrolled back up the page to El Puccini offering his rifle forwards with the rest of his battalion, red smoke misting his face. 'What a creep,' she said.

'I need to get down there.' I sat back hard. My tea splashed the couch. 'Oops.'

'Don't worry.' She mopped the spill with her napkin. 'It's waterproof. I also hate it.'

The adrenaline that had carried me through the day was sputtering out now, my blinks getting longer and longer. My eyes shut on pictures of Carlos' trashed apartment, and, when I tried to remember past those pictures, back to how it was before, I couldn't: all I could see was Lucio chucking the leather covering of the couch like he'd just skinned a fish.

Maya's hand was cool on my forehead. 'Want a break?'

I cracked open an eye. 'Lash on more *Gilmore Girls*?'

'I didn't know you watched anything that wasn't news,' said Maya.

'I have a rich interior life.' I grabbed a cushion to prop behind my sore back.

Maya huffed out a disgusted noise. But she pressed play again anyway.

'Thanks,' I yawned.

Swap the genteel dialogue for action-movie explosions, keep the body-heat beside me under a blanket, and it could have been Carlos' couch I was falling asleep on, could have been his movies I was falling asleep during, making me thankful for the dark, thankful for the laptop voices fraying into memories of Carlos.

14

Hard to say what set off that night's bad dream, but it ended when I thrashed myself off Maya's couch and onto the sitting-room floor, her purple Chiapaneco blanket still over my head, my pulse whumping in my skull, the breath quick in my lungs. In the dream, that blanket had been a plastic bag taped over my head by a guy with thinning chestnut hair and 'Z's printed on his teeth.

Whump, whump went the air, even though my heart was slowing down.

My breath sucked the wool nap of the blanket against my lips. I shook a cigarette from the box on the table to kill the dungy taste in my mouth.

Whump, whump went the air, cutting in and out against the sound of Maya's shower.

The whumping wasn't coming from my chest, so I whipped off the blanket, saw the palm trees tossing back and forth, and got up to stand by the floor-to-ceiling window, bare-foot, pantless, a cigarette dangling from my mouth, as a police helicopter veered low over the concourse outside Maya's building, rotors shuddering the air, the tinted-glass cockpit flinging back the high sun, the front light fixed on me, beady and insectile and red.

Whump, whump. Any second now the loud-hailer would spit static-garbled noise at me, order me to my knees with my hands behind my head.

Then the helicopter yawed south above Avenida Universidad, left me on the maple floor under a blue sky ribbed with cirrus-clouds.

Maya's bathroom door opened and she came out wearing a white bathrobe.

'Did you hear that?' I pointed back over my shoulder with my thumb.

'Hear what?' said Maya, towelling her hair. The air smelled warmly of Elvive. She handed me a fresh towel. 'Jesus. Are those your feet?'

'Think so.' I wiggled my toes. 'Why?'

'They've got beards. Even your toes have beards. Irish people are weird.'

'Hobbit blood.' I caught ash in the palm of my hand. 'Every one of us is part-hobbit. Matter of fact, hobbits invented Ireland.' I righted the blanket and lay down on the couch.

'You're full of shit.' Maya took a brick-pack of Lavazza from the freezer.

'It's not the volume of shit that should worry you,' I said. 'It's the fluency.'

Her electric kettle came to the boil. Maya unzipped the little doughnut-shaped wallet where she'd kept her Citalopram ever since her move.

'And you definitely didn't hear that helicopter? Definitely definitely?'

'No.' Maya poured water into the loaded cafetière, then shaved a sticky cone of *piloncillo* sugar in on top. 'But it's normal. They like to frighten men in their underwear.'

'Oh.' I put my jacket on. 'Yeah. Sorry.'

'Don't worry, I've seen worse. I think.' She handed me a cup of coffee. 'Here – you need this.'

She wasn't wrong. My reflection in the window was the pouchy, ashen *Before* face on a sleeping-tablets advert: hair rat-tailed across my forehead, scratchy beard, blood-rimmed irises.

On my laptop, the news from Poza Rica was grim. A Guardia Civil officer's head had been rolled onto a football pitch on the edge of the city. In retaliation, a state police officer had been shot in the head and dumped by a highway, dressed in a clown suit. The underside of my sternum itched.

'Shit. I need to get down there.' The towel slid from my shoulder to the ground. The photo showed head-blood matting rainbow curls, a cratered-in face, a mouth stretched in a yawn that wasn't a yawn. 'It's all kicking off – some kind of split, I think. Police are killing each other – look.' I turned the laptop towards her.

'So what?' Maya clawed away a web of smoke. 'It's kicking off everywhere. Finish your coffee.' She flung the towel at me. 'And close that. It's too early.'

After showering, I came out to find Maya plugged into her headphones, writing a transcript. Her laptop showed news photos of the approach road to the university, clotted with broken glass and rainwater. A roadblock of halved tyres smoked beside a trashed administrative building, with sheets caught in the branches of a fir tree.

'What has the students all riled?' I asked when she took off her headphones.

Maya scoffed and leaned back in her chair, rubbing her eyes. 'That kid you found, he's an icon now.'

'Really?' I said. 'Julián Gallardo?'

She nodded. 'Students' union called a strike. Solidarity thing.'

'Huh.' I poured myself more coffee. 'What are they saying about our boy Julián, then?'

'Pretty much what you and Carlos saw,' said Maya. 'Police collected his body from an alley – but then that body never showed up.' She held out her mug for a refill. 'Weird, though. Why would a Guardia Civil unit be cleaning up a body dumped by Zetas?'

In my head I saw the shot policeman in his bloodied clown-suit.

'Because they might be Zetas too,' I said.

'Eesh.' Maya made a face. 'But yeah,' she said, putting her headphones back on. 'That sounds about right.'

While she typed up her transcript, I read through some of the articles by Francisco Escárcega. One was accompanied by aerial photos of Ajenjo wells, circled and numbered, with graphs showing oil extraction figures diving from early peaks to near-zero flatlines, while the text talked about a major U.S. oil giant selling a horizontal drill, a monitoring booth, and trucks for injecting water and chemicals, in a deal close to eight billion dollars.

'Hey,' I said to Maya, waving my hands.

She took off her headphones.

'Here,' I said, turning the laptop, and zooming in the screen on the photo. 'What's all that look like to you?'

She frowned. 'Is that one of those fracking sites? Where is that, Texas?'

I shook my head. 'Poza Rica.'

Her eyes went wide. '*Neta?*' she said. '*Chinga, güey.*'

'We're on to something here,' I said.

Her eyes narrowed. 'What do you mean "we"?'

'Well, you're coming too, no?' I opened LinkedIn and went looking for people who'd worked for Ajenjo.

Maya laughed. 'You're joking, right? Like, OK, so it's more dangerous for Mexican journalists, blah, blah, but you're trying to poke around in some really dank shit, man.' She shook her head. '*Puta, güey*, I'd be dead if I even *thought* some of the shit you're trying to dig up. Like, you're the sober one, yeah? And so you're kind of meant to be good at this, like, self-analysis shit? And you can't see what you're getting into.' She blew on her coffee. 'Like, at all.'

'Yeah, well.' I turned the laptop around for her to see some LinkedIn search results of people who'd worked for Ajenjo. 'Who would you interview first?'

Maya shoved the laptop aside, but stopped short of pushing it to the floor. 'Andrew, are you even listening?'

'Well, no, like. I've shit to do.' I pulled the laptop back, clicking open a profile I liked the look of: a local-born driller for Ajenjo. 'This barista guy. You like the look of him?'

'What, physically?' Maya sipped her coffee.

'No,' I said, 'as in, like, is he too far out of the game? He quit in 2014. Became a barista here in Mexico City. Started a Motocross team – that's pretty cool.'

She gave a one-shoulder shrug. 'Sure. Whatever. Why're you rushing, anyway? It's Saturday, man. Chill.'

'Already got one of us killed,' I said, copy-pasting the address of the guy's café into an email to myself. 'Better get this done before they come back.'

Maya's eyes were still on me. 'That's fucked up.'

'What? It's the truth, like.'

'That is such shit.' She practically slammed down her coffee cup. 'He was his own man. A grown-up.' She huffed a laugh through her nose, flicking up her fringe. 'Kind of.'

Carlos on the bike, his middle finger upraised. The white chop-marks on his glass table. I didn't say anything.

Maya turned her coffee cup on its saucer. 'OK, so this might be rough, yeah? But you're going to have to do your own thing sometime, you know?' She plucked the sleeve of his – my – jacket. 'He's still got such a hold on you.'

'His ashes are barely fucking cold, Maya.'

She gave me a long, hard stare, put her headphones on and started tapping away at her keyboard again, like nothing had happened. There wasn't a single reply that I could think of that wouldn't sound petty and wrong, so I tried to soldier on with my reading, but I was so pissed off that it was like I had indigestion, and every noise from outside – the gas man's yawp, the knife sharpener's whistle, and one of those awful brass bands made up of off-duty football hooligans that clump around honking into people's intercoms in return for change – made the corner of my eye twitch.

When a camote-vendor's cart rocked up outside the apartment and let its steam shriek out, I slammed shut my laptop and leaned back in my chair, the heels of my hands kneading my eyes, uttering a low groan. When I'd finished, Maya was looking at me, her arms folded, her headphones around her neck.

'What?' I said. 'Did I interrupt you?' I folded my arms. 'I'm not sorry, before you ask. It's your fault I can't concentrate.'

'Jesus,' said Maya, recoiling a little. 'I was just going to ask if you wanted a break. But –' she turned around in the chair, already lifting the headphones '– *someone* still hasn't cooled down.'

'No, no.' I sighed. 'Fuck it, you're right.' I pocketed my wallet. 'Break time. I'll get us some snacks or whatever. You go pick something to watch.'

When I got back with some tamales, we nearly fought again, this time because Maya wanted to put on a gossipy documentary about the British Royal Family.

'What?' she said, plugging the SCART lead into her TV. 'Harry's cute.'

'Ah, Jesus.' I palmed my forehead. 'Honestly, anything, literally anything but them. Please?'

'Fine,' she said, killing the screen light on her MacBook. '*Gilmore Girls* again. But just two episodes, yeah?'

The day was bright, but frigid, so we brought our tamales over to the couch and drew Maya's blanket over both our laps.

'Very Queen Mother, no?' she said, tucking the edge of the blanket under her thigh and balancing the styrofoam tray that held her tamal on her knees.

'Stop it,' I said, a forkful of tamal halfway to my mouth, but I was just glad she was making jokes again.

With my eyes shut and Maya's cheek resting on the top of my head, it was almost like nestling in against Carlos. Sometime around the middle of the second episode, the weight of the tamal in my belly started to make me nod off. Next thing I remember was Maya tapping me awake.

'Sorry,' she said. 'You were beginning to drool.'

'Shite,' I said through a groan, rubbing my eyes. 'I don't get it. I'm so knackered all the time.' I sat up and let myself fall against the corner of the couch so I could stretch my back.

'It is tiring,' Maya said, pictures on the screen catching on her eyes in four pixelated dots that kept changing colour. 'The whole thing. Just having to think about it all the time, or else trying not to. Gives you a headache.' She got up to disconnect the laptop. 'And it's like you only ever think you're distracting yourself, you know?'

'Hundred per cent.' I leaned my chin on the heel of my hand. 'Probably I should crack on with work, I reckon.'

'Here, or?'

'Ah, no, my place,' I said, untucking the blanket. 'I'll just end up acting the prick again. I'm ratty as hell.'

Maya just stood there with her mouth open, mock-aghast, and darted her eyes back and forth. She had leaned forward a little.

'What?' I said.

'I wasn't sure if I was allowed to agree,' she said.

'Jesus,' I said. 'That bad, was I?'

She pinched her index finger close to her thumb. '*Tantitito*,' she said.

'C'mere.' I crossed the room and put my arms around her. 'I'm sorry. We're knee deep in the same shite and here I am acting like it's all about me.'

'S'OK,' said Maya, her voice muffled against my shoulder. She patted me on the back. 'Goes with the territory, doesn't it? All you stoical men.'

'Ugh. Sadly, yes.'

Maya walked me downstairs. It was already getting dark outside; across the road from her building, steam frayed up in crisp silver lines from an *esquites* cart. A father stooped over his kid's pram, blowing on a spoonful of corn kernels before feeding it to his toddler.

'*Ay, que pinche frío güey*,' she said, rubbing her upper arms and stamping her feet as I climbed into the car. She shooed me with her fingers. '*Vete ya*. I'm dying here.'

'You go back inside,' I said. 'Get your Queen Mother blanket back on.'

She raised her hand as if to slap me with the back of it. 'And you stay out of the deep end with that story, yeah?' she said.

'I'm only going back to do edits,' I said. 'Honest.'

Maya looked at me sidelong. 'You're really crap at lying, you know that?'

'Yeah, I suppose.' I scratched the back of my neck. 'Just don't want you getting dragged into anything, or whatever.'

'That's appreciated.' She leaned through the door, wagging

a finger. 'But don't pretend that I don't know what you're up to, yeah?' She gave me a kiss on the cheek. '*Conozco a mi gente*. Just be careful.'

'Always am.' I doused my cigarette in a quarter-empty coffee cup that stood in the driver door. 'Kind of.'

On the other side of the road, the father dabbed his son's chin with a napkin. The toddler laughed and kicked in the pram as his father loaded up another spoonful.

'I'll call you when it's over, OK?' I said. 'Promise.'

'When's that going to be?' asked Maya.

'Oh, pretty soon,' I said. 'Dominic likes a nice, fast turn-around time.'

Maya laughed. 'On top of everything else,' she said, 'you have to work to a deadline. Sucks to be you.'

'Could be worse. Take care, all right?'

'Yeah, you, too.' Maya shut the car door, crossed to her building, gave me a wave from the doorway of her apartment, and left me sitting alone under the concourse lights. The father feeding his kid on the road had been gone a long time by the time the rain tapping my windscreen reminded me that I should get home.

15

Back home, when I flicked on the light, Motita's eyes gleamed cobalt blue from under the cowhide-draped chair.

'Well, make yourself at home, anyway,' I said.

The noticeboard was busy now: Carlos' picture of Julián Gallardo, the tattered remains of the Díaz Ordáz acid blotter, a copy of *Proceso* with Carlos on the cover. The candles were veined with melted wax. The cigarette offerings I'd lit on the night Carlos had died lay snug in their ash.

My plants tinted the light a mellow green, and blue smoke uncoiled from my gold-filtered Sobranie, and I sat there in the forty-watt glow, house music low and pulsing against the beat of rain outside, the caffeine and sugar hitting my blood in rapid jags, and all of it was almost cosy, almost like before, to the point where I wondered if I shouldn't forget the article, forget the silver-toothed cop and his Salvadoran boss, if I shouldn't just get back to furniture and flower-markets and all the stuff that had filled my weekends since I'd gotten sober, but then my phone buzzed, my editor's number on the screen.

'Andrew,' he said, 'my sympathies.'

In the background I could hear the chatter of printers, the shrill chirp of phones. It wasn't hard to picture him at the late-shift desk, looking more lecturer than editor in his pilled slacks and trainers, his half-rimmed glasses, his cordless corduroy jacket, his faded Kraftwerk T-shirt.

'Sorry I couldn't make the funeral,' he said through a static-edged sigh. 'Wedded to the desk.' Talked more lecturer than editor, too, his arch diction rippled by a Dumfries burr. 'His mother's eulogy was tremendous. That "mistakes of history" line, *Reforma* used that as their headline. Splashed with her photo.' He cleared his throat. 'Anyway, enough of that. How're you faring?'

The fish in my tanks jerked back and forth, settling nowhere.

'Ah, you know,' I said, dusting sugar from my fingers. 'Keeping busy.'

'Hell of a land, what happened,' he went on gravely. A sheaf of papers rustled on his end of the call. 'But we've got your story, and Carlos' photos, and we should be able to run them day after tomorrow. How does that sound?'

My breath went in, hard, and stayed in. If he'd asked me that question a week before all this happened, I'd have run a victory lap of my apartment.

'Oh, yeah,' I said. 'Great. I mean, you know. Huge honour. First byline with the big guys.' The chuckle in my voice, even I could tell it was fake.

'First of many,' said Dominic. 'Trust me. Apart from a couple of minor edits, this is first-rate reporting. And Carlos' photos fit perfectly.' He went quiet for a moment. 'The news really hit us all hard. Can't get my head around it.'

Elvers of lit rain teemed down the glass. Motita nipped at dust-motes same as she used to jump at Carlos' dangling fingers when he'd sit where I sat now. When I didn't play along, she coughed out an amused non-miaow.

'Ah, cheers.' The doughnut chunk soured in my throat. 'Glad you called. I was thinking –' I pushed back my hair, eyes shut '– maybe hold the story?'

Dominic went quiet for a longer moment.

'See, thing is, I think I found something,' I said. 'Sort of big stuff, like.'

In the background, the printers went on whinging, the phones shrilling.

'What have you got?' said Dominic.

Motita clawed my dangling hand and missed. She looked at me, shocked. When I gave her the finger, she rolled onto her back, unimpressed.

'Ties in with Carlos' death,' I told Dominic. 'With organised crime. With multinational oil companies.'

'And you have testimonies?'

'Oh, yeah,' I said, my fingers crossed behind my back. 'Many, in fact.'

Another phone went off, nearer to Dominic this time. 'I have to take this, hold on.' His voice went small while he asked the caller on the other line to wait, and I used the time to look up the café where the driller-turned-barista worked. They didn't close for another twenty minutes. My knee started bouncing.

'Andrew, let's do breakfast. There's a spot near mine – I'll text the address. If I get out of here at nine tomorrow morning we can shoot for ten. Can you?'

'Hundred per cent,' I said, already out the door, a dough-nut clamped in my teeth, zipping up Carlos' jacket against the rain.

My jeep's tyres rasped against the tarmac. Up ahead, all around, brake lights shimmied and vied through the streaming dark. From the market above Metro Tacubaya rose the chug and boom of bootleg cumbia CDs, soundtracking labourers in wool-padded plaid jackets and baseball caps started on the long commute home, the pesero boys chivvying passengers onto the green and white buses, the mothers and grandmoth-ers toting loads and babies through the rain and yellow lights, their shoulders catching the charger-cables that dangled like vines from the stalls.

The insomnia twitch at the corner of my eye was strong now. The coffee cup I drank from could have been that morning's, could have been last week's, whatever, it was all fuel. The bloody lights of hotsheet motels and petrol stations spilled down the bonnet. Above the Metro Juanacatlán sign someone had sprayed a stencil of Emiliano Zapata above the words SEE YOU IN 2017.

The GPS said five more minutes, but the traffic said dif-ferent. My teeth found a hangnail and I tugged at it until the quick red zip of pain cut off my thoughts. When the cars budged and flowed, I cut down a quiet street of cobbles, plane trees, luxury apartments built in the '70s, past an arti-san bakery, past a restaurant behind tall metal security doors where yuppies and hipsters forked up Italian food. When I got to the café its shutters were down and a brown-haired woman dressed in black was dragging a couple of Acapulco chairs and potted ferns in from the terrace.

'Sorry,' she said, when I'd parked beside a shiny red Honda 450 dirt bike and gotten out of the jeep. 'We're closed.'

'I'm not a customer,' I said, goat-footing it through the drench and under the awning, my press lanyard held up. 'Guy work here called Leo?'

Her eyes took on a hard shut gleam. 'He's not here.'

'Isn't this his bike?' I pointed at the Honda. 'Motocross fan, I'd heard.'

A door slammed inside the café and I heard someone turning a tap.

She shook her head at me, then craned around the door. 'Leo? Someone's here. Some journalist.'

Footsteps clumped across the pale wood floor. He looked nothing like his LinkedIn photo: he'd gotten contacts, grown one of those huge lumberjack beards, shaved his head, covered his arms in bright, clean-lined Sailor Jerry-style tattoos – a cormorant, a seagull, a mermaid, an anchor.

'What's this about?' he said, drying his hands on a towel.

'Sorry for coming so late.' I handed Leo one of my cards. 'We're doing a story about Poza Rica. You have a minute?'

The woman came back out through the door, the hood of a pink rain-jacket pulled up over her head. She handed Leo a bunch of keys. 'I'm going to go, OK? I don't want to hear about that place again.' She walked away fast.

Leo tapped the card against his knuckles, looking at the writing. 'Well, I suppose you'd better come in. Coffee?'

'Bit late for me. Water's fine, thanks.'

'I might make one. Long day, you know?' He went around behind the bar and tipped beans into the grinder, flicked a switch.

'Nice place,' I said over the whining grinder. 'Lighting's nice and dim.' I tapped the windowsill. 'Scrap-metal's always a good look. You open long?'

'Year and a half.' He jetted hot water into a small white cup. 'Me and Erika and her boyfriend, we all lived in Poza Rica together. Got sick of the place. Her boyfriend, he's studied tourism, hospitality, everything like that, and Erika's parents used to do agronomy stuff for coffee growers. So I took out my savings, retrained as a barista, moved here with them.' He handed me a glass of water and sat down opposite me. A gust flung rain against the windows. 'You mind me asking what this is about?'

'Just a few general things.' I shrugged. 'Saw on LinkedIn you had oil-industry experience in Poza Rica, working with Ajenjo. Can I switch this thing on?' I held up my voice recorder.

'Do what you got to do, man.' Leo fluffed his beard. 'You want to talk about this?' He traced a 'Z' in the air with his finger.

I tried not to sound interested, just kept right on fumbling with my tape recorder. 'You know something about that?'

Leo stared past me. 'When you live in that town, that's all anyone knows about. Weeknights at home, weekends at the mall. Park's too dangerous, day or night. Nobody out after dark. Nobody calls it a curfew, but they might as well. Stuck in the shitty apartments they kept building. Inside, right,

everything was all shiny, all new, but the walls were like this.'
He tapped the table we were sitting at. 'Like you could put
your hand through them. Because a proper place with solid
walls costs more than an apartment in Mexico City.'

I sat back in my chair. 'Oh, I was shocked when I went
there. Everything is astronomical – food, rent, even the petrol.'

Leo raised his hands. 'Inflation. All that oil money washed
in, and nobody thought it'd ever wash out. But even after the
companies pulled out, the prices stayed up.' He snapped his
fingers. '*Puf* – just like that. Painters, builders, welders. Drill-
ers, engineers. Every job in the place, flat gone.' He scratched
his beard again.

'Mexico City prices, and no money coming in,' I said. 'No
wonder you got out.'

He clicked his tongue. 'Oh, that's not why we got out. It
was just too dangerous. You'd see bodies a lot, lying right on
the main avenue, real blatant, you know? Kids selling crack
by the Banco Azteca, out of their little kangaroo-pouch bags.'

'The cops let them do that?' I widened my eyes, tried to
sound amazed.

He snorted. 'The cops help them. If they're even cops at
all. Mostly they were just Zetas in uniform, shipping in all
that crap.'

'But which set of cops?' I flicked back through my notebook. 'There's the State Police, and there's the Guardia Civil.
Which ones help the Zetas?'

Leo shuffled in his seat. 'Both, I guess, nowadays.' He
shook his head. 'I mean, at the beginning, people said the
State Police were all bought by the Zetas, which was why

Guardia Civil came in –' he mimed air-quotes with his fingers '– "to clean up Poza Rica".' He gave a one-shoulder shrug. 'Wound up being the same shit.'

'I'll bet,' I said, and in my head I heard the clunk of Julián Gallardo's body in the flatbed of the pickup truck. I tapped my pen against my notebook. 'Last time I was down there, me and my partner caught three Guardia Civil guys lifting a body.'

Leo nodded. 'Sounds about right.' He blew steam from his coffee.

I pulled my chair in to the table. 'But this kid's body, it really looked awful. No face. No –' I gestured above my lap '– well, you know.'

Leo just nodded. 'Zetas did that a lot. But the Guardia Civil, too, after they came in. Did it to the Zetas. Or, you know –' he did the air-quotes again '– to "Zetas". A lot of the time, they just kill people – activists, poor people, indigenous people, even journalists – and say they're criminals afterwards.'

'But these new guys, these Guardia Civil guys – why would they help the Zetas get rid of a body?'

Leo shrugged. 'I mean, aren't they supposed to be cleaning the place up? Going to look bad for business if faceless kids keep turning up in alleyways, right?'

'But the kid we saw,' I said, 'he was the one that the pro-testers are talking about. Activist. Surely it's in a company's interests to have him disappeared, right?'

Leo clicked his tongue. 'Well, look, if you kick up enough of a fuss around there, someone will find a hole to put you in. Sure, they'll want him dead. But they might want it to be more discreet than in the past.' He sat back in his chair with his arms folded. His foot tapped the floor. 'You'd hear stories. How Zetas would go out to the villages, scare people off their land. Drown people in oil tanks. Rape. Murder.' He pulled a face. 'If the companies and the business guys and politicians want to terrorise people the same way as before, they'll have to be more discreet. And that would be the literal only change – that it'd be more hush-hush.'

'Jesus.' I scratched my chin, looked at my notebook, waiting for his silence to crack again.

Leo rubbed his hand over his scalp. 'It's a dirty city. Not just crime-wise. The things we did made every turtle in the region homeless. Plus you have all those places where the air hurts to breathe.' He folded his arms and leaned on his forearms. 'Coatzintla. El Chote. San Antonio Ojital.' He shook his head. 'Can totally see why kids like the guy you found would risk his life for better things.'

'Right.' I wrote down the place names. 'Anyone I should talk to down there?'

Leo stared at his coffee cup. 'Out of my crew, I think there's only one guy still there. Armando. Owns a grocery store in El Chote. I'll give you his number.'

'Thanks.' I slid the notebook across to him and he took out his phone to copy down the number.

After he'd finished, he looked at the page and scratched his chin, his frown deepening. Then he shook his head, blew out a sigh, and held up my notebook. 'Mind if I draw on this page? Quick science lesson.' Leo sketched an 'L', then drew an '8' on top of the vertical line. 'This straight downward line,' he said, 'is what a regular pipeline looks like – just a cement channel drilled into the earth.' He traced a finger along the drawing. 'The bottom of the "L", though, here? This is an extra channel. You put that in when you want to break open an old oil deposit.'

In my head I saw the article in *La Jornada de Veracruz*, listing the items that Ajenjo had bought from the U.S. company.

'Trucks for injecting water and chemicals,' I said. 'A horizontal drill. Monitoring booths. Eight billion dollars' worth – seems a lot.'

Leo nodded. 'It is, but it makes sense. Because that vertical channel, this one here?' He ran a fingertip over the page. 'It's a mile long. And you've got to shoot pressure all that way down, while keeping that pressure up high enough to carve open the old well.' Now he pointed to the '8' drawn on top of the 'L'. 'This is your wellhead, right? On the site we had, there were a bunch of pipes going into that wellhead.' He drew a long pipe, added a bunch of tiny dots. 'One for sand.' Next he drew another pipe, drew slightly bigger dots, said, 'This is for gravel,' then drew a third pipe and added tiny sharp triangles, saying, 'And these are ceramic chips.' Next to these he drew some large wheeled rectangles. 'These are your injection trucks, OK? Pressure chambers the size of this café. And they have to be. Remember –' he ran a finger along the 'L' '– a full mile down, a half mile across to the well. Ten thousand pounds of pressure per square inch, shooting jets of sand and gravel and ceramic, tons and tons, non-stop.'

His scribble grew furious – jets of sand, gravel, ceramic

– and he said, 'What you're trying to do is shred the rock encasing the oil deposit.' When Leo slid the notebook across to me he'd torn through three pages. 'Now,' he said, tapping the page, 'imagine what that would do to a body.'

From outside came the sound of a tamal-seller riding through the soaked night. A couple of cats yowled from a rooftop. The rain kept dumping down.

Leo leaned back in his chair, resting his hands on his head. Then he breathed the word 'OK' at the ceiling and took a long drink of coffee.

'So this was in May 2014,' he said, once he had swallowed. 'Just before the Guardia Civil came in to do their "cleanup". Town was a nightmare – men and women getting shot, day and night, everyone scared of the cops, because you couldn't know which one was a real cop or a Zeta in a cop uniform. Me and my friends called off our basketball league because nobody could make it to training. On one of my nights off, my boss calls me. He says there's been an accident. Says a jeep's on its way to my apartment. Boss sounds scared – and that gets me scared, because if he's scared, then it's something big. And if they're sending me out at night, it's going to be dangerous. But the jeep that shows up outside my house is a Pemex jeep, and the guy driving it is wearing union overalls, and my friend Armando's in the back, and he doesn't look scared. So I figure if he looks OK with it, then what's the harm?'

'The Pemex guy,' I said, 'how'd he look?'

'Kind of fat,' said Leo. 'Pretty short.'

'Curly hair?' I said.

'Yep. Dark guy, Campeche drawl, but didn't have the Campeche friendliness, you know? Not one single word the whole time we were driving.'

The name 'El Mangueras' floated up in my head from the spider diagram Maya had shown me.

Leo kept talking. 'Drill site was in the middle of nowhere – grass, hills, crickets, bunch of sick-looking trees. Foreman's there by the gate, and he looks like a ghost, because he has these cop cars parked behind him. When the Campechano guy tells us to get down out of the jeep, one of the cops waiting for us tells us to give him our phones, ID cards, wallets.'

'White guy?' I said. 'Beard?'

'Yeah, but no moustache,' said Leo. 'Sort of an Abraham Lincoln thing. *Norteño* accent.'

Another face from the diagram, tall, white, with a huge beard like a heavy-metal bassist or a high-school shooter, the name 'El Prieto' written beneath.

Leo kept going. 'They put me and Armando on our knees. Put guns to our heads.' He put a finger between his eyes. 'Right here. The mark didn't fade until like a day after. In these calm voices, like they've done things like this a million times before, they tell us to do what they say or they'll put us and our families into the ground.'

My pen tapped my notebook. 'And you think Armando can confirm this?'

Leo nodded. 'He was so messed up. Sobbing, man. Telling those Zeta-slash-cop-slash-whatever guys that he had kids. A family. He'll never forget that.' Leo shrugged. 'So they hit him. Kick him in the ribs. Leave him crying in the dirt. I felt bad for him, but mostly I felt bad for wanting him to shut up. Because I was pretty chill, all told. Maybe because I didn't know it was happening. Whole thing was like someone telling you about a dream they'd had – just couldn't relate to what was happening, even though it was happening to me. I just figured, if they're going to do it, they're going to do it. And the only choice you have, it's how you go down, right? It was kind of easy to just zone out like that.'

His fingers rapped on the table. 'But so the tall one, the white guy, he tells us to go over to the police pickups. Drags Armando to his feet. And I follow them. And in the back of the pickups, there's these bin bags – the heavy-duty kind, like you get out the back of restaurants. Bottom of the jeep's all wet. All red. Bags are wet. Smell from them like a butcher's shop.'

Leo checked his cup for dregs, drained them, then kept going. 'Those Zeta-cop guys ask which one of us is the systems guy. And that's me. So I open the prefab, switch off the pumps, get Armando to open the tanks. Then we start carrying the bags.' The rapping of Leo's fingers on the table grew louder. 'And, I mean – you know but you don't know, right? As in, you feel the weight jostle your leg. Slippery, making your hands red. Drops of wet on the plastic, on your boots, all red. The smell makes you know what it is, too. But your whole mind being on the struggle not to gag, you start thinking all sorts of things. How maybe the shapes bumping your leg are just fruit, big fruit. Jackfruit. Watermelons. The same flat thud. And the dumping of the bags requires the same motion as hauling trash, so you figure, "Yeah, that's all I'm doing. Hauling trash. A load of rotten fruit trash". And we wad those bags into the tank, with the water, and the sand, and the pebbles, and the ceramic chips, and down the chute go all those people.'

'Who were they?' I said.

'My guess?' said Leo. 'Villagers. Protesters. People who saw something they shouldn't. People the cops didn't like. People like the kid you saw.' He waved a hand. 'Could have been anyone. One of the bags Armando was carrying went and split. A tattooed arm fell out – a woman's arm, maybe, or a teenage boy's. Cut up all rough at the joint, it all looks the same: like steak or something.' Leo massaged his forehead, went to drink some coffee, remembered the cup was empty.

'How many?' I handed him my glass of water.

'Cut up like that, it's hard to know. But we were hauling bags a long time. Started around midnight. Moon was low when we finished. Switching the machine on was the worst. Sounded just like a normal job – same roar, same numbers on the screen, pressure, quantity, velocity, et cetera – like all we were firing into the ground was gravel or sand.'

Outside, the rain had eased. Drops plinked from the eaves.

'When we were done, those narco-cop guys tossed our cards and wallets and phones on the ground. Told us to get the fuck out of there. Not to breathe a word. The Pemex guy, the Campechano, he got in one of the cop cars. Left us to walk home. I barely could. Just put one foot in front of the other, all the way to the town, like a robot, or a zombie. Don't remember saying goodbye to Armando. Don't remember the bus-ride home. Just remember lying on my bathroom floor, cooling my belly on the tiles, too wiped out to move, too wiped out to puke.' His knuckles rapped the table. 'And, you know, what made me get sick, in the end, wasn't even a smell in my nose or the blood on my boots or whatever. It was just this this five-word phrase looped in my head – *It could have been me*. And, yeah, it could. Any one thing went wrong, it would have. I'd be in that hole. I'd be pulp. My being alive was just an accident.' He frowned, biting his lip. 'Like, life is shit-cheap in Mexico, man. We all know that, like, in theory. But to *really* know it, *really* feel it?'

He shook his head, then pushed back his chair suddenly. 'I need a coffee. You want one?' Leo crossed the room and switched on the grinder. 'Couple weeks later, we finish on that well. Switch off the machines. The goop oozes upwards, thick and brownish, same as ever. Oil and gas and people. Looking at it, you wouldn't know. It was just the usual dirty gunk. Nobody could tell what else was mixed in. Just me and Armando.'

Hot water rode the sides of his cup. The grounds seethed, thick and brownish.

'You know what,' I said, a hand at my mouth, 'I think I'm all right.'

'You sure?' He returned to the table. 'Anything else?'

'Just one more thing.' I took my laptop from my satchel, flipped it open, opened the photos of Puccini's pyramid. 'The Pemex guy, the Campechano – is this him?' I scrolled the document down to El Mangueras' photograph.

'Without the shadow of a doubt,' said Leo. 'Man, I will never forget these faces.' Leo tapped the photo of El Prieto.

'This one, too – the white guy with the beard, he's the guy who took our phones and stuff.' He eased back in the chair, holding his cup. 'And so where's this going to be published, anyway?'

'We can take your name out of the piece.' I pressed *STOP*.

Leo watched the steam rising from his coffee cup. He ran a hand over his scalp. 'Look, I mean, in Poza Rica, the streets know things before you know them.' His voice was dull. 'Plus, you know, you foreign journalists have been camped out in Mexico since I was a teenager, and nothing's changed.' His eyes rested on the coffee in his cup. He shrugged. 'But hey, what can you do. When you see Armando, you'll see what silence does to a person. I don't want that for me.'

'Thanks, Leo.' I slid the voice recorder back into my pocket and the notebook into my bag. 'I'll be in touch.'

'It's OK.' Leo walked me to the door. 'Tell Armando I said hello.'

The night had that clean pepper nip of wet hedges. Between the gaps in the cobbles the light glowed yellow as melted solder. Outside, Leo slung his leg over his Honda 450, shook my hand, and then he was gone, roaring away into the dark.

16

Next morning, I headed to the breakfast place Dominic had chosen – crumbling pink Art Deco stucco on the outside, winking cutlery on the inside. He was sitting on the terrace at a wrought-iron table, beside a terrapin pond, the screen of banana leaves around his table half see-through with sunlight. When he saw me, he gave up trying to flag down a waiter for a refill and stood up to shake my hand. *Concha* pastry crumbs littered his saucer. His glass of *jugo verde* was half empty.

'Shit, you've been waiting ages,' I said. 'I'm sorry. Traffic.' I pulled out a chair.

'No trouble, old soldier,' he said. 'Not the best time of day to cross the city.' His eyes were pouchy from working all night, in that seasick time zone where breakfast is dinner and your head starts to ache like evening just as it's getting bright.

A copy of *Proceso* lay on the table. On the cover was Carlos' byline photo.

'I'm truly sorry for your loss, Andrew,' said Dominic.

'Yeah.' From the magazine I lifted my eyes to the terrapins

kicking through the pond near our table. 'Strange to see it all written down like that.'

Dominic made a face like he'd pulled a muscle. 'I wouldn't read that, if I were you. Toxicology report came out, and the prosecutor has made hay out of Carlos' – ah, leisure activities.'

'Classic behaviour.'

A slim young waiter handed me a menu.

'Mind if I smoke?' I asked.

Dominic sipped his *jugo verde*.

'I'd prefer if you fortified yourself,' said Dominic. 'When my old man died, my appetite died with it. Looked like a ghost for days. Had to force the food down in the end. Had to tell myself I could eat a nun's arse through a tennis racket.' He shrugged. 'Eventually felt like I could.'

'Actually, I probably could eat a nun's arse through a tennis racket.' I opened the menu.

'That's the spirit. Get what you want. This is on the Baron's dime.'

The Baron – his name for his agency, founded by a rich German in the nineteenth century.

At the next table sat a young couple, a man and a woman, wealthy types – '*mirreyes*' we called them, the kind of people who wore padded designer waistcoats over their chinos; who never wanted to hear about the news; who took about an hour to complete a single vowel.

Looking at the menu, at the two-hundred-peso eggs and fifty-peso juices, what I wanted to say was, 'I'm glad the Baron's getting this.'

What I said was, 'I'll have what you're having,' and shut the menu.

'Very good.' Dominic flagged down a waiter to order two plates of *chilaquiles*.

'With two eggs,' he said, 'on this guy's. That's very important.'

The waiter laughed, handed us our coffees. 'Very good, sirs.'

Dominic thumbed open a *bolillo* loaf and handed me the bread basket, then lifted the copy of *Proceso* to pull out a type-script hooped and flecked with red pen.

'That's a lot of red,' I said.

Dominic turned the pages. 'You know me. There's always a lot of red. But it's solid. No holes. Nice colour, too – I like the refinery chimney disguised with plastic palm fronds.'

'Bit florid, I thought.' My eyes were on the happy couple, who were trying to pick the right angle for a selfie in front of a large bird-of-paradise flower growing by the pond. Dew-drops hung from the flower's purple and orange petals. Me and Carlos, we'd taken our fair share of selfies, sure, but never in places like this. Our last post had been a shot of us on the worst beach in the world, just outside Coatzacoalcos, a slick of oil-killed mackerel behind us, our faces wild with fake joy.

'No, but it fits.' Dominic put down the typescript. 'All of it. And that's why our phone call pulled the rug out from under me a tad, old soldier.'

The food arrived, plates heaped with fried corn chips in green tomato sauce, topped with cream, white cheese, fried eggs, refried beans on top.

'You weren't lying about "fortify yourself",' I said. 'Enough for a food coma.'

'Conveniently,' said Dominic, stabbing an egg yolk. 'I had a sleep pencilled in for after breakfast.' He looked at me. 'Notice I said "had".'

'Yeah, all right,' I said, wadding down the food before my stomach turned again. 'I'm sorry to pull the rug out from under you. But I have a new angle.'

His fork stopped halfway to his mouth. 'Go on. And don't mention the fracking thing. You have it here, and it's a rabbit hole. The Baron isn't going to care. Corporate malpractice in Mexico is old hat.'

'That missing student isn't old hat.'

On the bank of the pond, terrapins clambered over one another, blunt dinosaur heads clashing.

Dominic clicked his tongue. 'It's sad, certainly. But what's he got to do with oil companies?'

'Me and Carlos found his body.' I sat back, flicking ash. 'We were driving back. Stumbled on him. Watched some cops take his body away.'

Dominic's eyes didn't move from mine. 'You're serious?'

'That's why Carlos stayed. He found out what happened. Seems to have spread the word, because, later that day, a protest broke out. Zetas in cop uniforms were right there, machetes out, swinging them at kids. Carlos got photos.'

Dominic scratched his chin. 'The problem is photos on their own won't do.' His nine o'clock shadow rasped. 'We need testimonies.'

'Got one last night,' I said. 'A driller saw bodies being

disposed of at Ajenjo sites, with known narcos in police uniforms giving him the orders. One of them was at the protest Carlos took photos of.'

Dominic's eyebrows went up. 'Can you corroborate it?'

In the pond, two terrapins cruised through underwater gloom. My leg was jigging under the table and the space under my ribs was all cold white electricity.

'Got the name of a witness down in Coatzintla.'

'Means a return trip,' Dominic said through a sigh, swabbing up egg yolk with a torn-off hunk of *bolillo*. 'Means a budget request from the Baron. A fixer's fee.' He chewed slowly, swallowed. You could nearly hear him twisting the information around in his head, kinking the arguments, gauging their strength. 'And you definitely have sources on the ground?'

'Got an itinerary.' I flipped open my notebook to show him.

'When would all this be?'

'Today, ideally,' I said.

'Thought as much.' Dominic drained his *jugo verde* and leaned back against the chair, his eyes were on the terrapins. 'Go for it.'

A chunk of ash fell from my cigarette.

Carlos, if you get this, we've got this story.

Dominic stuffed money into the little wicker basket that our bill had arrived in. 'It's worth drilling into, if you'll forgive the pun. Pack a bag.' He counted on his fingers. 'Do the city again, nice and fine-grained, focusing on why those whistle-blowers go in the grinder.' Dominic was tapping his middle finger now. 'Now, the Holy Grail. Americans sold Ajenjo the drilling gear, yes? So, if you can prove Ajenjo's CEO knows what's happening on his watch – or is even, shall we say, *encouraging* such things to happen on his watch – then we have US multinationals making some of their profits, in part because of death squads.' He shrugged. 'Unwittingly, of course.'

'Sure.'

Dominic scratched his chin. 'Look, end result of it all is you might need to move country – but you'd have a hell of a story.'

'I see no downside to this.'

'Well, yes.' Dominic frowned at the place where the money had been, rapping the table with his knuckles. He folded his napkin onto the clean plate. 'Now, I think it's time I hit the hay.'

We got up from the table. The couple – they'd finished their selfie – went to cross the terrace. Now me and Dominic had to wait for them to finish up their kiss before we could pass. Back outside the front of the restaurant, I lit a cigarette.

'Thanks, Dominic,' I said. 'Really.'

'A pleasure.' He was polishing his glasses on his Blue Cheer T-shirt. 'Good luck, old soldier.' He set off the other way, under the canopy of ferns and palms and cypress above the walkway that spined Avenida Amsterdam.

The *viene-viene* sitting by the entrance to the parking lot was reading *El Universal*. Page one showed Carlos' mother on the crematorium steps, staring into the silver ripple of flashing cameras, beside the A2 photo of Carlos.

Driving home, passing a newsstand, its metal lattice clothes-pegged with copies of *Reforma* and *Proceso*, Carlos' face looked down at me in multiple, rippling in the draught of passing cars.

'Looking good.' I flicked ash. 'But I'd sooner you make page one with, you know, photos *by* you, not photos *of* you.'

Carlos' face looked down from a copy of *El Metro* that lay on the dashboard of a bus driving beside my jeep along Nuevo León.

'But, then again, who wouldn't.'

At a quesadilla stand on Baja California, the vendor was using a crumpled-up page one of *La Razón* to dry her hot-plate. Carlos' face wrapped her knuckles.

17

You travel as often as I used to, you never really unpack.

You have your iPad and your laptop and your camera and your spare camera and a whole lot of blister plasters.

You have six days' worth of clothes: mostly comfortable, mostly weatherproof, but also a pair of slacks that could pass for neat, a shirt that could pass for formal, a tub of boot polish, a brush.

That's why I never owned a washing machine: even a three-hundred-peso hotel will do your laundry for you if you're nice about it.

You have a long-sleeve shirt for dry heat, a Hawaiian shirt for wet heat.

You have a jumper and a leather jacket against outdoor cold, but mostly against shitty-hotel cold.

Meaning that when I got home, the packing took all of six seconds, leaving me time to book a hotel in a tourist town outside Poza Rica, book a meet-up with Francisco Escárcega, and get back on the road.

Before leaving the city I stopped for a coffee at the Teatro de los Insurgentes, lit up white against the midnight dark, leaning against the bonnet of my jeep, smoking cigarettes, my flask of LSD and water turning the view into Carlos' first day in Mexico City, when I'd taken him to the university campus for a walk and a joint, before making our way to the theatre murals.

Towers loomed high above us, their black glass fronts shining like iPhones.

'When I was a kid,' I said, pointing at the mural above the doors to the theatre, 'I used to look at photos of this place. My grandad had all these old encyclopaedias, with this like properly '70s colour palette on the pictures inside.'

At the centre of the smoke and fumes and scarlet drapes hung an opera mask decorated with a sun and a moon. Red-nailed fingers held that mask up above a space of fire where revolutionaries and emperors and Aztec duchesses twisted like dancers.

A gentle rain fell through the light, the fine white drops chased by the draughts of passing cars into the shapes mackerel form when threatened. Carlos shivered in his jacket.

I pointed. 'The sky in the background had this powder-blue tint that made everything look like morning.'

'You mean you found the only scrap of blue sky in Mexico City?' Carlos' voice was fake-amazed. He pointed. 'Love that Devil in the corner. So sleepy. So hungry.'

'He's really good,' I said. 'But I'm all about that blue. Used to sit at the back of class, stare up out of the window, watch planes cut through the sky, and wish they were lifting me all the way here. And then, years later, I *did* wind up here.

Landed on the rainiest, greyest, most hungover Sunday morning in the history of life. But the trees, they were rinsed green, and their shine was as glossy as the ones in that mural. All I had was two hundred words of Spanish, two hundred dollars in my wallet, and the address of some room the school had found for me, and so I showed the taxi driver the address on my phone.' I pointed with my cigarette. 'And he dropped me off at a house two blocks behind the mural. That picture, the one I'd always had in my head, suddenly I was living right around the corner from it. All day, every day, bouncing around town, underground on the Metro, through every traffic jam on every shitty bus, teaching English to nobody whose name I can remember, I'd carry that picture in my head, all the way back home to the stupid peeled Corona chair on my terrace, and I'd sit there with a book and a pack of smokes, looking up at that mural, home at last.' The long drag I took on my cigarette was one of those perfect drags that make your body feel like it's going to scatter in a rush of atoms.

Carlos nodded like he'd barely heard, looking at his cigarette. 'Shit, my head hurts. All those weird drinks we had, *vato*, I swear.'

'Which ones?'

'The Elvis Presley,' said Carlos. 'That was the first of your corruptions.'

'All you had in your hotel room was Xanax and whiskey.'

'That's not true,' said Carlos, and dunted me with his shoulder. 'We had vitamin C tablets as well. That's how we made the Enola Gays.'

I shuddered. 'The second night, what was it we were drinking?'

'Thom Gunns.' He bared his teeth like his head still hurt, tendons cabling in his neck. 'Cognac and speed. Did any of them actually taste good?'

'I'd give the Thai Orchids a solid seven out of ten.'

'What were they?'

'Jameson and coconut milk. After a stripclub near my university.'

'You had a stripclub near your university?'

'And a methadone clinic. I used to work there.'

'The stripclub?'

'The clinic, you bastard.'

'Huh.' He leaned forward and spat deliberately into the curb. 'Jesus,' he said, peering at the clot of phlegm. 'Look at that Chernobyl green. I'm ruined.' His shoulders folded in around his body like wings. He pushed his hair back from his eyes, shaking his head, his face turned towards me.

Except, now, in the memory, trying to call up his face, all I could see was his smushed nose, his kinked and broken fingers.

'Hell of a trip, all this.' He gestured vaguely.

Now, in the memory, his shirt was holed with two star-shaped burns. The whites of his lost-kid eyes brimmed with red.

Petechial haemorrhaging, Teresa had told me.

'You'll be OK, man,' I said.

Even in the memory, my hands under his shirt didn't run over his tattoos – the two swallows below his ribs, the black-letter curve of the nickname 'Flacucho' over his stomach – but over a 'Y' of autopsy sutures.

He looked at me steadily. Smoke crinkled out from the holes in his chest. Then he laughed. It sounded like a cough. 'You sure?'

Between third and fourth rib on the right side, fatally puncturing a lung.

'Positive,' I said, even though I wasn't. 'Come here.'

Between fifth and sixth rib on the left side, destroying the heart completely.

Against my throat, my lips, my tongue, I felt his smashed teeth, tasted his pulped lips. His throat wore a scarlet collar of bruises.

A reverse chokehold, Teresa had told me, *fractured the hyoid bone.*

Back in real life my eyes stung and blurred and my knuckles whitened around the doughnut bag, alone outside the mural, smoke unfurling from my lips. The people who'd killed him hadn't just taken the man: they'd taken my memories of him, too, Carlos moving into my arms in that hotel room in El Paso, Carlos slamming to the floor of that Poza Rica alley, Carlos on the mortuary trolley rattling down the apartment steps.

Then I balled up the half-eaten doughnut in its bag and stuffed it into the door and slammed the jeep shut behind me. After that I ate at a sad blue diner on the edge of the city then hit the fog-shrouded highway, heading east.

18

The poolside terrace of the Hotel El Tajín was loud with a mixed group of teenagers blasting cumbia and ranchera songs on their phones. They wore counterfeit Ralph Lauren swimsuits and fake Ray-Ban glasses and their flirting consisted mostly of yells and shoves. Francisco Escárcega sat at the far end of the pool, in the shade beside the bar, looking like his *Opinión de Poza Rica* byline photo: slim, dark, and with a sceptical, acne-pitted face.

'Good choice,' I said to Francisco as a girl ran screeching across my path to escape a boy who'd charged from his room after her. 'No one will hear a thing. Not even us.'

Francisco shielded his tamarind juice flung up by the spray of the two teenagers hitting the water one after the other, then shook my hand. 'Sorry, Andrew. Summer holidays. How was your drive?'

The front page of the paper at his elbow showed how a Poza Rica nightclub shooting had left four bodies twisted in a pool of Coca-Cola, grape soda, and syrup-thick head blood.

'Hard place to get to, Papantla,' I said, raising my voice

over the teenagers, who had bobbed up, yelling. 'Lot of twists and turns.'

'We're pretty cut off here,' Francisco said. 'Island without a sea.' Then he tsked. 'I was sorry to hear about your friend. Brave guy.' He gave a chin-jut. 'Saw him at the protest.'

The machete, the blood, the silver teeth flashing in the sun.

'He approached me at the end,' said Francisco, turning his glass on the table. 'Asked me for a few names of the people he'd seen. Asked me to get him to the bus station. So I hid him in my car, lying down behind the front seats.'

My throat was chalkdust-dry. 'You really put your life on the line, man.'

Francisco shrugged. 'Oh, it's there anyway.'

The teenagers in the pool had reconciled, kind of: the girl was slapping the guy in the chest while he laughed.

'We owe you, too,' Francisco said. 'Weren't for you and Carlos, we wouldn't have found out about Julián Gallardo.'

'Protest looked bad,' I said. 'Be better if we'd said nothing.'

Francisco lifted his hands like he was weighing something. 'Look, I mean, it did get nasty. Lot injured. One girl hit with a machete, went missing. Cops said she fell. Said she caught her leg on some metal. Said they took her to the hospital. Said she went missing after she was discharged.' He gave a bitter laugh. 'So precise. The police – Mexico's greatest fiction writers.'

Carlos' photos of black drops of blood falling from the blade, a girl on the ground clutching her opened leg.

Francisco shrugged. 'But, hey, unless there's a revolution, crackdowns at protests is all we've got.'

A Totonaca man in clean white linen trousers and a shirt

emerged from the hotel and skirted the pool, holding metal key rings of the Tajín pyramid out to the kids, smiling a silver-plated grin. One by one they shook off his pitch.

'Ah! American!' said the Totonaca guy, in English, when he saw me, jangling his pyramids at me. 'Welcome, welcome. Souvenir, souvenir.'

'I no want.' I waved my hands, pretending I spoke no Spanish. 'No. Wanto.'

The Totonaca guy held the pyramids under my face. 'Good price.'

'No. Wanto,' I said.

At last he was deterred, and swept from the terrace and out the back door onto the street with a flourish of his broad-brimmed straw hat.

Francisco made a crease of his mouth, nodded. 'You never know who's involved.' He gestured at the door to the street, where a *viene-viene* was whistling a car as it reversed to the curb. 'Even these car-minding guys get a couple hundred pesos a week from Puccini's boys to keep an ear out.'

'How do you stay safe?' I offered him a cigarette.

Francisco shook his head. 'There is no *safe*. Three reporters dead in town this year.' He counted on his fingers. 'A camera-man, an editor of a paper bought out by Zetas, a guy who did sports.' He sipped his tamarind juice. 'So much for the clean-up.'

'About that.' I pulled out the map I'd bought from the stationery shop across the street. All day, I'd combed the local news outlets to do a notch-and-cross tally of the people murdered in Poza Rica for the last eight years, with separate columns for people killed by Veracruz State Police, by suspected criminals, and by the Guardia Civil. 'This look OK to you?'

Francisco nodded. 'Yeah, the narrative's there. Puccini's boys basically did here what he'd done in Salvador. Anywhere people felt cagey about fracking, his boys went in.' He flicked his hands. 'Burned houses. Killed people in their beds. Disappeared the bodies.'

'I've heard.' I flicked back a couple of pages. 'An Ajenjo guy I met, he said Puccini's boys used to put bodies down into fracking wells.'

'Other places, too. A bridge right outside town. Lot of rocks. Lot of strong currents.'

For a moment I rested my fingertip on the page that Leo had shredded for his science lesson. Another kid splashed into the pool.

Francisco tapped one of the rows. 'But do you see this? Since 2014? Eight dead Zetas for every dead cop. These aren't shootouts: they're massacres. Death squads. Sentence first, evidence never. Not just for Zetas – students, protesters, indigenous people. This was the same year that local companies started trying to get foreign companies back into Poza Rica. Same year the Guardia Civil went after the Zetas, making room for whatever new gang of cops and criminals the companies send after protesters from now on.' He shrugged. 'Not that anybody'll complain, long as the last gasp of oil makes it into the right bank accounts.' He signalled the waiter for another tamarind juice. 'How long you here for? Got much lined up?'

'Few days. Main thing is I wanted to go see this guy out in El Chote.'

Francisco sucked his teeth. 'Yeah. That's a polluted spot. An old waste tank left by some American company started leaking a couple years ago, right into the river.'

'Huh.' I turned a page. 'Here's the other places this driller guy mentioned. Could be our next couple of days,' I said, passing Francisco the notebook.

He tapped the page. 'This place, San Antonio Ojital, we could go in the morning. Some people I interviewed once live round there. After that, we could do a drive around Poza Rica. I'll have to leave you then – it's school-run and then the night-shift for me now. But we can get breakfast before all that. I want you to try *zacahuil*.'

'I don't know what that is, but sure.'

The whole group of kids were in the pool now, their laughter kiting up in brilliant red flags.

'There was one other thing.' I scratched my chin. 'Reckon I could talk to Julián Gallardo's mother?'

Francisco cocked his head from side to side, balancing it up. 'I mean, I'll try, but after all she's been through? We'll see.' He grabbed his car-keys from the table. 'You're in for a pretty boring evening, hey – it's not safe after seven around here.'

'Oh, I love boring.'

Francisco laughed. 'Well, then,' he said, getting up from the table. 'Enjoy.'

19

Next morning, Francisco couldn't convince me to try the *zacahuil*.

'It's traditional.' In the passenger seat his fork scraped against a styrofoam burger-shell loaded with an orange mess of shredded corn and chillies. 'Very ancient.'

'Yeah, well, then you shouldn't have told me how people made the first *zacahuil* out of the body of a defeated sex murderer.'

'Just sharing.' Francisco held up the empty container. 'I leave this where?'

'Honestly, wherever.'

Outside the white church, six Totonaca guys in white linen pants and embroidered floral tabards climbed a tall cedar-wood pole, ropes tied to their heels. The clouds were a lead hood over Papantla. Day labourers shivered on the park, waiting for pickup trucks that might come, might not. The GPS sent us out of town, past a rubbled house whose chunks of wall were scrawled with letter 'Z's, then up a gravel track lined with red-trunked palo mula trees whose leaves looked burned. The jeep's tyres growled against the stone track. We rolled down a hill past a primary school with a cedar-wood pole standing in its yard.

'Guy broke his neck diving off that one,' said Francisco. 'Ten days ago. Totonaca guy, like the souvenir guy yesterday. They do this ritual where men climb the pole and dive off, sort of a slow bungee-rope thing, banging drums, playing fifes, trying to attract the rain-god's attention. Started years ago, during some drought or other.'

'Did it work?'

'Legend says it did, yeah.'

'So why are they still doing it?'

Francisco shrugged. 'Tradition?'

The ceiba trees on the other side of the road didn't look good, either, their oval leaves holed with yellow. We parked in their shade, because by now the clouds had burned off, and the seven a.m. cold wouldn't be around much longer, and then headed down a white path through an arcade of singed-looking banana leaves.

'We're not too early?' I hauled two ten-litre bottles of water from the boot.

'It's practically lunchtime for these guys.'

Francisco led us down the sloping path as far as a gap in the banana stems, their fruit spotted with rot, knocking against my shoulder.

'Take a look,' he said, parting the stalks so I could lean through. A well had been cut in the ground and lined with halved bricks.

'Smells like petrol.'

'There's a drill-site near here,' Francisco said. 'Soil's poisoned. Trees, too.'

After I'd snapped a couple of pictures, Francisco led me forwards into the clearing, where a thin Totonaca man of about fifty, wearing a vest and faded jeans, hacked at the stems with a long machete, outside a house walled with clapboard and roofed with dried palm fronds. When he saw us he stabbed the machete into the dirt and wiped his hands on his jeans.

'Tomás,' Francisco said, 'meet Andrew.'

He studied me from the shade of his faded baseball cap. 'A pleasure.' His voice was wary as he held out a calloused hand.

'We wanted to talk about what it's like living here.' I raised the bottle as best I could. 'Heard you had some problems with water.'

Tomás pushed his cap all the way back. 'Very kind of you,' he said tonelessly.

'Where do you want me to bring it?'

'Through to the kitchen, if you don't mind.'

He held the door open, and we stepped into a wide, clay-floored space with a metal cot in one corner and plastic chairs in the other. A woman in a polyester dress stood beside a sink's metal skeleton, scouring a plate with water from a plastic basin.

'Apolonia,' Tomás said, 'we have visitors.'

The woman gave me the same hooded look that her husband had. 'Welcome to our house,' she said, in a voice as dull and guarded as her husband's, drying her hands on a frayed tea-towel and then patting her pinned-back grey hair. 'Please, sit.'

Francisco and I crossed the clay floor, past a framed photo of the Virgin of Guadalupe decked with lilac orchids and dried mandarins. I stowed the water under the sink and sat down on a chair with no table. Tomás poured out plastic glasses of orange juice from a small jug, handed them to us, and sat down with his arms folded, beside Apolonia.

'I'll tell you what I tell them all,' Tomás said. 'We're poor, but we're not stupid. You can't eat money, and you can buy less with it every year. It's a fraud. Not like the land. The land never stops giving. That's what I tell them.'

'Who do you tell?'

'Foreigners. *Mestizos*,' Apolonia said. 'People who want us off our land. People who poisoned our well, made the water almost too thick to draw.'

Francisco took a sip of his juice. 'Tell Andrew about the company.'

Apolonia laughed, and put a long-fingered hand over one eye. 'Our owners?'

'The new laws,' Tomás said. 'If there's oil under your property, the government can sell it under you. Suddenly you're the company's.'

'We didn't take the money,' Apolonia said. 'And the man who offered it hasn't come back.'

'What if he does?' I asked. 'The companies are returning soon.'

'Fight them, I suppose,' Tomás said with a bitter laugh. 'I've got a machete. A catapult. Apolonia can throw oranges at them.'

'Look, whatever about the money,' she said. 'We could

take it. We could move. But where?' She pointed at the hearth. 'They buried my umbilical cord here when I was born, tangled up with my mother's, and my grandmother's, and her mother's, all the way back. If I sell this place, what will my family tell me when I meet them again?'

'But they're sending police,' I said.

'Police?' Tomás laughed. 'They've sent worse than that.'

A chill crept my neck. 'What? When?'

'A couple of months ago,' Apolonia said.

'Longer than that,' Tomás said. 'Spring. I'd gone to town to get weed killer.'

'Left me to deal with them,' Apolonia cut in, with a mocking glare. 'Two weeks after we refused a compensation cheque from Ajenjo – that much I know for sure. Because no more than fifteen days after he was gone, the Zetas came.'

'How did you know it was them?'

She spread her hands. 'This was something we all heard about. How they'd go to a village, kill people, dump bodies on the outskirts. We knew we'd be next.'

'What uniform did they wear?' My breath was going like a piston. 'Veracruz State Police?'

Apolonia nodded. 'But they talked like narcos. "We made a generous offer, and if you're here when we come back, you're all dead".' She leaned her chin on a seamed hand.

The chill spread from my neck to my shoulders. 'And could you tell me –' I slid my iPad out of the satchel and tapped open the photos of Puccini and his lieutenants '– were any of these men there?'

Apolonia studied the screen. 'This one doesn't come

around. They say he's in charge.' She tapped Puccini's face, then moved her finger to El Prieto's. 'This frightening one isn't someone I've ever seen.' Finally her finger rested on Sharktooth's face. 'This one, with the teeth. He came here.'

The chill crept down my shoulders, over my back.

'Just to be clear.' I flipped back through my notebook pages. 'After you refused a compensation deal from Ajenjo, you were threatened by members of an organised crime group.'

'Yes,' said Apolonia. 'Twenty thousand dollars, they offered, no more.'

'And these gang members, they were masquerading as police.'

'Correct,' she said.

'And you know they were masquerading as police, because you recognised one of them as a members of Puccini's cell of the Zetas.'

'Also correct,' said Apolonia.

'And you're sure you want to go on the record?'

'You can use our names,' said Apolonia, running her fingertip along her eyebrow. 'If they're going to do something, they'll do it, whatever you write.'

'OK.' I stood up on jellied legs. 'Thanks for having us.'

'Thank you for the water,' said Apolonia, but her eyes were already somewhere else. Tomás slipped out the front door, and Francisco picked up my orange juice for me and brought it to the sink. Then we went back to the jeep and started driving, and I was glad that my licence plates were too dirty to read.

20

Driving in to Poza Rica jacked my heart-rate right up. The noon sky was brown and louring, the dashboard thermometer read forty Celsius, and the breaths I drew were warm and thick as bathwater.

Francisco had me drive past the union building for a few photos. The green glass facade shone in the dull afternoon light. To one side, beside the words SECCIÓN 30, a smog-browned concrete frieze showed a muscled oil worker toting his spanner in the shadow of an oil derrick. A second frieze retold Mexican history as a straight line from conquistadors battling locals via some priests and revolutionaries as far as a petrol-worker's family dressed up like it was 1950s America.

'The guy I want to talk to,' I said, snapping a picture, 'his friend said a union official drove him to the body-disposal site.'

Francisco nodded. 'Sounds about right. This is where a lot of money gets laundered – there's some pretty high union rates. Really it's just workers being given parcels of cash to pay into the union.'

'Huh,' I said, my camera lens drifting over a group of beaten-down-looking men and women peering at chits and waiting to be called. Among them stood union officials wearing the kind of suits and watches that union officials can't usually afford.

After that, we continued to the edge of town so we could see the Zeta-controlled neighbourhoods. Scrolling by, fast, in the rear view: electric wires rat-tailed in puddles; rainbow maps of spilled-out cooking fat, detergent, petrol.

Outside a rundown pink convenience store sat a mother and son. The son had dreads, a Rasta-theme Adidas zip-up, cracked bifocals, and he and his mother gave a start when they saw our jeep. We could have been the cops, or local bosses seeking their weekly war tax, or why not both.

A bunch of men in vests and jeans lounged outside a row of grey degraded shop fronts and mechanics' yards. Beside some of the doorways stood Santa Muerte statues garlanded with flowers and rosary beads.

'Those shops don't look too active.'

'They are,' said Francisco. 'But only in the mornings, when the night's haul comes in. Your car gets stolen in Poza Rica, next morning, you can buy back the parts right here.'

We passed the open doors of a Jesús Malverde temple, its inner walls pasted all over with prayers scrawled on dollar bills. Some of the prayers were threats: '*Brother Malverde, help me to chase down the dogs of the colonia Zapata.*' Just outside sat a man heating a crack pipe. A tall Santa Muerte altar loomed over him, overhung with black and yellow triangles of bunting.

'That altar's a drop-off point,' said Francisco. 'You leave guns, drugs in under the flowers, and nobody'll touch them.'

The skeleton saint grinned out from under her purple cowl. Her glass box was like a vertical coffin, crept all over with a vermicular spackle of airborne dirt.

The man in his beer chair gave a cagey backward nod when he saw us.

'Is there an international sign for "I'm not DEA"?' I said to Francisco.

'Looking like you do, no.'

The guy was still looking, so I gave him a big cheery thumbs-up.

We cut down off the avenue, drove through an alley of trash and cinder-block housing. Then a siren cut the air and put a spike through my navel.

'What's that?'

'Probably another raid,' said Francisco.

When we got to the top of the alley, a whole fleet of Guardia Civil vans were parked across the road, outside a rundown coral-pink *vivienda*. From inside you could hear the quilted pop of gunshots.

'You aren't worried about those guys?' I asked Francisco.

He shrugged. 'Always. But what can you do?'

Six Guardia Civil guys in ski-masks and sunglasses were marching a line of about fourteen kids from the *vivienda* towards two big, mesh-windowed police wagons, kids with Neymar haircuts gelled crisp as toffee apples, Barcelona and América jerseys, big fake Nikes, not one of them older than seventeen. Through the glass, you could hear one of the cops yelling, 'You're fucked now, boys! You and your mothers!' while the rest whistled.

Francisco and me, we just started filming. My camera's mic caught the thunk of gun-butts against kids' shoulders from where we were parked. The kids' poker-faces started to strain as they neared the police wagons. One caught my eye: frowning, pudgy, around fifteen years old, climbing into the mesh cage of the riot-van. That's all I saw of him, but what I could feel was his life in that *vivienda*, hearing cries catch and warp against the walls all day and night, years and years between walls that were too tight and too thin for him to get any homework done, and what I knew was he went stressed-out every day to a school that was no more than a holding pen.

Me, if I'd been that kid, I'd have dropped out too. I'd have taken the hundred-sixty-dollar weekly wage to watch a block for the boys who owned shiny jeeps and shiny guns like the posers on Bandamax TV, instead of turning chickens on a spit sixty hours a week for a hundred dollars a month.

While Francisco finished filming, I peered at the kid on my screen, at his bleached Mario Balotelli mohawk, at his wide, lost face.

Could have been the face of a lookout. Could have been the face of a kid who drank a few cans or snorted whatever lines of cut-to-shit coke he could cadge from his friends so that maybe they'd stop making fun of him. Or it could just have been the face of some poor fat kid born in the wrong city.

A cop slung shut the police wagon, and I lidded my camera.

★

'Good luck with the school run,' I said, dropping Francisco off at his newspaper. A couple of kids with pinched faces and baseball caps eyed us from a doorway, their hands in their hoodie pockets.

'See you tomorrow, for more *zacahuil*,' said Francisco.

After that I headed for the address Armando had given me, my eyes locked on the rear-view mirror, waiting for a State Police truck to slip behind me, my blood a scurry of ants, the highway snaking through a humid green nowhere.

With no cars chasing me the sweat began to cool on my back, and I dropped down the approach road to El Chote, quiet, lined with ceiba trees, with nests of vines hanging from its telephone wires. El Chote itself was a barely there town with a bar about double the size of a shed, a straggle of low houses screened by bluish ocote pine, a group of kids jinking their ragged football across a field the colour of rust, with a wellhead stuck up through the centre circle. Between the pines you could make out a slow black river thick as blood. A high ammoniac sting pricked my sinuses even with the windows up.

The *abarrotes* shop Leo had mentioned stood beside a junkyard. Faded Telcel and Sabritas sponsorship logos hung above its door. When I parked outside, a man stepped out from the rusted security cage, peeling a mandarin.

'You the journalist?' he said when I got out of the jeep. He had an indoor pallor, and his thin hair was mussed like he'd been lying down. 'Yeah, Leo told me you might come here.' He tossed a chunk of mandarin into his mouth. 'Be careful taking pictures. Photographer came round here once. People didn't like him taking pictures of the kids. They left him in ribbons.' His skin breathed days, weeks, years of frightened sweats and bad sleep, a madness that isn't a madness, a paranoia that's not paranoid, because, living in a place like this, if you're paranoid, you're probably right. He flung the handful of mandarin peel into the grass. 'How can I help?'

The air seethed with insects. The long grass rustled. In five minutes, I told myself, I'd be out of there, speeding back to the quiet furnished cave of my apartment.

'Leo told me about your time working for Ajenjo,' I said.

Armando nodded. 'Those were bad times. The worst times. After those times, I quit. Then my wife left. Took the kids to Puebla. There's a military academy there. My boys, they're good boys. They won't fall into vice – not like the boys around here.' Armando gestured at the grass that edged the football field. 'Everything talks here. The grass. The crickets. They know things before you even think about them.'

My thighs and groin tensed with fear.

'All right,' I said. 'Could you identify some men if I show you their pictures?'

He lifted the hem of his T-shirt to wipe his face, revealing a leopard-mottle of burns all over his skin. He huffed a laugh through his nose. 'I tried, I really tried. Wasn't enough petrol.'

'I'm going to need a yes or no answer here,' I said.

Armando stared at a point above my shoulder.

Turning, I saw a Veracruz State Police car roll slow past the poisoned river, past the pines and the bar and the football field. The windows dropped. The kids didn't even stop kicking their ball around.

In the driver's seat was a man with a long beard and a pale face. His picture from the iPad flashed in my head: El Prieto, the white guy who'd been there when Leo and Armando had gone to the well. Beside him sat another man, muttering into a phone, his arm hanging through the open window, his tie loosened, his eyes brimming with sleepy patient violence. He was heavyset and curly haired. His voice was a Campechano drawl.

'Here's your "Yes",' said Armando.

Something like that happens to you, your bladder swells up planet-sized. The piss runs right to the tip of your dick. You want time to skip into thirty-two-speed fast-forward, except you also don't, because you don't know how long you have left.

Armando clanked shut the gate behind him and went back to his couch, the blanket pulled over his head. Mangueras gave me a slow salute, the gravel crunched, and they drove on into the dark, while I ran for my jeep, the phone at my ear, already calling Francisco.

'Everything OK?' he said.

'Met a couple of our friends.' I swallowed.

Francisco clicked his tongue.

My eyes flicked from the road ahead to the rear-view mirror. No jeeps up front, no jeeps behind: just a motel built to look like a castle, a couple of kids in school uniforms punting a Coke can along the verge.

On the other end of the line I heard Francisco rap his knuckles against his desk.

'Which friends did you meet?' he said.

Up ahead, parked by the roadside verge, stood a Veracruz State Police car. My back ran cold.

My foot pressed the gas. The cops in the car looked up. One of them spoke into his walkie-talkie, but the car didn't move.

'Andrew?' said Francisco. 'Which ones?'

'The lawyer and the white guy.' I swallowed. My throat was drier than it had been on the morning Carlos and I had found Julián Gallardo. 'Look, if anything happens to me, you never knew me. You never saw me. I was never here. OK?'

The doors of the police car opened. The two cops climbed out. One was videoing my jeep on his phone.

'Shit,' I said. 'I have to go. Be safe, OK?'

After a long pause, Francisco said, 'OK,' and hung up.

The narrow streets on the outskirts of Papantla were choked with people – a religious festival, kids dressed in white, candles held under their chins, San Judas Tadeo riding a litter heaped with yellow and green flowers – while cars and mopeds inched behind, hazed in exhaust fumes. Bass drums thumped louder than my heart. Trumpets squalled.

'Jesus, come on,' I said to no one, and rubbed my fingertips against my forehead, willing the procession to move faster. A firework thoomed and streaked the dark.

Outside the machine shops and *abarrotes* stores stood men in dirty vests and women in string tops. They weren't watching the parade: their eyes were locked on the forecourt of a Pemex across the street. One woman chewed a fat gum-wad, her jaws working fast, and the tension in her gaze watching the petrol station should have told me to worry, but I was too spooked to think straight, and the police car I'd seen on the highway pulled out of an alley and rolled across to block the gap of space between me and the rest of the traffic jam. Before I could kick into reverse a pickup rolled off the Pemex forecourt to block the way back. The kid riding the moped behind me didn't even honk.

Mangueras opened the door of his pickup and walk slowly towards my jeep, rolling up his sleeves, stretching like he'd had a tough day locked behind the desk.

'Andrew,' said Mangueras, and leaned against my open window. 'We met earlier. You never introduced yourself.'

The policemen who'd filmed me opened the driver door and gestured for me to get out. When I climbed out into the street the onlookers slunk back into their shops and their houses.

'You've been poking around,' said Mangueras. 'Mostly in the wrong places. We can take you to the right ones.'

The white guy with the heavy metaller's beard, the guy they called El Prieto, he got out of Mangueras' pickup, held out his hand for my keys, and I handed them over before he had to pull out a gun.

'*Sale, pues,*' said Prieto, and shoved me into the passenger seat.

The procession thumped its way around the corner, leading the cars and mopeds behind it. Then it was just the tremble of crickets, the shudder of my breath.

Prieto climbed in on the other side. One trained an FN-259 on me. The other turned my keys in the ignition. The Fidel Castro key ring jangled.

'My boss said it would be a big noise if you were to go

missing around here,' said Prieto, driving. 'Me, I'm not so sure. It's never a big noise when anyone goes missing.' He raised his hand from the wheel. 'But who am I to say, hey?' He chuckled. 'He's the boss.'

We'd gone back the way I'd come, then out a side-track, past a junkyard so overgrown with ferns that they sprouted from the open, empty bonnets, and then on to a tyre-rutted tarmac road.

'So my boss, he says we have to do something special for you.'

The seat ran with my sweat. Shakes hit me in bursts, like my body was a washing machine on its last spin. The coffee cups rattled at my feet.

'And I'm like, sure, whatever. You know best. That's why you're the boss.'

Mangueras' police car drove just behind us, headlights glaring white on the cracked glass facades of the big oil company headquarters zipping past, one by one, security guards watching the grass that poked through the parking lots.

'But it's not my bag. No, sir. If it was up to me, you'd be dead by now.'

The grass verge was littered with plastic bags, sweet wrappers, rat-looted heads of corn. Beyond the headlights the night was humid and empty.

'You know how long it takes for a body to go bad out here? In all this heat?'

The chatter of my teeth did the replying for me.

'And it's a wet heat out here, *cabrón*. Four days, you wouldn't have a face.'

When the lights of a house came into view on the right, Mangueras flashed his headlights once and Prieto slowed the car to roll up a dirt track with tall rows of corn on either side, as far as a red-brick house surrounded by scaffolding.

Prieto clicked his tongue, said, 'Idiot couldn't wait until he'd finished his house,' then pulled up at the door, braking so hard and fast that we skidded to a halt right outside, loose grit pinging the undercarriage. Mangueras parked just behind, then hopped from the police car to open my door. Prieto kept his gun trained on me so I didn't bolt. So did two men in State Police uniforms, their ski masks pulled up, AR-15s primed and ready.

'Get out.' Mangueras hauled me from the car into the dirt. My arm nearly popped out of its socket as he dragged me into the tiled hall. A smell of fresh blood kicked me in the nose, and, when I saw where the smell was coming from, my guts lurched and I sprayed the back of the white leather couch where Abel Carranza, alias Sharktooth, alias Z-35 sat with his head blown off and his silver teeth melted into his exposed bottom jaw.

Mangueras dealt me a shove that knocked me over, sent me sliding face first towards scattered shards of Abel Carranza's skull. 'This is the man who killed Julián Gallardo, the man who killed your friend.' He nudged me in the ribs with his patent-leather shoes. 'And we caught you before him and his bosses could. Stopping him is the last favour we'll do for you.'

What I wanted to say was, '*Last* favour?', but Mangueras was already dragging me out the door. Prieto and the cops raised their gun at me again.

'Now, get the fuck out of here,' he said, climbing into the police pickup.

Prieto threw the keys at me. Fidel Castro's beard caught me full in the temple.

Then he sat in beside Mangueras, and the two cops took up positions in the back, the headlights raking over me one last time as they turned in the driveway and drove back the way we had come.

For a while I lay there waiting for my pulse to slow down from a heart-attack sprint, then dragged myself into the driver's seat with the keys in my fist and my jeans stained with the blood from cuts I didn't even feel yet. In the red glow of the dashboard light my shoulders had the same bullied hunch as the kids I'd seen during the round-up that afternoon.

The steering wheel was wet when I lifted my face away from the moulded plastic. A hand that didn't feel like mine placed a lit cigarette between my lips while the other hand keyed my home address into the GPS, its red navigation line a miles-long snake unkinking toward the highway.

'Just be glad that bastard's dead.'

Moths clouded my high-beams. The day's pictures flickered in the dark: Apolonia with her head in her hands, the sad fat kid in the back of the police van, the burns stippling Armando's torso, the unreflecting calm in Mangueras' eyes as he dug me in the ribs, the dark pool of blood and brains on Abel Carranza's couch. My story was a ragged collage that made no sense.

Another five tabs of the Díaz Ordáz blotter sloshed at the bottom of the flask. The bitter pulp slid down my throat.

Smoke floated from my pulped lips as my tyres droned against the road.

The first time I zoned back in, the mountain fogs had rolled in over the car. Bolero songs played on the radio, a Pemex zipped past in the rear view, and the road lines ticked by like white dashes.

'Where it all went wrong,' I said to no one.

The second time I came round was in Mexico City: bad traffic, brown air, sour drivers. My eyes scanned over all that morning rush but all I saw was Abel Carranza's unlidded skull, his shot-out molars, the silver teeth welded to his jaw forever.

My street looked like nothing had happened. And nothing had, not for the older women sat waiting in the beautician's beside my apartment building, or for Gustavo the Rastafarian *luchador* sweeping up outside his fruit shop, or for the moustached old guy in the cowboy outfit selling lottery tickets outside the HSBC.

Inside my building, the ground floor apartment's wide-screen TV cast blue lights over the palm tree and the pebble bed at the bottom of the light well. The usual morning chatter filtered from the doorways: radio burble, parents hurrying along their children, the clink of grabbed keys.

Those sounds of normality, they were the closest thing I'd known to safety in I didn't know how long. My gait was baggy as a sleepwalker's heading up those stairs.

But when I got to my floor, the door swayed open, one of its panels kicked in. The lock was buckled, gouged, stripped of paint.

The queasy feeling I'd carried all the way from Veracruz got worse now, my ears ringing like I'd stayed underwater for too long. No noise came from inside: not the trickling fish tanks, not the hum of the fridge, not the gurgling of the pipes.

The Mexican papers have this way of writing the passive voice. When you don't know who did something but you know what happened, you just say *they did it.*

So when a man gets shot, the headline reads, *Lo tiraron: They shot him.*

When a woman turns up stabbed to death, *La acuchillaron: They knifed her.*

. When eleven bodies turn up chopped up by a roadside, the headline reads, *Los descuartizaron: They chopped them up.*

Yeah, I know: *they* and *them* in two separate clauses.

What you lose in clarity you gain in immediacy, I guess. That's the thing about reporting in Mexico: clarity's in short supply. All you know most of the time is that something happened, and that *they* did it. That's how it is, reporting in Mexico: you only find out the truths you don't want to know. Truths you *do* want to know, you'll never find out.

And that's if you're lucky. If you're not lucky, those truths find out where you live.

Whoever *they* were today, they had pulled the shelf of cocktail-glasses from my wall, left broken glass drifted like snow across my table, floor, chairs.

A landing plane whooshed low overhead. The room and my skull shuddered.

'They really hated my art.'

The display cases had been tipped over, my strobe-lighting

169

Kalashnikov stomped in two, my Guatemalan pagan idol's bright skull punched in, and each one of the five faces of Michael Jackson I'd kept framed on my wall had been torn in two.

'Thorough,' I said, nudging the smashed halves of the William Howard Taft mug with my toe. 'Too scared to wreck the saint stuff, though, eh?' I picked the Jesús Malverde plate up from where they'd left it on the table in a space cleared of broken glass, beside the Santa Barbara and Santa Muerte statues.

In the kitchen I climbed over the tipped-over fridge and leaned under the sink to the cupboard where I kept my cleaning supplies. When I swung the door open Motita coughed out a yowl and jumped into my arms.

'Someone was shy.' I hefted her until she stopped trembling. She swatted my face with her paw, gave me a look that said everything was my fault.

'Let's go see the damage, fatty,' I told Motita, carrying her through the sitting room. The metal-framed chair lay buckled under the weight of my heaved-over palette and plants. They'd shattered my pots and pulled the branch down from its ceiling wires to lie snapped on the floor, as ugly as Abel Carranza's bared jawbone. Peat-moss starred the floor, the reed mat, my cowhide throw, the sheepskin rug.

They'd had trouble with the desk: it weighed half a ton, after all. Some of the drawers had been beaten in, my folders scattered everywhere, and my iMac was gone. They'd torn down my map and snapped the noticeboard in two, but the acid blotter was intact enough to fold into my jacket pocket.

They'd flung the yellow ashtray right at the fish tank, let the water come flooding out, sucking the java fern and Amazon sword plants and the pebbles onto the floor.

'Saves me dealing with the snails, I guess.'

The fish were hours dead, their scales faded, beginning to fur. Julián Gallardo's printed-out photo lay pasted to the ground, so I knelt and picked it up, placed it to dry on the slashed upholstery of the chaise-longue.

Motita hopped from my arms to the desk, her tail jerking, her fur on end, and swatted some loose pages to the ground, where they soaked in the wet. The upholstery of my chaise-longue had been slashed with what I guessed was a machete, but I sat down anyway to unlock the desk's bottom drawer, which they'd kicked in, leaving it so buckled I had to grip the sides to jimmy it out.

'Come on to fuck.'

At last the drawer gave way and clanked to the ground, the handle falling off, tipping the old tapes and notebooks into my hands: small, black, hand-sized, the elastic beginning to wear and snap, their hard covers dinged and faded, and I flicked through pages sallowed by the drag of my hands, breathed in their yellowish smell, and ran my fingers over the tight, neat scrawl, the scribbled maps, the names, the dates, the phone numbers, before standing up to spill the lot into my satchel.

'There it is, Motita. Our stories. Our interviews. All the stupid shit we did that never made the actual copy.' I ran my finger over the tape labelled 'CARLOS // EL PASO // 30 / 12 / 2012'.

Motita coughed.

In my bedroom, the lampstand had been snapped in half and my macramé God's-eye hauled to the ground to lie pooled with the curtains. The bedclothes were rucked, the clothes in my wardrobe pulled apart at the seams, and a huge letter 'Z' slit into my mattress. What was left of my fingernails ground against my hand.

'We should go,' I told Motita, collecting Julián Gallardo's photo from where it dried on the chaise-longue and folding it into my jacket pocket. 'They might be watching.' Then I walked to the bathroom, and brushed away heat-killed flies to lift the cistern-lid. The gun was taped to the inside of the water-tank inside a Ziploc bag.

'Never lift the lid,' I said. 'Burglars always take a massive shit after they trash a place. It's, like, tradition.' I peeled the Ziploc free of the water-tank and unsealed it, took out the gun, let the bag fall to the floor.

We went to the kitchen, where I propped the fridge on a pulled-over shelf and opened the freezer. The two bullet-filled bags of Café Garat clanked into my free hand. Motita nosed the ice that clung to the inside of the freezer.

'Come on.' I picked her up again. She didn't resist much. 'Going to see your Aunt Maya, aren't we?'

Motita coughed, and I kicked my way through the drifted trash as far as the door and headed downstairs through the building's morning noises.

'Don't know how they didn't hear anything,' I said to Motita, shutting the door behind me. 'Although maybe they did.'

When I opened the back car door for Motita to hop in she

recoiled from the trash and pages littered over the seats. 'Come on, Motita, there's a good girl.' She gave in, but curled up as small as she could, like she didn't want to touch anything.

The sun that morning was livid red, round and swollen as an octopus' head. The tapering red jet contrails could have been tentacles. After not a very long time I couldn't look at that shape and lowered my eyes to the road, my head empty of everything but the high grey song of my tyres on the blacktop, all the way to Maya's apartment. She wasn't in, and Motita didn't like being dropped off there, but the security guy thought it was all right: his grin showed almost all of his braces.

After that I drove to the airport, past drenched palms and the smashed-ruby glitter of brake lights. When I parked, I locked the gun and bullets in my glove compartment, left the car in long-term parking, and headed inside the airport, where I stood with my back to a pillar, near two security guards, and had to take eight steadying breaths before I could work up the guts to call Dominic. Families, spring-breakers, sports teams all hurried past, hauling bags, surfboards, cardboard boxes. My whole life lay in three bags at my feet.

'Andrew,' Dominic said in my ear. 'How's the story going?'

'Ran into some trouble.'

A tall suited man stopped four feet from me, squinting like he recognised me.

My breath stopped.

Then I remembered the flight-times monitor above my head.

'What kind?'

The man in the suit walked away, his Samsonite rumbling on its little wheels.

'They, uh, they found out where I live. Did a job on the place.'

'Jesus. Where are you now?'

The two security guards standing nearest to me walked up the concourse, so I shunted my bags over my shoulders and tried to stay in their sightline.

'Airport.'

The security guards stopped outside a convenience store. One of them went inside. The other turned her back to call out to him what she wanted from the shop.

Dominic's sigh huffed static in my ear. 'That's hardly ideal. They get much?'

'Ah, they did, yeah. Story's safe, though.'

'Well, I hadn't wanted to ask, but that's something of a relief.'

'Yeah. Here – you can't get me out of here, can you?'

The security guard still had her back turned, and I was sure that now, right now, some kid would sidle out of the crowds, press a muzzle to my navel, waltz off before the burn-circles on my shirt had even finished smoking.

'Well, we're not really in the habit of doing that, but needs must.' Dominic's nine o'clock shadow rasped on the other end of the line. 'Where were you thinking? Back home?'

What I wanted to say was, 'After eight years, "back home" is here.'

What I said was, 'Anywhere safe, Dominic, genuinely.'

'OK. Go somewhere public. Give me fifteen minutes. I'll

call the Baron. See if we need a job done somewhere nearish by.'

All the while I waited for Dominic to call I walked within sight of the guards, sipping on my flask, sweat pinpricking all over my skin.

When my phone buzzed this time, Dominic's voice was almost cheerful.

'Andrew,' he said, 'did they get your cameras?'

'No, they're right here,' I said.

'Great. Well, you're in luck. There's a huge blizzard about to hit the south of Uruguay. First time some parts will have seen snow since 1960.'

The security guards stopped to give directions to a stressed-out older couple.

'And we need pictures. Our woman in Argentina, she's held up in the north – something about mining. She can't get back down to cover the snowstorm, but if you can get us a few shots, that's our excuse to have you down there. TIFF format, no cropping, nothing fancy.'

'Dominic, you're a lifesaver.' I changed course without stopping and quickened my pace towards the Avianca desk.

'Don't be so literal, old soldier. Put it on the credit card. Send the receipt. And –' he cleared his throat '– send the main story when you can.'

'Will do.' I was already at the desk, passport open, the credit card's blue weight between my fingers bringing me back further than I expected, all the way back to my old boss Helen's fingers tapping on her laptop keys, back to her blond bob lit up in the screen's bluish glow, back to the night she booked my flight to the city I was now leaving.

The clerk's voice cut through the memory.

'Is that your total luggage, sir?' she said.

'Yeah, that's everything.'

'Have a safe flight,' said the clerk, handing my tickets. 'Security's over there.'

All the way through security, immigration, check-in, boarding, pictures I didn't expect came bobbing up through my head: snow over the River Liffey on the night that I'd met Callum and Helen; a beach of sand the colour of bone where Helen and I sat toasting my impending escape with a bottle of Sancerre and a couple of stolen Ambien; the scared, lightened feeling when she'd dropped me at the airport.

Then I was on board, belted in safely, and the plane jerked forward, sped, rose. Below me the city I'd craved to live in for so long dropped away from me: its roads like long black veins, its blocks packed like cells, a city whose teeth had clamped around me and shaken me limp. When the plane levelled in the air and the chime went to unclip our belts, I could've slid all the way to the carpet, an empty sack of tired skin.

The air steward handed me a glass of orange juice, and by the time she had served the next passenger I'd glugged it empty.

Even though I didn't know it then, only fourteen hours remained before I saw you for the first time.

If I'd known, maybe I'd have been something like happy.

Probably, though, I'd have felt the same: scared, and too light, and all alone.

21

We landed in Buenos Aires to rain edged with sleet. My eyes were sticky and my armpits were rank but even still a lightened feeling started to quiver in my chest, one that wasn't entirely due to the last dregs of the tabs in my flask.

In the arrivals hall the TV weather showed snowstorms circling like tank formations. We'd been lucky: passengers clustered around monitors that read CANCELLED. Within that press of people, oblivious, an older couple, two women, sat hooked up to a shared pair of earphones, watching opera on their laptop while they waited, a single blanket pulled over their knees. I snapped them for Dominic.

'Well spotted,' I imagined Carlos telling me. 'Sentimental, but well spotted.'

'Fuck you, Carlos,' I said.

From the taxi, zipping through the wet fog, past the Plaza de Mayo, I got shots of Malvinas veterans laying down sandbags around their tattered military tents.

Under a big highway overpass I got the driver to slow down so I could take a picture. Rain tipped down from the buckled highway overpass in a phosphor seethe. In the shadow of the overpass, MISSING posters hung on stakes, arranged in a shape like the chalk outline you'll see at crime scenes, each one glowing in the white light of a single electric bulb.

'What's this place?' I asked the driver, zooming in, raising my voice over the roar of that pre-dawn storm. Bright piles of hail drifted over the names and faces.

'Used to be the Club Atlético police station,' she said. 'Fifteen hundred people disappeared there.'

'You remember any of that?'

Her eyes met mine in the rear-view mirror. 'Of course. I was sixteen.' She looked towards the shape losing its outline to the sleet. 'Get your picture?'

'Oh. Yeah. Thanks.'

The word TERMINAL glowed red through the murk. If I'd felt self-conscious at the airport, with my rat-tailed hair and pisshole-in-the-snow eyes, here I just blended in with the backpackers as we climbed through the boarding tunnel onto the deck. The Mar del Plata ramped against the ferry.

Wind chased my cigarette smoke over the bay, and the boat shuddered down the slipway and out of the dock, its motor pulsing. When the cold reddened my knuckles, I ducked inside to get coffee, across a red carpet and stained brass fittings that hadn't been updated since the years my taxi-driver had talked about. Two families sat at faux-marble tables, counting stacks of credit cards held together with elastic bands, downwardly mobile middle-class types, the men in pilled Ralph Lauren gilets and the woman carrying handbags that they'd repaired more than once or twice.

When the kid at the counter – handsome, with a big '70s bouffant and a pirate earring – brought me my cup I asked him about the people with credit cards.

'In Uruguay, the casino ATMs feed out dollars,' he said. 'So you bring credit cards from everyone you know, withdraw all their daily limits, then exchange the lot back in Buenos Aires, at these black-market change shops.'

'Snow doesn't put them off the trip?' I pushed aside my coffee to take a note.

The guy laughed. 'If you lived in Buenos Aires, a plague wouldn't put you off. Economy there is –' he gave a thumbs down. He leaned closer to peer at my notebook. 'What's this for?'

'An article. You OK if I quote you?'

He shrugged. 'Sure. Put my name down as Charly. No big deal. Even the cops do the credit card thing, when they can.'

'Wow, interviews here are way easier than in Mexico,' I said.

Charly laughed. 'Then you should stay.'

I didn't say anything, and took a seat on a red leather banquette by the window. The horizon was an empty mercury shimmer under the white mell of snow. Zeros of spume spread breaking across the water.

The snow had yet to hit when I arrived, but the sky shone white. After collecting my bags at the terminal I got a bag of roast chestnuts and walked along the beach toward the hotel, the hot bites stinging the cores of my teeth, sand hissing underfoot. Two streams braided across the sand, feeding the estuary with red Virginia creeper leaves.

From my boot I shook a straggle of seaweed brown as film reel. The clean air seemed to rinse the tar from my lungs. More pictures of Dublin broke upwards through my head, from the days after Helen had vanished: drinking vodka from Lucozade bottles on the coastline DART; the mornings spent in class, the evenings with data-entry work open on one tab and juddery football streams specked every forty seconds by ads on the other, a Moosehead in my fist and the ballsack odour of my drying work-pants all around me, my stomach concave from too much drink and too little food; drinking to fall asleep, sleeping to kill the time between drinks. By the time I reached the end of the beach, the memories had me as dizzy as the weed and booze of my Dublin years.

'Weird to think of you here, Carlos.' I opened the map I'd screen-shotted, then cut past old colonial buildings whose stucco fronts had that nibbled, undersea look, over cobble-stones that gleamed like wet lead. 'It's pretty. Quiet. Not very you.'

The map sent me as far as an empty square lined with plane trees, a statue of the independence hero Artigas standing at the centre, and I stood outside a converted warehouse built out of rough limestone blocks.

You stood in the driveway, stooped over a brown Labrador who had a stick clamped in her jaws. With one hand you held back your long black hair. With the other you tried and failed to wrestle the stick from her.

'Good luck with that,' I said to you from the gate.

Way you looked in that brassy strike of morning sun, the shine it put on your hair, your poppy lips, it tightened my chest like I was back in Poza Rica.

'Joke's on her,' you said, not looking up. 'I've got plenty of wood. And she's got only one set of teeth.'

Behind you, beside the door, stood a pile of chopped logs, their rinds of frozen sap shining like orange zeros.

'Good point.' I shucked my rucksack and red rubber sailor's bag from my shoulder. 'She a real Labrador?'

'Oh, yeah.' Finally you gave up, but threw aside the stick so hard that the Labrador rolled over on her back and huffed out a disgruntled noise. 'One of those wood-eating ones. Very rare.' You wiped your hands on your jeans and looked up at me. 'So you need a room, then?' Your skin was shellacked with health and your boots were as scuffed as mine. 'I'd shake your hand but –' you held up your palms '– very doggy. Need help with your bags?'

'Ah, no. It's just these.'

'Someone travels light.'

'Lately I tend to,' I said, and followed you through the door into the dim, cool hall. The floorboards were dark knotted oak, and from a fire glowing orange in the brick fireplace smoke spooled upwards, thick and dark as your raw wool jumper. The deep bay windows looking out over the park were lined with red leather banquettes and cushions, and near the centre of the room stood a huge maple table lined with neat rows of tourist brochures.

'Nice place,' I said. 'Floor's cool.'

'It's real easy clean.' You stepped behind the desk and

flipped open your laptop. 'What you do is you tell yourself the grime is part of the aesthetic or whatever.'

'That work on the owner?'

'Works on the guests.' You held out your hand. 'Passport?' When you looked at the front page I said, 'I go by the middle name.'

'Who calls you your first name, then? Just your family?'

'My family doesn't call.' I scratched the back of my neck. Lifting my arm made me remember that my last shower had been in Poza Rica. 'Bit wiped out after the flight and all – water pressure any good here?'

You handed back the passport. 'Yeah, super strong. You need laundry, too?'

'Very much so.' I slung you the red sailor bag.

You looked at the passport photo a little more.

'Yeah, so I've aged terribly.'

But you just smiled and handed it back, then took a set of keys from the row of hooks behind you. 'And, since you're the only one here, we'll give you an upgrade.'

You led me through the hall as far as a flight of dark wood stairs that creaked underfoot. At the top floor you pushed open the door on a bright, white-walled room. The skylight's blue square was right above a fat bed, and a screen door opened onto a bright terrace.

'Bridal suite. You look like you need a good week's sleep.' You opened the bathroom and leaned into the dim, terracotta-tiled space. 'Roll your sleeve back.'

Hot white needles stung down from the showerhead, dimpling my skin.

'Strong enough for you?'

'Yeah, I think so.'

'There.' You switched off the water. 'I'll let you unpack. You need anything, I'll be downstairs. Oh, and technically you can't smoke in here.'

'Oh. Sorry.'

You smiled. 'Technically, though, I'll bring you an ashtray later.'

Then you left me alone to empty out my bags: the note-books, the worn copy of *Proceso* with Carlos on the cover and Julián Gallardo's face folded up inside, the tape recorder, the cassette holding mine and Carlos' first meeting.

The plan was to listen to it again, all the way through this time, but when I lay down on the bed, I had barely enough time to get my phone plugged in before the blood in my arms and legs felt as heavy as the water in my old fish tanks, and when I shut my eyes the dark behind my lids became a dream of Carlos, of snow over a floodlit cove, of his cover-photo rippling and softening in the water, and the sleep that came afterwards held no further pictures.

22

If Maya hadn't called, I don't know when I'd have woken up – ten days later, probably.

'You're dead,' she said, her voice low with fury.

'Oh, hey, Maya.' I slugged from my water flask and lay back on the pillows.

Motita coughed in the background.

'Your reactionary, misogynist cat.'

The clunk on the line was Motita smacking herself against one of Maya's cupboards.

'You dumped her on me.'

'Yeah, well, I also skipped the country, so there's nothing you can do.'

'What? Where are you?'

'Uruguay.'

'Are you serious?'

'Yeah.' I held up the phone. 'Hear that? Uruguay.'

'You have a lot of explaining to do. And even more apologising.'

'I'm sorry, Maya. The Motita thing, it's only for a few days, I swear.'

She didn't say anything for a second. 'You sound tired.'

Above the skylight the clouds had darkened, become a green ocean.

'Dominic tell you?'

'He just said you were OK. What happened?'

'Remember your break-in?'

Maya didn't say anything.

'Something like that.'

A light patter started on the glass above my head. A voice rose in my head, a voice from eleven years ago, a voice that brought back a nape that had smelled of wealth, eyelids that had ticked under my lips like birds' heartbeats.

'Sucks, doesn't it?' said Maya. 'I almost feel sorry for your cat now.'

'Oh, don't,' I said. 'That's how she'll get you.'

The white flakes stuck to the glass and didn't melt. That numb, desert-trail emptiness I'd felt sitting at the wheel outside Abel Carranza's house dropped over me again.

'Do you want me to let you go?' said Maya.

'Yeah. I just have to take some photos.'

'See you soon?'

'Promise.'

You were right about the water-pressure. The blast lifted the blood and sweat and dirt from my skin, sent them swirling into nowhere, raising a steam thick as fog. In the mirror, my skin had colour in it again. Even the dark bags under my eyes had been scoured a fainter shade of purple.

You were sitting at the maple table when I came downstairs,

stooped over the receipts, your hair shining dark blue in the light.

'Well, hey, Lazarus,' you said.

'You didn't want to go look at the snow?'

'I'll look in the morning,' you said. 'You going out in that?'

I still had Carlos' jacket on. 'Well, yeah. Warmest thing I have.'

You shook your head. 'No, no.' You got up from the table, walked behind the desk, and opened a closet. 'Take this.' You held out a long double-breasted wool trench coat. You pulled a mustard plaid scarf from the pocket. 'We're the same size.' When you handed me the coat and scarf, you squeezed my shoulder. 'Almost.'

'Thanks.' Your broad gold odour of gardenias washed around me when I buttoned on the coat. I headed for the door. 'I'll be back in a bit.'

'Take your time. I'll be here all night.'

What I wanted to say was, 'I hope so', but instead I just waved and went out into the shin-high fog and the snow's oblique swirling punctuation.

The story was easy. Most people were kind of flattered, posing beside the names of their hotels or their restaurants or their casinos or whatever. None of the Porteños cared who knew about their dollar-runs.

By the time the orb-lamps on the main square glowed through the wet fog, and a red evening sun blotched the water, I had enough quotes to write up the snow story in a tiny café decked with nineteenth-century photos. Storm-noise and tide-hiss rinsed the windows, and, when my head nodded forward, I jerked from my doze to guttering candlelight, wishing the coffee was stronger, or spiked, or why not both.

'Fuck this.' I slid some money under the saucer and went out into the dark, down streets far from the tourist area, where dead ivy scrawled out the commemorative plaques, and the fanlights had been looted, and the balustrade pegs on the balconies lay keeled-over and poked through by cords of weed. Yellow plane-tree leaves drifted the curb, softening with the snowfall, and I slipped, and when I righted myself my foot caught a loose cobble and I went down hard on my shoulder. The strap of my satchel snapped and my laptop skidded out.

'Fuck.' The laptop was fine, but your coat was ruined, the sleeve all pulled and damp and muddy. 'Just when I was all clean.'

The bruises on my ribs and my back rang with pain, and the cuts on my knees leaked blood into the one clean pair of jeans I had. Slowly I got to my feet and kept walking, the wind making swallowtails of your coat's hem.

White-knuckling, they call it, when you're sober but you don't do meetings, and that's because however hard you grip, your grip's got to slip sometime, and down you'll fall, all the way back down to the places you swore you'd never go again.

The snow was coming down hard now, and in that whipping cold every bar, every restaurant, every beer-ad glowed like the lights of a rescue boat.

Any one of them would have done, every one of them.

And I would have cracked, I know I would have, but those

lights, they were too harsh, too yellow, when what I really wanted was to get lost in the mellow forty-watt glow of your hotel.

Meaning you saved me, kind of.

'Fuck you, Carlos,' I said, and chucked the flask of LSD away, then I ran through the snow – ribs burning, knees screaming – all the way back to you.

You'd moved to the couch by the time I got back, staring at the fire and pouring hot water from a Thermos into your maté cup.

'I'm so sorry.' I raised one arm. 'Sleeve's out of shape.'

You crossed the room and took the cuff between your fingers. 'It's just wet.'

'But the mud.'

'Andrew, I run a hotel – I know one or two dry-cleaners. It's fine.'

'I'm so embarrassed. I never do this.'

Taking your coat back from me, you saw my jeans and you made an 'O' of your mouth. 'Ouch. That was a bad fall.'

'Different fall.'

You looked at me and frowned. 'What happened to you?'

Through the window the snowfall had become a storm. When a draught rocked the door it could have been Carlos' ghost roaring to be let in.

You draped the coat on the armchair nearest to the fire. 'Want to sit down for a bit?' Then you sat back on the couch. 'It's miserable out there. Come dry off.' For a second I wasn't sure if I should join you on the couch, but then you held up the maté cup. 'Thermos is still warm,' you said, pouring out another cupful of hot water from your flask and holding the maté out to me.

'Is it always so quiet?' I sat down beside you and sucked a tart mouthful through the metal straw.

You laughed. 'I wish.'

'Keep it this way. Tell guests it's cursed.'

'I have heard of better business models than this. Oh, and before I forget.' You collected an ashtray from the table and handed it to me.

'Technically you're not supposed to let me.'

'Technically, I don't really care.' You took back the maté. 'You're all right, you know. Most of the people who come here, they're real demanding.'

Dark chunked logs burned in the hearth.

'Strange question,' I said. 'I knew this guy. Came here when he was a kid. Said he stayed at El Sur. You remember him?'

You frowned, sucking on the straw. 'When?'

'Oh, shit, like, seventeen years ago.'

You laughed. 'See, that's a problem. I was fourteen. And I'm from Rocha.'

'Oh. Well. Worth a shot, I guess.'

'What happened to your friend?'

'What do you mean?'

'You said "I had this friend". You broke up?'

'Not quite.' I took the worn copy of *Proceso* from my satchel.

You took the magazine from my hand and looked at the

date, then back up at me. 'This isn't so long ago.' You flicked through the pages. 'Jesus. What a sad time for Mexico. Seems like everyone has a tragedy in their lives.'

'Yeah, well.' I was slumped halfway down the couch now. 'Call him mine.'

Another page turned. 'That's really hard,' you said. 'What was he like?'

My eyes crept towards the window. 'A good guy, mostly. Troubled. But OK.'

'You're shaking.'

A sheet of ash slid from the log.

'Yeah,' I said, and swallowed, shutting my eyes. 'I still . . . I see him.'

The magazine rustled shut. 'When?'

'Sometimes. Often. He's –' I huffed out a sigh, and when I blinked I saw Carlos' poppy collar of bruises, the hole in his forehead, the bullet stigmata that marred his hands '– he's very much like a ghost.'

'You miss him,' you said. 'My grandmother saw my grandfather after he died. A lot at first. Then less, and less. And then once more, when she was dying, she said he'd come to say goodnight. Went the next day.'

'You saying it's normal?'

'I'm saying it happens.'

'I don't want to be mad.'

'You're not. You're just someone who's lost somebody. And you've probably seen some things. And you like strong water pressure.' You swatted my shoulder. 'And you're really bad at taking care of coats.'

'Do you think the coat's OK?'

Your hand didn't move. That warmth, that soft weight took the cold from me.

'I think the coat's probably fine, Andrew.'

When I opened my eyes you were looking at the fire, but your hand was still warm on my shoulder.

'You're still shaking.'

'Lean there long enough, there's a rhythm.'

You gave it a couple of seconds. 'Incorrect.'

A snow-edged gust wind chased a 'V' of crows past the window, and your throat was a 'V', too, as you leaned in honey-slow to pull us both down.

Afterwards, in my room, we sat half-wrapped in the bedclothes.

'Had it been a while?' you said, and bit my shoulder.

'What?'

You looked at me sidelong.

'Oh. Yeah. Kind of. Why?'

'You seemed very . . . euphoric.'

'Jesus. That's embarrassing.'

After a while we sifted through my old notebooks. You ran your thumb over the words like each letter was a tiny blue scar. With you beside me, walking your fingers from my throat to my navel and back, the room's warm blue dark on our skin, it was easy to tell you all of it.

'Where were you for this one?' you said, opening the one with all my notes from Poza Rica inside.

'Worst place of them all,' I said, and lit a cigarette.

'Oh, you'll eventually feel nostalgic about it,' you said. 'Trust me.'

'Yeah?' I said, tapping ash. 'When?'

You lay there, looking light and untrammelled, with your tanned and bird-alert face and your hair spread all around you black and wild as a cloud of starlings, smiling at the ceiling.

'One year,' you said, 'I didn't go back to university. Went on a boat instead.'

'What? How?'

'It's easy,' you said. 'You go search for boat crew on the Internet. And you fill in a form. And then you're on a crew. Easy – except for storms.' You laughed. 'And now I even miss them.'

In my head, Mangueras' car pulled up outside Armando's house. My hand found the small of your back and the picture vanished.

'I mean, the storms are bad,' you said. 'You've got these waves like towers above you – they've even got shadows. Drops rain down from them. Wet your face. And then they hit –' you clapped your hands '– and you think you're going to flip. All you've got is your black box, and your GPS, and your six crew members, and that's it, that's all you are. And when you don't flip, you feel so light. So unbreakable.'

My eyes moved over the three bags that were my life now.

'The calm, afterwards – that's delicious,' you told me. 'You lie on the deck. All you have are the stars, the boat rocking, the feeling of your own body pulsing under nothing. The sea, afterwards, it's like a mother carrying you on her hip. Gets me so nostalgic that I even miss the storms.'

'Huh.' I lit another cigarette. 'And what'd you do all day? When you weren't playing Captain Ahab.'

You rolled over and put your head on my chest. 'Read Proust. Perfect time to. As long as there's no storm, you can just watch the water. Read. Maybe that's what you should do, after you're done.'

'What, go on a boat?'

You propped yourself up. 'No – go somewhere quiet. Stare at nothing.'

What I wanted to say was, 'I'd rather stare at you', but I just kissed you instead.

After you fell asleep I slid into my pants and sweater, borrowed an umbrella, and crept from the hotel, the snow creaking underfoot all the way to the park. Bergs of dead plane-tree leaves flowed down the curb, carried by the currents of meltwater, and I reached in my bag for the El Paso tape, slotted it into the recorder, skipping four hours in, to when me and Carlos were making roaches from his old business cards and he was doing a frame-by-frame commentary on Elvis' 1968 *Comeback Special*.

'Man, look at the arm-waving,' Carlos said over the orchestral billows at the end of 'If I Can Dream'. 'So gospel. This note is rad. Wait, no. Next note, next note.' He blew out a sigh. 'After that thing with the cops, man,' he said, 'I just looped this song for hours. In my room. I don't think I was me any more, you know? Took loads of my mother's pills. Zolpidem. Temazepam. Names like Aztec gods, man.' His dark cackle jagged up out of the speakers. 'The fucken sun-god, man, to go by the sweating. And then one day, I drove out into the desert in my mother's car. Way, way out, down into the canyons, boiling up dust behind me, until I came to a rise of boulders. Neon cactuses towering around me. Lay there in the smoothed-out rocks.'

His voice was deep and slow and rhythmic, like he was chanting. 'The carves of some old gone river had left shapes in them like emptied veins. And I just lay there, and smoked a bowl, and the pink-lit clouds in the sky were the dying thoughts of God, seemed like, and the rocks I lay in were the lap of some beautiful corpse.'

He sucked on the joint and his voice came out croaky and strained. 'The clouds were history, and history was God's dreams as he died high and paranoid in the sand. After that I dreamed I was dead.' More smoke puffed against the mic. 'And I didn't mind at all.'

Carlos cleared his throat. 'And that didn't scare me. Just made me feel a bit ill, a bit embarrassed for the person who had to come clean me up. I looked down on myself, laid down on the rocks, split from hip to rib, laid in hay, my heart glistening apple-red like a prize for the ants. A wind scattered my bones' white nubs like dice.'

Then you could hear the rustle of his bedclothes as he sat up. 'Ah! Here it is. Way Elvis hits this note. This one right here.' His tenor grew reedy with passion. The orchestra boomed behind him and he pumped up the volume. The tape buzzed.

Somewhere, out in the cold distance, a car raked past.

'Troubled,' I said. 'And probably not OK at all.' I stopped the tape.

You half-woke when I came back into the room, rolling over, your eyes shut.

'Out with your ghost?' you said, in a voice thick with sleep.

The boot stopped halfway off my foot. 'You heard?'

'Mmhmm.' You stretched. 'Saw it, too. Was asleep. Was nice.'

'You mean you were dreaming?'

'Close the door, won't you?'

The beach was white when we headed out the next morning.

'You don't seem impressed,' I said. 'This blizzard is, like, historic.'

'I work ski-seasons in Bariloche. You get all the snow you could ever want up there.' You kicked a drift. 'More, even.'

On the sand stood a chunk of whitewashed wall reading *PARALLEL UNIVERSE ENTER HERE* with a squiggled line pointing at a door.

'Bit trite, that.'

'One of the better ones around here, unfortunately. Let's go to a bar. A warming whiskey, I think.'

'Ah. I don't do that any more. Quit.'

You laughed. 'A journalist who doesn't drink?' You slid your arm through mine. 'Well, then. Glass of . . . milk?'

I kicked a heap of snow. 'Ah, God. At least offer a coffee, like. So I don't feel like an absolute child.'

On the far shore cranes swung in the dusk. Brine stung my nose. A large black dog trotted across the sand, his moustache a sandy droop, blood thick as ketchup dotting his flank. He threw himself down in the snow-covered sand, panting like he'd never stop. When he saw me he flinched upright, growling. You leaned towards him, arms out, murmuring under your breath.

'Careful. That dog has no chill.'

'Oh, he's all right. Just don't give him that look. Watch.' You knelt beside the dog with your hand out. His tail slapped the snow, throwing up white dust. Then he whimpered and rolled over on his back with his tongue out.

'You ever pass a dog you didn't greet?'

You rubbed his dreadlocked belly. 'God, I hope not. You got pets?'

'Kind of.'

'What do you mean, *kind of*?'

'Just moved house. Gave my cat away. I mean, she was kind of a wanker sometimes, so it's probably all right, really.'

When you'd had enough, you wiped your hands on your jeans and kept walking beside me. The dog sprinted off in the other direction. 'Will you get another?'

'Haven't decided where I'm moving yet.'

'Oh, you have to. I couldn't live without pets.'

'Think a pet's about all I'm fit to live with. Or a plant. A sturdy one.'

You tidied my hair back from my face. 'We'll train you. We've got nine days.'

Except we didn't have nine days. We had barely nine hours.

That night, coming back from the bathroom, I saw the green notification light flashing on my phone. When I swiped it unlocked, there were twelve missed calls from Francisco, the most recent one from ten minutes before.

The covers rustled as you pulled them around you. 'Andrew, the door!'

'Won't be a sec.' I shut the door and went downstairs with the phone pressed to my ear. 'Francisco, what's happening?'

'Ah, you're OK,' he said. 'Phew. When I heard they got Carranza, I was worried. Word of it came so soon after you called.'

'Still here, man,' I said. The hearth still smouldered. I leaned against the warm brick arch and flicked my cigarette butt into the hearth. 'You all right?'

'Same as ever,' he said. 'Nobody seemed to mind that you were down here.'

'No, everyone was very helpful,' I said.

'Glad to hear it. Hey, so, I've got some good news, too,' he said. 'It's Julián Gallardo's mother. She said she'll talk.'

I sat down on the armchair. Your coat fell to the ground. 'And she won't talk to you?'

'She won't talk to local press,' he said. 'And she's afraid they'll tap her line. Going to have to be face to face, I think.'

'Ah. Right.' I pressed the heel of my hand to my forehead. The cigarette I'd flicked into the hearth had begun to smoke, a long, grey taper as smooth as the line of Carlos' smoke rising from the crematorium, and I knew I had to be the one to finish this. 'Here, let me get a plane sorted. Meet you in Papantla day after tomorrow, how's that?'

'A plane? Where are you?'

'Think it's fair to call this place the opposite of Poza Rica.'

Francisco tsked. 'It's well for some.'

'Yeah, well, see you in a bit, OK? I'm going to pack.'

You were sitting up when I got back into the room. 'Everything OK?'

'I have to go.' I started turfing my things into a bag.

'Did I do something wrong?'

'No, not at all.' I put my arms around you. 'Work called.'

You looked at me with big-eyed fake amazement. 'But your laundry.'

'Security deposit.' I zipped shut my backpack.

You pushed back your hair. 'Are you seriously leaving now?'

'There's a flight out of Montevideo that hasn't been cancelled.'

'You won't get there in time. No buses.' You grabbed your jumper. 'I'll drive.'

'What, really?'

You shrugged. 'What? This is the most exciting thing to happen to me since the boat.'

When we pulled in at the departures building you stretched like a cat in the driver's seat and put your hand in the back of my hair.

'OK, you're semi-trained,' you said, and pulled me in for a kiss. 'We can finish the rest when you're back.'

'What's the rest?'

You shrugged. 'Small stuff. Fetching logs. Taming dogs.' You plugged a cigarette in my mouth. 'Now, go get your plane.'

I twisted the bag-strap on my shoulder. 'This was nice.'

You smiled. 'And it will be.' You took off the handbrake. '*Te espero acá.*'

In Spanish, the verb *esperar* means 'to hope', 'to wait', and 'to expect'. Which of the three you meant, I didn't know, but I prayed it was all three.

23

After that came fourteen hours of migraine-colour light and air that made my throat sore, but enough of your gardenia smell had caught on my clothes to keep the dread at bay until I landed at the squat concrete airport outside Poza Rica.

Francisco met me at arrivals, where he stood next to a small spry man with a large moustache and a faded baseball cap.

'Welcome back,' he said. 'Andrew, this is Lombardo, the *agente municipal* for Zapata. He spoke to Julián's mother for us.'

'Thanks for setting up the meeting.' I shook his hand. 'You sure you won't get in trouble being seen with me?'

'Ah, don't worry.' Lombardo waved a hand. 'We'll just say you're my cousin. On the Chihuahua side of my family.'

'There's a Chihuahua side to your family?'

'Sure there is,' said Lombardo.

Francisco led us out through the doors to an ambulance that stood parked on a mostly empty, weed-pocked lot.

'It's the town's,' said Lombardo. 'Present from Pemex.'

'Is the doctor OK with this?'

'Cousin,' said Lombardo, clapping me on the back, 'I am the doctor.'

We drove through thick woodland, past a grass verge dotted with rusted signs for Pemex wells, as far as a deep gorge crossed by a huge rusted bridge. A Guardia Civil pickup stood at one side. Four men in plainclothes stooped over the edge with AR-15 rifles under their arms. Lombardo just kept driving.

'Another kid went missing in Papantla last night,' said Francisco.

The ambulance rucketed over the bridge and we headed down a tree-hooded road tight and dark as a tunnel. The uneven surface rattled the trolley and drips in the back. A tall, shimmer-edged refinery flame wavered in the distance.

'Those cops weren't looking very hard.' I turned around my chair.

'That's because they threw him in,' Lombardo said simply.

Slowly the refinery flame grew taller and taller, until we could hear its roar through the windscreen. Lombardo lowered my window.

'Sounds like a plane taking off,' I said.

'All day, every day,' Francisco said as we passed outside a reed-and-mud fence that surrounded a whitewashed bungalow roofed in tin. Men and women dressed in Pemex overalls, jeans, and plaid shirts stood clustered in the yard, eating pork and tortillas from plastic plates. Beside them the clean pink halves of a pig hung from a wood frame, its parts bobbing in a tin cauldron over a wood fire. The refinery flame towered above us in the blue air.

'Our whole village is a victim of the oil companies,' said

Lombardo as we crossed another bridge. Pipes traversed the gap, some of them dripping, tainting the water with oil-stain rainbows. In one yard a woman sat on twelve-inch pipe, fanning her cooking-fire with a dried palm-frond. Francisco and I leaned out to take pictures.

'Is that safe?' I asked.

Lombardo shook his head. 'Not really. We've counted them – a hundred and eighty-two pipes cut through the town.'

'How many people are there?'

'About a hundred and eighty-two.' I pretended to take a note. 'I'm joking, I'm joking. Jesus. You got the slow blood in the family, eh, cousin? We're living on top of a bomb. Whole village burned down when a pipe exploded in 1962.' He gestured out the window. 'All this was rebuilt.'

The hilltop road took us above a grove of mandarin trees, their leaves burned-looking, their fruit pitted and scrotal on the branch.

'And what about crime?'

Lombardo laughed. 'Don't get me started. I'm the only doctor for miles. A country doctor, treating war wounds in the middle of the night.' His voice was light. 'You get used to it. And, you know, I do my best work for those Zeta guys.'

'Well, you'd have to, wouldn't you,' said Francisco.

The road tapered through a centreless maze of rusted spigots and crumbled concrete walls, bleached by the high noon sun. Thick ferns bobbed in a light wind. A graveyard feeling breathed from the wreckage.

'The old village,' Lombardo said, stopping the ambulance

for a moment. He clicked his tongue. 'I wasn't born. My father remembers.'

'What'd he say?'

'"You ever see pictures of Pompeii?"' He took off the handbrake and drove as far as a house on an outcrop above the valley. 'Here she is,' he said gently.

A woman of about forty wearing sweatpants and a purple spaghetti-top stood outside. She looked different to her son's Facebook photo. The red streaks in her short hair had faded, the smile on her face had gone, and her eyes had a broken look.

She was already walking towards me as I climbed out, her arms open. 'I want to thank you,' she said, and clasped me to her, 'for what your friend did.'

'I'm so sorry for your loss,' I said.

She talked on like she hadn't heard. 'He was so brave.'

'So was your son.'

We stood looking out at the green empty countryside seamed by the distant river. The refinery flame roared and smoked above it all.

'Tell me about Julián.' I took out my notebook.

'He was a good kid,' she said. 'For a kid from this town to go all the way to university is a big thing. Lombardo threw a party for the whole village. We were so shy, but we went.' She smiled. 'And for the first year of university, it was like a celebration, every day. He worked so hard. He'd get the bus to Poza Rica, come back from the library after dark, even though it was dangerous. We lit so many candles. But he was always careful. He hadn't any vices. But then his father died.

My husband.' She swallowed. 'He was a personal driver for one of the Ajenjo engineers. He'd take him around the wells at all hours of the day, morning, noon, the dead of night. Sometimes they'd sleep there. Sometimes he'd come home pale, and wouldn't tell me why.' She waved her hand. 'But we all knew. We all knew where the bodies went.'

She coughed out a bitter laugh, took her phone from her pocket, and started swiping through photographs. 'One night, halfway through Julián's second year, his father went out late at night with the engineer – some emergency, he said, but something that wouldn't take long. He said he'd be back in an hour.' She shook her head. 'And, you know, Ajenjo, supposedly, they had a protocol around this. They tell you within ten minutes if they can't locate somebody, then they update you every hour. But they didn't tell me a thing. Julián and I went to the offices, and all we got were stony looks and words that don't mean anything: "We're investigating to the height of our capacity, we've involved every element of law enforcement", everything like this.' She held her phone up for me. 'Then, two weeks later, the company sent us this photo.'

The screen showed two bodies lying beside an oil-tank, their faces masked in oil, the lines of their lips dark, their eyes full, their hair like brown eels, the thick glar heavy in the folds of their clothes.

'They said the engineer fell in first, and that my husband fell in after him. That they both drowned. That it was an accident.' She shook her head. 'A lie. I've seen these tanks. They're not deep. And even if you do fall in, there's a metal rod you can hold on to for someone to pull you across to the ladder. And somehow it took them a fortnight to find them in the tank. Here, give me your number. Have this photo.'

I handed her my card.

'They told me I could claim him,' she said, tapping on her phone, 'but when I went there, they hadn't washed him. He had no autopsy stitches, you know the ones? And the marks on his face, the bruises, the broken nose – you don't get this when you bang your head.' She zoomed in on the picture for me.

'And this was in 2014, right?' I said.

'August of that year,' she said. 'A week after the Guardia Civil came in. One of them was there when they gave the body back. A tall man. Silver teeth. Brown hair.'

My pen stopped moving.

Carlos, if you get this, what the fuck?

'Your husband saw something he shouldn't have,' I said. 'And either the company or the Zetas or both decided he couldn't go public about it.'

Nodding, she leaned against the chipped wooden lintel of her door and finally let herself cry. 'And this is what killed Julián. This is why he started to organise, to rally, to work. To find the people who killed his father. And I tried to tell him to keep quiet, tried to tell him that I knew what would happen, that what always happens would just keep happening, like it happened to his father, like it happened to those poor Ayotzinapa students, like it happens to anybody in this company since forever.' She cut herself off, waving her hand. I handed her a tissue from my pocket.

'So the company sent the same man after your son,' I said. 'And got the police to cover up his murder.'

She nodded again, her eyes shut. 'And, you know, part of me is proud of his sacrifice. But the rest of me just wants his body.'

The weight of the airline pastries was cold as oil in my gut.

'Señora Gallardo,' I said, 'I don't want to take up any more of your time. But we're going to take your son's story to everyone we can.'

She wadded the tissue up in her hand.

'It's not justice,' I said, 'but it's something like revenge.'

In that flickering orange refinery fire I saw Carlos wreathed in flames, smoke pouring from the bullet-holes in his chest.

'It's all I want,' I said. 'The ones who killed your son and your husband killed my friend, too.'

She put her hand on my chest. 'I'll light a candle for him.'

'He'll need a few more than that.' I slid my notebook into my pocket. 'He was a complicated guy, Señora Gallardo, I'm not going to lie.'

'So was Julián.' She stared at the refinery flame. 'We need complicated people.' She shut the door behind her and I climbed back into the ambulance.

'All set?' said Francisco.

'All set.'

Lombardo took off the handbrake and drove down the hill. 'Back to Chihuahua, then, cousin?'

'I was thinking further south, actually.'

★

The first flight back to Mexico City wasn't until the following morning and we couldn't trust the night buses, so Lombardo dropped Francisco and I at the hotel in Papantla.

'You know, this place is all right,' I said to him, as we sat down on the restaurant's banquettes. 'You should move here.'

'The *voladores* would drive me crazy,' he said, pointing through the window at the six men in their tabards and white linens diving from the pole by the church.

'Ah, c'mon, man,' I said. 'Embrace the tradition, or whatever.'

He gave a fake shudder. 'I'll stick to *zacahuil*.'

The sharp white fife notes cut through the glass as the *voladores* dropped backwards to the ground on their long ropes.

'Fair.' I pointed at his empty glass of tamarind juice. 'Another?'

'Think I'll be heading back.' He patted his stomach. 'All those tacos, plus a hotel dinner. I feel like a python. Going home to sleep for a week.' He stood up.

'Yeah, same.' I hugged him. 'Here, thanks for the *zacahuil*. Kind of.'

'Reporters are a dying breed round here,' he said. 'Have to stick together.'

When he left, I headed back up to a room so tight and airless it was like being sealed inside a plastic bag. Dominic had emailed to thank me for the photos from Uruguay – and to badger me about the oil story. The blank document pulled my thoughts all the way back to you, its cursor a lone coated walker, the fan a wind edged with sleet, the letters skinny as holly branches. All I could think of was how snow over El

Paso and a blizzard over Uruguay had become this sweltering hotel in Veracruz.

The slow ceiling fan chopped my cigarette-smoke into long blue festoons. Through the open window the evening sky was a thirty-two-degree hyper-saturated red. My cursor ticked across the screen, and the tin roofs outside ticked and contracted with the day's fading heat. As the colour died from the air I watched them hammer their tambours and toot their fifes as they dropped backwards, their music shrill enough to make me want to saw down their stupid UNESCO World Heritage pole, but I gritted my teeth and bashed out a draft before slamming shut my laptop and walking into the humid night.

The hotel's red lights smouldered through the evening mist. Dun flocks of chachalacas scattered above the park, empty now except for an old couple sitting on a bench by the bandstand. The Totonaca guy I'd seen at the pool with Francisco had come into some luck at a restaurant: a salesman type and his wife marvelled as he held up a replica of the church and its diving pole, complete with four model *voladores*. When he caught my eye he nodded and smiled.

After that I walked downhill into a maze of streets I hadn't gone down before. The only lights on around here came from a whitewashed bar on a corner with the words EL TALIBAN written in tall blue letters above the door. Instead of a door the bar had a red curtain. Bolero songs rippled out to me through the gap.

White-knuckling is the name for what happens when you're sober but skip out on meetings, when you grip anything and everything that's not a drink, because really you're just a drunk without the alcohol.

But now the man I'd been white-knuckling was gone. The LSD flask I'd been white-knuckling was gone. The story I'd been white-knuckling all this time was almost gone. Soon I'd be left gripping nothing at all, and then I would only slide.

My cigarette flew through the dark and I was through the red curtain and into the bar's warm aortic dark before that flicked butt hit the curb.

There weren't many of us in there: just a table of teenage boys hunkered giggling at a video playing on one of their phones, and a couple of Totonaca builders with the shins of their jeans white with the dust of a long day. At the bar I sat beside a scrawny guy in a Pemex outfit. Behind the bar a large woman dressed in a bodice and lace tights fixed her makeup in the smeared bar-optics.

'*Chela, güerito?*' she said in a deep, velvet voice.

The flutter in my throat was so loud and so strong that all I could do was nod. The bottle cap hissed against the opener and tinked to the ground.

A six-foot oil painting of Osama Bin Laden watched me through the gloom in the corners, hung with cobwebs thick as cotton gauze.

The bottle sat in front of me. A bead of moisture slid from neck to shoulder. Before I took that first swig, I got up and crossed the room as far as the jukebox, flicked back through the menu as far as the Elvis songs, found 'If I Can Dream', slid in ten pesos. Trumpets rose, sad as a last-stand bugle, toy piano notes played on my own back's bones, and the washes of electric organ were the same green tone as the crematorium music two weeks before. I shut my eyes and Carlos slowly formed out of my cigarette smoke, wearing the slim leather shoes and suit that I'd found in his ruined wardrobe. The smoke darkened and curled into the gentle brown waves of his hair, the jukebox speakers buzzed like wasps, and his voice rose in my head.

But before I could get back to my stool and drink my beer, the curtains whispered apart, the lace-clad woman stopped fixing her hair in the mirror, the teenagers stopped giggling and the Totonaca builders went rigid in their chairs. The scrawny guy in the Pemex uniform, he turned around all right, but then he turned away again once he saw who had come in, and emptied his beer, and then everybody in the bar got up almost in unison to spread their hands on the wall, their feet shoulder-width apart, their eyes aimed at the ground.

'I'm terribly sorry for the interruption,' said a voice behind me. The accent wasn't Mexican. The aspirated 'h', the dropped 's' were pure El Salvador. 'Ordinarily, we'd invite you to sit and enjoy a drink with us.'

Someone's feet squeaked against the grit of the floor.

'But we have to speak with this man in private, so we must ask you to leave.'

A couple of heads craned, then went back to staring at the wall.

'Please allow me to take care of your bills. Now, if you don't mind . . . ?'

The lace-clad woman, the scrawny guy on the chair, the teenagers, the builders, they half-jogged from the bar, leaving me alone with Osama Bin Laden and Mangueras and El Prieto. Beside them stood the vendor with the pyramids and the clean white linen trousers. His face looked carved out of wood.

When I saw the other man with them, the man who'd spoken, a sound rose from my throat that was too tired to be a sigh, too shallow to be a groan.

His face had loomed out of my sleep most nights since the first time I'd seen it, peering sombre out of the photograph of an army battalion surrendering its rifles on a soccer field in 1992, oval, olive-skinned, with a shapely nose and a neat black crew cut.

Puccini had aged well. His hands could have been a teenager's, the skin was so unbroken, and no grey hairs flecked his crew-cut. Except for the scar that bisected his face, his expression could have been a teenager's too, all relaxed floating bravado, like none of anything was a big deal.

'Is that him?' Puccini asked.

'That's him, *jefe*,' said El Prieto.

'I asked our colleague.'

The Totonaca guy nodded.

'Very good,' said Puccini, and shook his hand. 'You can go now.'

The four guys behind him parted the curtain to let him pass, his brass pyramids jangling in his hands.

'Search him,' said Puccini.

Mangueras crossed the floor nice and slow, scratching his stubble, looking at me like I was an idiot. His pats were practically punches. Then he slid a gun from a shoulder-holster and clouted me across the jaw, the crack bright and loud,

TIM MACGABHANN

and the grit on the bar-room floor cut my cheek. A cloud
of receipts and plane-tickets and small bills flurried around
my head when he pulled the gun from my pocket. A foot
clumped down hard on my neck and turned the bar-room
into a long black tunnel of white shooting stars, whooshing
like deep space.

The gun in Prieto's hand clicked wetly as he cocked it at
my head. Next there'd be a bang I wouldn't hear, I'd twitch
once in a pool of brains and teeth and hair, and then I'd be
gone for good: just like Abel Carranza, just like Carlos, just
like Julián Gallardo, just like two hundred thousand other
names I'd never know.

'Bag him,' Puccini said, over the jukebox's explosion of
orchestra and choir.

Prieto walked forward with a plastic-coated hemp sack
marked CAFÉ DE CÓRDOBA spread in his hands and
pulled it over my head.

The room went dark, and I breathed air that smelled itchily
of dirt and coffee.

That's what really killed me, knowing that the smell of the
bag would be my last breaths, and not your broad gold odour
of gardenias, or the leather sting of a cigarette, or the chloro-
phyll tang of the plants in my apartment, or the cold nick of
woodsmoke in the air above your town.

Then I felt it. The rabbit-tremble of Carlos' pulse under
my thumb in the car that time, it was under my skin now.

A rough hand grabbed my wrists, zipped shut a plastic tie.
Hands reached around my neck, I thrashed, my feet caught
nothing, and one of them kicked me so hard in the ribs

that all I could do was curl around myself like a prawn.

'Not so tight around the neck,' said Puccini.

The tie zipped shut: loose enough to breathe, sure, but barely enough; the breath rasped through the pinched hole of my throat.

'Feet,' said Puccini.

The bones of my ankles knocked together hard, and the hem of my pants rode up over the plastic, and the plastic pinched my leg hairs.

'OK, we're good,' said Puccini.

They clunked me against the door on my way out but I was too dazed to wail, and then my body slammed to the floor of the police pickup, a pair of boots squeaking behind me.

'I don't get you, *cabrón*,' Prieto said above me, his foot on my neck. 'We do you all the favours in the world, and you throw it back at us.'

The jeep's engine roared and we were gone, through the noise of Papantla's main streets at night on to the silent back roads, every bump in the road slamming my head against the floor.

The jeep stopped.

There's a dozen ways to make a body disappear.

You throw them off a bridge.

Prieto took the foot from my neck and knelt over me, his knee on my shoulder. He whipped off the bag. A fantail of my sweat sprayed the warm night air. Above us, half lit up by the police jeep's headlights, the pyramid of El Tajín loomed down like a pile of empty eyes. Puccini stood behind the pickup in his Veracruz State Police uniform.

You dump them in an oil-tank.

'I want to apologise for the nature of your transit,' said Puccini. When he scratched his cheek I saw that the MUFC tattoo across his knuckles was the stick-and-poke kind. 'You may get down out of the pickup,' came a southern United States drawl. 'Prieto, help him.'

Prieto hauled me by the oxters until my ankles hung above the bumper.

You chop them up, jam them into a fracking well.

'I've got it from here, thanks,' I said. The words came out in a bubble of blood.

He threw me to the ground, onto my sore ribs. My breath skittered gravel.

Puccini knelt over me with a long clean hunting knife in his hand and snicked off the wrist-ties with the tip. He did the same for my ankles and went to sit down on a fallen column engraved with snakes and stained green with moss.

'Sit.' Puccini indicated the space beside him. 'Cigarette?'

'You got water?' My voice was a rasp. I shunted across the grass-spined dirt track as far as the fallen column and sat in the halogen glare of the headlights.

He handed me a flask. The gulps rocked my throat.

'Since you can't grasp it by yourself, I will tell you this now,' he said. 'You won't find a paper trail on my relationship with Ajenjo. Our relationship was verbal. We held one meeting with their CEO, at a small restaurant in Narvarte, in April 2011, and his instruction was clear: to break local resistance to their plans for the region. By what means, you know already.' He lit his cigarette.

My wrists were welted pink from the ties. My head rang. Prieto and Mangueras watched the track with their rifles.

'Your guys,' I said. 'They talked about favours you did us.'

Puccini nodded through a broken screen of smoke. 'You know by now that we didn't kill your friend, or Gallardo.' He held the pack out to me. 'In fact, we protected you from the people who did: Abel Carranza and the Guardia Civil.'

'But he was one of yours.'

'Was.' Puccini shrugged. 'Mexico is full of talkers,' he said, his eyes on the empty track that led from the pyramids back to the main road. 'Word got out about the pact with Ajenjo, and it looked bad for the state. A show was made of going after us, but really the Guardia Civil is doing what we used to do, with a stamp of state official.' He ground the cigarette out with his boot heel. 'We were replaced. Didn't look good for the state or the companies that we were working for them. So they brought new people in to do what we did – the kind of people who could hide behind a badge.'

'And then Abel Carranza betrayed you.'

Puccini looked at me and nodded. 'He saw which way the wind was blowing, took his men to the company director, and said he could help the Guardia Civil do their thing. And they hunted us down like dogs, and Abel became the new disposal man for every activist in the city. He'd bring the bodies, and the Guardia Civil would vanish them. Took them to the army barracks crematorium, apparently.' He shrugged. 'Nothing to do with us. Me, I wanted your friend alive. I wanted Gallardo alive. They could have made enough noise to cause problems for those bastards in Ajenjo.' He took a drag. 'Collapse their share prices, I don't know. Anything to get back at them. Taking our help, then cutting us loose when they felt like it.'

'You'd have killed us three years ago.'

'Oh, no question,' Puccini said. 'But the protests and your story might do worse damage to Ajenjo than we could. So we let you keep going, as a favour. And when Abel went after you two, we went after him.'

Rats scurried in the long grass. The empty sockets of the pyramid watched us, breathing their river-smell of forgotten history.

'And so,' Puccini said, crossing a leg and sitting back on the stone bench, 'you owe me two favours.' He took a piece of paper from his pocket and handed it to me. When I unfolded the page the neat blue cursive had the address of a restaurant in Narvarte written on it. 'Tomorrow night, at eight thirty, the CEO of Ajenjo is going to be expecting you to arrive at this address for an interview. I got some kid who speaks English to call him and pretend he was your personal assistant.'

I looked up from the paper. 'Where's the favour to you here?'

His eyes moved to meet mine. 'Just interview him. Be out by nine p.m. When you're done, you go home, you publish your story, and you never so much as think my name again.' He held up a finger. 'That's the first favour.'

I could barely feel the mosquitos strafing my arms, my body was so tense.

'The second is you smoke another cigarette with me.'

When we'd lit up he said, 'I hated every minute of this life, you know. In the battalion, they used to cut us if we failed an exercise.' He ran a finger down his scar. He squinted, rolled his cigarette between his fingers. '*Scarface* was big at the time. Everyone started calling me Al Pacino. All most people could say was "El Puccini".'

Colonel Monterroso on the edge of the football field, his acne-pitted cheeks catching shade from the booming flares.

'Fail twice,' Puccini went on, 'and they'd leave you in a cage with the mastiff dogs we used on raids, and the dog would rape you.' He looked at me. 'I only failed once.' He took a drag. 'They told us it was to help us serve God, country, and family.'

In my head I saw the *L.A. Times* article again, saw the photo of Alfredo Cristiani, with his neat moustache and neater suit on the edge of the football field: '*You served a transcendental mission in the armed conflict.*'

'After the war,' said Puccini, 'if there was a god, he was worse than the Devil.'

'*You fought with mysticism and discipline, courage and valour.*'

El Puccini pursed his lips, shook his head. 'And then there was no country. With my pension, I helped my cousin buy his auto-repair shop. Set us up forever. That was the plan. And then?' He clapped his hands. 'Eight days, two Yankee boys fresh off the deportation plane shoot him down from their bikes.' Puccini leaned forward.

'No God, no country,' I said.

When Puccini ground out his cigarette the steel toecap of his boot winked through the worn leather. 'In those years, people were killed like chickens. Still are. Economy was dead, too. Still is. Only job I could get was driving a bus. Fourteen hours a day, hands gloved in dust, red eyes going home. Could have joined the police, the interior ministry, the secret service. But better a tired father going home in the evenings than no father at all.' He took my wrist. 'Here. Touch here.' He pressed my finger to a pit in the back of his neck, just behind the ear. 'You feel a lump?' He wagged his finger. 'Eight years in the army. Ambushes, shootouts, you name it. Wasn't even grazed. And I drive a bus for three weeks in San Salvador, two kids get up on the footboard, and plug me in the skull.' He laughed. 'Didn't hear the gunshot. No tunnel, no heaven, no light. Woke up with blood and teeth pooled around me in the bus seat.'

He went on. 'Dragging myself out of there, the pain in my head was no worse than a smack to the head – the endorphins, you know, they rush in fast. But when I get to the public hospital, they won't treat me. Too scared: they think the kids are going to come after me.' He scratched the scar bisecting his face. 'Thing with head injuries is they look worse than they are. You're not likely to faint as long as your brain is in one piece and you can resist the shock. So I drag myself to the private hospital.' He took a drag of smoke. 'Bill was enough to ruin my family. So I caught a plane to Atlanta. Paid my medical bill in dollars, working construction. And I stayed, because those dollar paycheques meant my daughter could go to a safer school. Not that this means anything any more.

'My daughter. She was smart. Really good kid. On Skype, she'd show me the tests. A, A, A.' His eyes were aimed at the hissing undergrowth. 'Then she turns thirteen. Kid turns up outside our house. Playing a voice message from the local gang boss. Tells her to go to his house. She ignores him. Next day, the kid comes back. Says she doesn't have a choice this time. This kid, he brings her to a safe house – about four blocks from ours. Down a street we always told our daughter not to go down. And that's where they keep her.'

The voice telling me all this, that voice was dead.

'No family,' I said.

'Goes on for a year. Nobody tells me. When I come home, that girl is someone else.' He shook his head. 'A kid, with a soul more ruined than those of the two men guarding that road.' He swatted the air. 'And that's when I made my mistake. Told the police. But the kid who'd raped her, he was a minor. Sixteen. All they could do was give him a caution. But, knowing my background, they did me a favour. Gave me a gun and a patrol car. Gave me a week to kill him.' He shrugged and gave a bitter laugh. 'Couldn't find him. So my daughter and I drove to Guatemala before they could find out I'd ratted. Left her with the nuns.'

'After that, to stay safe, my family needed a lot more money than building work could bring in. So I went to find a fellow veteran working in the city. And then I started working for him.'

'That's certainly one way of putting it,' I said.

He just looked at me like I'd been rude, and continued as though I hadn't said anything. 'After a few years, my boss sent me to Tabasco. The governor here in Veracruz liked what he saw. So did the company. And so they brought me to Poza Rica, tripled my wages, and every penny I made went back to Guatemala, to my daughter, and back to Salvador, to her mother.' He sat back. 'And now that's all over, and I'm here, with a handful of men, the entire police force after us, and no God, and no country, and no family.'

My cigarette had burned out. A long tusk of ash hung from the filter.

'Can I offer you another?'

'I think I'm all right.' I raised his flask.

He held up the back of his hand in deference. 'Please, go ahead.'

When I'd emptied the thing I set it back down, wiped my mouth, and said, 'Can I quote you?'

Puccini laughed. 'Make that interview tomorrow, and you can quote whoever you want.' Then he got up from the fallen column. 'We're done,' he shouted at Prieto and Mangueras. 'You two, in the back. He's riding up front.'

Back at the hotel my sleep was dreamless and total. Next morning, I zombied my way from the hotel on to a plane, then back to the car park at the airport in Mexico City where I'd left my jeep, and the coffee cups, the fug of stale smoke, the gun in my glove compartment. Even though the air was warm, I shivered in my jacket and drove through thickening traffic to the address Puccini had given me. The sky was the colour of smoke when I parked around the corner from the restaurant, and I killed the hour until the appointment with a meal of bad doughnuts and worse coffee snatched at the wheel, the AM radio playing boleros while I ate.

The restaurant where Puccini had sent me was about four blocks from my old apartment, with a dark oak door and windows that looked in on a bar like Los Angeles in the 1950s. Outside the hipster *mezcaleria* on the opposite corner stood kids with neat haircuts and pressed clothes and mon-eyed brays.

A Lexus SUV was parked at the door, leaving a lot of space for mine. When it was two minutes to eight thirty by the dashboard clock, I crawled my jeep around the corner, a hand raised to the large suited man standing by the door. He nodded and let me park, then patted me down at the door.

'Thank you.' He swung the door open. 'My employer is waiting for you.'

Roberto Zúñiga sat at a red leather banquette, with a bottle of Centenario Reposado and a half-full tumbler in front of him. He looked more imposing than the business pages made him out to be: six foot four, hale, and white-skinned, his hair full and grey as his moustache. He switched on his smile like it was a set of high-beams.

'Andrew,' he said, 'so good of you to come.'

'The pleasure is mine, Don Roberto.' I extended a hand.

'Please, have a seat.' He filled a second tumbler for me.

The pale amber liquid rose up the glass. My heart ticked in my throat. We were alone apart from a suited bodyguard standing watch beside the toilet.

'I don't think I'll need to take up a huge amount of your time.'

'Oh, be as comprehensive as you like. We want the world to know what we're doing,' he said through a gentle laugh. 'Poza Rica went from a field to a city in just five, six years. Up as far as the early eighties, our people suffered from cholera, dysentery – diseases to shame any modern nation. And what solved that? Oil money.' He sat back against the studded banquette. 'It's what we want to do now. We want to put the people of Poza Rica first once again.' He raised his glass. 'A toast to that.'

But I ignored the glass and held up the voice recorder, and said, 'May I?'

'Go ahead. Like I said, we want the world to know.' Don Roberto held up a hand. 'But, before we begin – your accent, is it American? British?'

'The opposite. Irish.'

His laugh was a deep, unctuous ripple. 'Wonderful symmetry. The story of Poza Rica begins in 1898, you know. An Irishman struck oil there. Refined it as kerosene.' That laugh again. 'And then, of course, the English took it from him.'

'What can I say. It's tradition.' I settled back in my chair.

Don Roberto laughed. 'So, what did you want to talk about, specifically?'

'Where to begin.' I scratched under my chin, idly flicked a page. 'Well, I guess it's just that the new oil rush could be a big moment for your city.' I switched on the voice recorder. 'Could you tell us about your hopes for Poza Rica?'

Don Roberto smiled. I'd started him on safe territory. 'The day the expropriation was announced,' he said, 'was March 19, 1938. If you went to our union building, you may have seen the bust of our esteemed President, Lázaro Cárdenas. He is the grandfather of this city. Before his great gesture, there was a lot of abuse of the worker. Unions were forced to hold their meetings in silence, in secret, and, when the American companies found them, they would be beaten, kidnapped, tortured, killed. That very brutality –' he raised a finger '– is the very reason why our president decided to nationalise our great country's petroleum assets, and make them the property of all Mexicans.'

I wrote nothing down. I'd heard these lines before, read them before, in interviews with him going back years. 'So the city owes you a favour.'

'Well, I wouldn't be so presumptuous.' Don Roberto relaxed in his chair, on autopilot. 'After 1938, the oil belonged to Mexico, and, some of it, to our company. The war brought wealth to us.' He counted on his fingers. 'We sold to America and Japan, to Russia and Germany, to France and Italy. And, afterwards, we had a workers' paradise made by and for Mexicans.' He spread his hands. 'Oil flows in our veins. Poza Rica is the union, and the union is Poza Rica.'

'So what about the decline of the city?' I flipped a page of my notebook. 'You know, people talk a lot about crime rates, the oil thefts, displaced Totonaca people.'

His easy smile froze. 'Oh, it's all very sad. The decline of Poza Rica is the decline of oil itself.' He shrugged. 'But, as you say, new investment means a new hope.'

'Are you not afraid of a return to the situation in the '30s, though? I mean, you just mentioned abuses by foreign companies. There's a lot of it about.'

'It's a different time.' Now his voice was a blade. He took a curt sip from his tumbler.

'No, but this workers' paradise you talk about.' The air

in the bar turned jungle-humid against my skin. 'I mean, it's basically hell for other people, right? Totonaca people cleared off their land, poisoned water, poisoned air.'

Don Roberto's frown deepened. 'We made reparations to those affected.'

'Oh, like in San Antonio Ojital?' I asked.

He coughed into his tumbler. 'What about it?'

'I spoke to the mayor,' I said. 'You offered her a low sum for her land.'

'We offered her the market value of her land.'

'But how much oil did you expect to pump out? How much was that worth?'

'It's impossible to say,' Don Robert said. 'We had yet to explore the wells underneath her land. It could have been a lot. It could have been very little. We offered her the sum we believed to be fair.'

'Twenty thousand dollars.'

'Something like this, yes.'

'Did you also think it was fair to send a death squad to her house?' I asked.

His eyes narrowed and he leaned on the table. 'Excuse me?'

I swiped my iPad unlocked and tapped open Abel Carranza's mugshot.

His reply was instant. 'I have no knowledge of this man.'

'What about these two?' From my bag I slid the printout of Julián Gallardo's peeled face onto the table. 'You had him killed.' On my iPad I opened the photo Gallardo's mother had sent of her dead husband. 'And you tried to disappear his father.'

Zúñiga fingered his tie, his face still. 'I have no knowledge of these events.'

'OK.' I flipped through the pages, as far as my interview with Leo. 'A former employee alleges that bodies were disposed of in your company's fracking wells.'

He scoffed. 'That's an issue for his line manager.'

The bodyguard by the toilet uncrossed his hands and took a step forwards.

I took the worn copy of *Proceso* from my bag and flung it to the table. The glass of tequila Zúñiga had poured for me tinkled to the ground, leaving a stain across Carlos' face.

Carlos stared up at the man who'd had him murdered.

'Recognise him?'

Zúñiga didn't say anything.

I tapped the magazine cover. 'He was mine.' I shoved the magazine at him and said, '"We want the world to know".'

Zúñiga uttered a disgusted sound as the magazine hit him in the paunch, then he stood up from the table.

'With the greatest respect,' he said, 'I must ask you to leave.'

'Cool,' I said, then pocketed the notebook and the voice recorder, folded the copy of *Proceso* up like a fly-swatter, and made for the door, Roberto Zúñiga's eyes lasering into my back, Carlos' face snug against my chest.

'Safe driving.' He emptied his tumbler down his throat.

Be out by nine, El Puccini had told me.

It was eight fifty-eight by the grandfather clock in the restaurant lobby.

★

The man and the car guarding the door had gone when I stepped outside. The sudden draught of a passing vehicle slammed me against the jeep before I could open the driver door. The car that had passed was a black Lexus SUV.

Through my open window I reached for the glove compartment. The gun was cold and light in my hand. I hunkered down, flat against the car door, and watched the SUV's reverse lights wink on four blocks away. Then it screeched in a wild circle and righted itself, and its high beams were a white dazzle.

The engine roared and the SUV leapt forward, three blocks away.

Osito's words in my head: 'Laser-sight switch is on top of the stock.'

Two blocks.

I flicked the switch and took a deep breath.

One.

A pheasant rising from a hedge in Ireland, a rabbit springing across a field, and my finger pulling back the trigger of an air-rifle in the field behind my house.

The boom of that SUV's blown-out tyre swallowed the crack of my handgun, and his brakes squalled, dragging rubber over the tarmac, but it didn't work: glass shattered, and the SUV crumped to a halt against the wall of the hipster *mezca-leria*, making the kids out front shriek, while the horn blared under the pressure of the unconscious driver's forehead.

Don Roberto stood alone at the window of the restaurant, his mouth open, his eyes on the wreck. I didn't look at him, and just climbed into the car.

The kids were already running to help the guy in the car, phones at their ears.

'Fucking three-point turns,' I said, reversing backwards and swinging onto the roundabout. When my foot hit the accelerator, a coffee cup bounced over my feet.

Don Roberto's face in the rear-view mirror shrank and was gone. I accelerated, and the sudden speed was a heel pressed against my stomach. Passing the Parque Delta I texted Maya and told her to get to Dominic's, the headrest wet against my skin.

First bin I saw, I pulled up, dropped the gun in a coffee cup and dumped them both.

A few blocks from Dominic's house, I dropped the two Café Garat bags of bullets to the curb, pulled off my licence plates, and slid them into a discarded pizza box that lay propped against a bin, then pulled the key from the ring and left it in the ignition with the door unlocked, then walked to Dominic's with my bag on my back and a cigarette wagging between my lips.

24

Dominic answered the door looking rumpled and tired.

'Weren't you in Uruguay?' he said. He ushered me through to a sitting room wallpapered in frames from *Tintin*. The long table was a sea of business cards and printouts. He shoved a space for me. 'What happened?'

'Car tried to run me down,' I said.

'Did they follow you?'

'Don't think so. The guy crashed. Knocked himself out.'

'Let me get you some water,' Dominic said. 'I'll get the guard downstairs to call a patrol car.' He returned to the table. 'This is good timing, sort of. I was going through last night's draft. Have you got anything else? This thing about cartel death squads doesn't quite stand up.' He paused. 'You're smiling.'

And then I took out my notebook and my voice recorder, and by the time I had finished explaining Dominic sat slumped forward with his hands on his temples.

'Fuck,' he said, and turned his laptop around and pushed it towards me. A drift of business cards and pages rustled to the ground. 'Fucking fuck. You write this up. We need this on the wires by the morning.' He stood up. 'And I need a drink. Want anything?'

The feathery twitch in my eye was back. 'You couldn't do us a coffee?'

The door buzzed.

'That's Maya. Uh. I was just. You know. Trying to be safe, or whatever.'

'What, you want a posse or something?' He opened the door.

'Before you ask,' she said to me, 'I didn't bring the cat.'

'She has a name, you know.'

'What's this all about?' said Maya. 'The shooting in Narvarte?'

'What?' said Dominic.

My spine froze.

Interview him.

'Yeah,' said Maya. 'Your Ajenjo man got himself waxed.'

And be out of there by nine.

'Twitter says it was three guys in a Veracruz State Police car,' Maya said, looking at her phone. 'Shot up a restaurant in Narvarte, right on the roundabout.'

'Only one victim, though,' Dominic said, reading over her shoulder. 'Roberto Zúñiga. CEO of Ajenjo. One bodyguard had a concussion after crashing his jeep, another took a bullet to the shoulder.'

'Look at all these bullet casings in the photo,' Maya said. 'Lead-free.'

229

'Think we all need a coffee,' Dominic said.

'Beer, if you have it.' She sat down on the couch. 'So, when did you get back?'

My fingers clittered on the keys. 'Hard to say.'

'He's got to do a story,' Dominic said. 'We're both his boss tonight.'

'Well, he's been an abusive employee,' Maya said. 'He tell you about the cat?'

'He's told me everything else,' Dominic said from the kitchen.

'Dumped her on me.' She pointed at me. 'The second you're done with that article, I'm throwing you off Dominic's balcony.'

Dominic slid the coffee in at my elbow and handed me a pair of headphones. 'You might need these. I have a six-pack in the fridge.'

Maya and Dominic kept me going with hits from the coffee-maker before the six-pack they'd gotten through left them dozing. By the time the early-morning gas-man yawped his way down the block, the story was done.

'Hey, so,' I said. 'Uh. I think we're done.'

Dominic fixed his glasses. 'Oh. Terrific. Let me just . . .' I turned the laptop towards him. His eyes scanned the document and I went to lean on the balcony beside Maya, who was asleep under a blanket in one of the Acapulco chairs Dominic kept there.

The skyscrapers on Reforma glowed brass in the dawn. The cigarette I smoked made me shiver all over. Through the morning haze the apartments looked like little caves of dark wood and mellow light.

'This is sterling work,' Dominic said from behind me, holding a printout with no red ink on it. 'We may need a follow-up.'

'It's all here.' I clamped the cigarette in my teeth and handed him the USB.

Dominic frowned. 'So what you're saying is you won't be available by email.'

'Technically, yes. But – well, you know.'

Dominic shrugged. 'I suppose you never did finish that holiday.'

'Where you headed?' said Maya, yawning on the chair.

Carlos, if you get this, your mother scares me more than El Puccini, Mangueras, El Prieto, and all those boys put together.

'Guatemala,' I said. 'Antigua.'

'Nice place to relax,' said Dominic. 'Go see the churches.'

'Which church?' said Maya. 'There's three hundred of them.'

'One of the old ones,' he said.

'Again: three hundred of them.'

'I'm not pressed for time.' I turned the tape recorder over in my pocket.

Dominic's BlackBerry tinged.

'That's the Baron.' He looked at the screen. 'Your story's going out in twenty minutes.' He pushed his glasses up and rubbed his eyes. 'More coffees, I think.'

'I'll make these,' I said.

'Would you?' Dominic sat down slowly on the couch.

Maya followed me to the kitchen. 'So, Guatemala, then.'

'Yeah.' I rinsed out the moka and tamped in coffee-grounds. 'Carlos' mother.'

'Give her my best.'

'Oh, I will. She likes you.' I put the moka on the stove and lit the flame.

'Likes you, too. At the drinks after the funeral, she wished you'd been there.'

'To cut my head off, is it?'

Maya swatted my shoulder. 'Don't be like that.' She huffed out a sigh. 'Go see her, yeah? See what happens.' With a last squeeze of my shoulder she went back to the sitting room.

The moka whistled on the stove and I switched off the gas, but I couldn't even pour the coffee out, I was crying so hard there at the sink.

25

There's a flight every couple of hours from Mexico City to Guatemala, and so four hours after leaving Dominic's I was sitting on the roof-rack of a converted US school bus painted turquoise and red, talking shite and smoking fags with the baggage guys, and looking over Guatemala City from the hilly forest road to Antigua.

Behind me cheeped a bunch of baby chicks in cardboard boxes. The bus suspension was loose as old bedsprings, so that cheeping got pretty wild every time we hit a bend – and that was pretty often. The draught buffeted my face and killed every thought in my head but the wind on my skin, the dappled light through the trees, the smell of petrol and warm tarmac and humid vegetable life beyond the verge.

We arrived at the market by late afternoon, where I tipped the baggage guys and walked off through the yellow late-afternoon glare, dusting roadside grit from my fringe and carrying my whole life in a single bag.

At the hotel, I got online to text Maya and say I'd arrived

OK – which was when all the buzzing started – congratulatory texts, shares, retweets, all of that.

'*Great tribute to Carlos,*' wrote Sadiq.

I clicked open the link Dominic had sent and scrolled through the article – the story me and Francisco had finished, the story that had finished Carlos, the story that everyone was talking about, the story with his name and Francisco's name and my name at the top.

'*The Mexican business world is in a state of shock this morning after Roberto Zúñiga, 61 – the CEO of fast-growing oil company Ajenjo and a fixture of business pages talking up Mexico's "oil miracle" – was gunned down at a restaurant in the middle-class neighbourhood of Narvarte.*

'*A police spokesperson refused to speculate on the motive behind the crime, but eyewitnesses report that gunfire from a Veracruz State patrol car strafed the restaurant where Mr Zúñiga was drinking alone with two bodyguards – both of whom escaped with injuries that are not believed to be life-threatening.*

'*"We're devastated," said a representative of Ajenjo who declined to be named. "Roberto Zúñiga did more to transform his home city of Poza Rica than anybody."*

'*Ajenjo's US-based contractors refused to comment on the incident, stating that "while tragic, the event is an internal matter, and our thoughts are with Zúñiga's family and his outstanding legacy for the company."'*

My phone buzzed again. Kelleigh: '*Kept that one under your hat!*'

'*But questions linger over the nature of that same legacy for Mexico's crumbling oil capital, Poza Rica.*

'*An investigation conducted out by this outlet has uncovered a web of cartel muscle, union corruption, and intimidation stretching from Zúñiga's boardrooms to the high-profile disappearance of environmental activist Julián Gallardo, the murder of photojournalist Carlos Arana, and the assassination of two other Ajenjo employees, all of whom tried to blow the whistle on the company's attempt to crush protests against the pollution choking the region's air and waterways.*'

Another buzz: Pau from CNN. '*How did you do all that?*'

'*A local cartel figure, veteran of El Salvador's civil war, Evelio Martínez – who goes by the* nom de guerre *"El Puccini" – went on the record about a verbal pact between his faction of the notorious Zetas cartel and Mr Zúñiga himself, established in 2011.*

'*"You won't find a paper trail on my relationship with Ajenjo," Martínez said. "The relationship was verbal. We held one meeting, in April 2011, and his instruction was clear: to break local resistance to their plans for the region."*

'*That testimony is borne out by the mayor of the Totonaca hamlet of San Antonio Ojital, whose wells and plant-life carry the tell-tale signs of oil pollution: shrivelled mandarins, water thick as molasses, and air that tastes of smog.*

'*Apolonia Xanat Benítez claims that two weeks after refusing a compensation offer from Ajenjo for her land, a known member of local organised crime – masquerading as a Veracruz State police officer – attempted to force her family out of their home.*

'*"He told us, 'We've made a generous offer, and if you're here when we come back, you're dead'," she explained. "But we'd rather die than leave."*'

Yet another buzz: Jon. '*You bastard. Now we all have to go to Poza Rica.*'

'A drilling crew formerly employed by Ajenjo have also attested that fracking equipment – purchased from a US multinational oil concern for use at a site outside Tamiahua – was used to dispose of the bodies of people murdered by Puccini's local Zeta faction.

'"We stuffed binbags full of people's limbs into the wells and switched on the motors," said one former driller. "Cut up, it's hard to know how many bodies there were."

'Both the driller and his colleague confirmed that a Zeta employed as a lawyer by the local petrol workers' union and another gang member, who had infiltrated the local police, oversaw the disposal operation, which took place in May 2014, just before the elite Guardia Civil police force was called in by the state government to deal with spiralling violence in the city.'

Francisco left a voice note. You could hear the relief in his voice, and the wheels of his car speeding on the road.

'Great news,' he said. 'Everyone wants to talk. I'm off to see a bunch of oil workers now. Later, I'm off to the port – some documentary makers flew in from Colombia.' He paused. 'You know, Carlos really did something amazing.'

'Cartel members have attested to the continued alliance between Ajenjo and local law enforcement, with murdered gang member Abel "Dientes de Tiburón" Carranza being involved in the murder of Mexican photojournalist Carlos Arana, and the disappearance of student activist Julián Gallardo, dashing Poza Rica's hopes that a clean-up on crime might lure investment and employment back to Mexico's former oil capital, as well as confirming fears that pollution and a nexus of organised crime and corrupt members of the elite Guardia Civil police force will continue to poison civic life for some time to come.'

Flicking through the tabs on my browser, I saw that all the main news websites were running us as a top story – me and Carlos, our names everywhere, in places we'd always dreamed of.

After not a very long time, I switched my phone off before taking my coffee up to the roof terrace, then shut the window and sank back against the metal frame of the chair, my head in my hands.

'I'm so not ready for this,' I said, turning the tape recorder over in my pocket.

From the terrace I could see right through the door of a semi-derelict church on the corner. Red wax dripped and fumed and caught fire on a tray by the altar. Opposite the church, beside a portico ruined in the 1773 quake, Mayan women sat with corn and chayote and chillies spread out on red-pink blankets zigzag patterned like the crop fields all around the town. Watching them calmed me down enough to head downstairs and make for Veronica's house.

Antigua's a central node of the region's backpacker trail, so the clubs were already loud with the yawp of happy tourists and the thud of dance music, but Veronica's street was a solid dozen blocks from all that, backing onto a lush hillside. The only sounds were the odd motorbike blatting past, the pulse of crickets, birds chittering from their nests in the hollowed-out ruins of churches. Under the sodium lights the collapsed naves and domes could have been the little gravel arches my poor dead fish used to swim around. The sky's eastern corner was all mute white flashes from the Pacaya volcano erupting in the distance.

The house lay at the very end of the street – a colonial-style villa painted blue, behind a huge seamed wood door, whose knocker was a massive steel ring that hung from a lion's mouth.

'Three knocks is enough, right?' I said to nobody, then did what I'd flown all this way to do.

Veronica didn't take long arriving at the door. When she did, she had a tea towel in one hand a mug in the other.

'Andrew.' The look on her face was pretty much what you'd expect: three kinds of *What the hell are you doing here?* – angry, surprised, touched – all mixed in together, but she pulled wide the door all the same. 'Well, come on in.'

'Thanks, Ms Arana.' I followed her into a high-ceilinged stone hall bristling on all sides with small wooden school chairs. Pointing at them, I said, 'These chairs, they're one of your exhibitions, right? Carlos showed me a photo once. Turned out great.'

She nodded. 'From late last year. For the anniversary of the ceasefire. They're all from Nebaj.'

'Where the massacres happened.'

'That's right.' She put her hands on her hips. 'Schools couldn't afford furniture up in that neck of the woods, you know. Used to have to bring their own chairs. One for every kid murdered in Nebaj during the war.'

The breath she sucked in sounded hot, and she turned her eyes on the floor.

'I never thought—' She cut herself off. 'Excuse me.' She turned away for a moment, pinching her nose, her thick-rimmed red glasses resting on her fingers. 'OK. I'll make coffee.'

We walked past a door in the hallway that opened onto her studio. Part of a large wooden Pieta stood at the centre of the room. Mary's face was stained black. The hair cascading from under her blue wimple was real. She had no son in her arms.

'It's from 1541,' she said. 'First year the city was destroyed. This was all they could rescue from the cathedral after the eruption.'

On my left side the terrace lawn was a lush green, pocked with deep purple azaleas. A fountain splashed at the centre. More saints hung on the walls: Saint Lucia offering forth her eyes on a plate, Saint Sebastian's mute groan and livid wounds, Saint Jude's brass medallion of Jesus in profile.

'Must get pretty quiet around here,' I said as we skirted around the terrace to her kitchen.

'That's the way I like it,' she said. 'Usually.'

Huge yellow clay bowls hung on hooks all over the terra-cotta tiled walls, beside old cast-iron skillets, tongs, pokers. The stove in the corner was an Aga. A wooden Jesus with hinged limbs sat on one of the chairs.

'Sorry about this guy,' she said. 'He's too heavy to hang on the walls.'

I sat down next to Jesus. His lapis lazuli eyes glittered in the kitchen's dim wattage. 'That's the rest of that Pieta, right?'

'Yes,' she said, clanking a pot onto the stove. She stood there, wordless, until the water boiled, then said, 'How was your flight?'

'Slept all the way,' I said. 'Didn't expect that.'

'Oh, I'm not surprised.' She carried a brimming cafetière to the table. 'You had a hard couple of weeks.'

'I don't know,' I said. 'Nothing compared to . . . You know.'

'Pain is pain.' Veronica pressed down the plunger and poured us a cup each. For a moment she stared at her coffee, her long white hair shining in the light. She and Carlos, they had the same strong-boned face, fierce eyes, sceptical eyebrows.

Carlos, if you get this, you take after her like you wouldn't believe.

'How have you been?' I said.

Her gaze slowly lifted to the Jesus statue sitting next to me, then moved across to meet my eyes. 'I don't know.'

The fountain's splashing grew louder as a fine rain began to fall.

'Every morning,' she said, and took a breath. 'Every morning, all those years he was working, I'd check for a message from him. First thing I did, every single day.'

The coffee cup on the white saucer was the pupil of a staring eye.

She looked at me sidelong and raised the cup to her lips.

'You can smoke if you want, by the way,' she said.

'I think I'm all right.' A shiver uncoiled from the base of my skull, and I rapped my knuckles on the table until I was ready to say what I'd come to say. 'I'm sorry for what I did to your son. If I hadn't gone to him four years ago, we wouldn't be here. And he'd still be here.' I folded my arms, stared at my lap. 'I took him from you. Like he was mine.'

Her long-boned hand was cool on my forearm.

'Well, he was yours,' she said. 'Naturally, I was happy he'd found someone, but the thought of him going back to that kind of work?' She shook her head. 'Of course I blamed you.

And I thought I'd never stop doing that.' Her voice went quiet. 'But then I started to see him. Nights like these –' she pointed out the window '– the rain, it'd be his voice whispering. Telling me it was OK. To go to sleep. That he was safe. That he was something like happy. And, you know,' she said, 'you get to my age, you think everything's early-onset dementia.' She laughed. 'Or maybe it's not even that early any more. I don't know.' She shook her head. 'Last few days, I've been waking up with his hand on my head, stroking my hair. Telling me you'd probably turn up here sometime. That I should be nice about it.' She sighed through her nose, her eyes shut, shaking her head. 'And look, really, I knew you didn't have to twist his arm for him to leave El Paso.' Her smile didn't reach her eyes. 'You and me put together couldn't have kept him away from his work. Day he stole his first camera from my studio and came back with a copy of the paper, with his photos, that's when I knew. The look on his face when he showed them to me. Like a bird of prey.' She made a crease of her mouth. 'No way to coop that up. No, he wanted to solve the world or die trying. And in Mexico, you die trying.' She stared at the table. The tears brimmed but didn't flow.

My knuckles tapped the table in time with the rain blattering on the roof. 'I didn't know you knew about – you know. Us.'

She smiled. 'When it's your son, the closet is see-through. I think I knew how he felt before you did. The day after you met, I couldn't shut him up on the phone. All came spilling out of him – "Ma, I met this writer, he's even more desperate than me, he's polite enough for you to approve, and we're going to save Mexican journalism".'

'Sounds about right.' I scratched the back of my head. 'I mean. You know. Like something he'd say.'

'It sounds about right, too.' She looked up at the rain teeming the glass. 'I read the story. You boys did well.'

'We did OK.'

I took my tape recorder from my pocket and laid it on the table.

'Is that . . . ?'

'Yeah. Day we met,' I said. 'Beyond a certain point it's just the sound of us making terrible drinks, to be honest. But, you know. It's his voice, or whatever.'

She picked up the recorder and pressed play.

There it was again: the door shutting on Room 404 at that El Paso hotel; Carlos sniffling with his cold, swearing about his hangover, asking, 'Is that thing on?'; and the sound of a lighter flaring once, twice.

'Can we listen to it?' his mother said over the hiss of the tape's wheels turning.

'The whole thing?'

She nodded.

'Sure.'

Outside, the night darkened, and Jesus' statue cast a shadow on the floor. Carlos' mother, she laughed, smiled, cried a little at times. Me, I just patted her hand and listened to our story go tapering up into the light, gentle as candle-smoke.

'This is my favourite part,' I told her, about an hour into the recording.

'How did you get into the job?' I heard myself ask.

Carlos' voice was cottony with held-in smoke. 'So back when I was young, my mother was so careful with me. Never let me outside. Understandable, you know? My dad wasn't in the picture, she'd moved from Vermont, and so I was the only home she had. But when you're sixteen, you're an ass-hole. All you want to do is your own thing. And I'd ask her, "C'mon, I want to hang out in town." And she'd say, "Not if they pay me." And one day I asked her, "What if they pay me?" And she said she guessed that was fine.'

Carlos' mother laughed, sniffed.

'So what I did was I took one of her old cameras, started walking around Juárez looking for cool faces,' he said.

'The brat,' said Carlos' mother.

'And me, I knew a lot about the narcos,' said Carlos. 'Way most kids know footballers is the way I knew narcos. My room was this, like, cave of posters of those bastards. I had Carrillo Fuentes, I had Arellano Félix, I had El Güero Palma. I wasn't allowed have El Chapo, but I didn't like him, anyway.'

She held her face in her hands. 'That room was horrifying.'

'That first day in Juárez, with my mother's camera, first face I find, it's this old lieutenant from the Carrillo Fuentes years.'

She watched the tape turn in the deck. Her smile was warm and absent.

'One of the old generation,' said Carlos. 'One of those guys like they used to have in every town, right up there with the priest, the mayor, and the teacher – except this guy, this kind of narco, he'd plough real money into the town. Fly weed bales across the border, fly back with bales of dollars, and sit in his house all day waiting for people to ask for his help.'

'I was furious when he told me,' his mother said. 'But so proud, too.'

'So this guy I saw, he was one of them. And he was just working in a car park. Old and leathery and moustached. And I just walked up, asked him for a photo, and he was so flattered that we did an interview. Sent the pics to the *Diario*. And the rest is history.' He sucked smoke. 'I got a glittering career behind me, *cabrón*.'

When the tape clicked off it was nearly dawn. Veronica heaved a sigh so long and deep that you could hear kilos of grief lift and drop inside her.

'You can keep the recorder,' I said.

Her eyes flicked to meet mine. 'No,' she said. 'I couldn't. That's yours.'

'Nah,' I said. 'Honestly. I have my ways to remember him.'

She turned the recorder in her hand. 'Are you sure?'

'Yeah. It's nice to have his voice around. Most of the time,' I said. Outside, the roar of the pre-dawn storm was falling quiet.

She got up from the chair. 'I have something for you as well.'

Her footsteps creaked up a dark wood staircase lined with more saints: Maximón with his drooping moustache and sad gaze; placid, bearded Hermano Pedro; Saint John gripping the shoulder of Jesus.

'Here you go,' she said in the doorway, yellow light spilling over her from behind. She held out an envelope-shaped cardboard parcel tied with a rough wool string. When I took it from her hands the contents sifted into the corner.

'Not all of him,' she said. 'I want to scatter some in the desert.'

When we hugged she shook crying in my arms for a long time, and I kept my eyes on the parcel in my hands, running my thumb along the smooth cardboard, and for a moment it was the three of us all together.

The sky was sheer Kodachrome blue that morning on the terrace of my hotel room, the mist and cigarette smoke and my own sleepiness so thick around me that I could nearly imagine Carlos sitting beside me on the other wrought-iron chair, his eyes red, his neck ringed in bruises. The envelope of his ashes lay on the table beside my phone.

He pointed at the envelope with a broken finger. 'You know where to go with that, *vato*?'

A cloud of starlings scattered through the air. Down below, a couple of white tourists snapped pictures of the ruined portico where the women had been selling their wares the day before. The starlings formed a 'V' in the air above the soaked green hotel garden of palm trees and banana leaves.

'Shit, man,' I said through a yawn, hugging his jacket around myself. 'I'm really going to miss you.'

Carlos exhaled smoke, and his outline shivered. 'You know I'm not really there, right?'

The star-shaped holes on his chest, the ones rimmed in blue fire, those holes widened now, and sent grey smoke fraying up to join with the cigarette between his shapeless tapering fingers.

'But that manager of yours might be.'

He was a cloud now, floating above his chair, and then his cigarette was between my lips like it had been all along, and it was just me and the waking town.

The dial-tone went for ages, seemed like.

'No way,' you said at last.

'Ah, yeah. Story's done. On holidays.'

'Well, congrats. Whereabouts?'

'Guatemala,' I said. 'My room still free?'

There was a smile in your voice. 'Could be. Thinking of coming back?'

Carlos' last threads of smoke widened and frayed and were gone.

To get from Guatemala to Uruguay, all you have to do is get the night-flight on LAN as far as Chile. Then it's a one-hour hop to Montevideo and a bus to Colonia.

'Kind of.'

'When?'

The starlings rose breaking into empty blue air. I was fifty-five kilos of blood and muscle, a single backpack, and a couple of impending paycheques.

'Well, today, to be honest.'

'Wow. Well, OK,' you said through a laugh. '*Te espero acá.*'

In Spanish, the verb *esperar*, it means 'to hope', 'to wait', and 'to expect'. Which one you meant, I didn't know, but I guessed it was maybe all three.

READ AN EXTRACT FROM
ANDREW'S NEW ADVENTURE

I

On the morning that the phone calls started, I dreamed that Carlos and I were back in Poza Rica, back in that place where nobody had asked us to go, back where nobody had asked us to look. This was where my mind lived at night – in a bar with riveted portholes for windows, a slow ocean of fog breaking against the windows, the river slopping black against the glass leaving a thick drag of foam. An oil derrick clanked behind the bar, pumping stout into a pyramid of glasses, while the dead kid we'd found, Julián Gallardo, lay on the bar at the centre of an altar we had made around him.

It's like I told you before: nobody had asked Carlos and I to look at that body. But we had, and then everything had fallen apart. Julián had been an activist, murdered by corrupt local police. We'd never known him when he'd been alive, never even met him, but nobody had changed my life more. Carlos and I had found him lying dead and faceless at the bottom of an alley, and only I had lived to tell the tale.

There's no need to tell you how big a news story that had been. That story was the reason I'd had to leave Mexico.

Two shots, the forensics technician had told me, outside the apartment where Carlos had died, *the first between third and fourth rib on the right side, fatally puncturing a lung.*

In the dream Carlos stepped up beside me. Smoke crinkled out of the bullet-holes in his chest.

'Jesus' – his fingernail clinked against my glass – 'of all the ways to crack, you pick *Carlsberg*? *No mames, vato.*'

Three years since my last drink or line, six months since I'd gone around dosing my grief with swigs of diluted LSD from a dinged metal water flask, and yet here I was, a pint in my hand, saying, 'Hey, come on, man, it's a premium lager.'

'Doesn't taste like it, *vato.*' He lifted the pint and took a deep gulp. Something hissed wetly inside him as he swallowed.

The second shot between fifth and sixth rib on the left side, destroying the heart completely.

Carlos tucked his shirt back in and leaned forwards to reach for one of the glasses in the pyramid. A poppy collar of bruises ringed his neck. In the creamy whorls of reds and browns I saw oil, blood, smoke.

A reverse chokehold fractured the hyoid bone.

'Try this instead, *vato,*' he said, and held the glass out to me. His vibe was different from before, stand-offish, cold, like those white marble statues of Ancient Greece, of Orpheus or Eurydice or someone, I don't know. 'It'll kill you. But gently, you know?'

The fizz spritzed my face like drizzle.

'It could all be over if you just let yourself drown, *vato,*' Carlos said. His voice was gentle, his fingers were broken, and his eyes were pinkish with petechial haemorrhaging.

Three years.

Six months.

But now my mouth was dripping with the thirst, and my throat became a long ache. A sob rose and fell in my chest. My hand was lifting the glass all by itself.

Then gravel crunched. A siren cut through my skull. Police-car lights washed over Carlos and me and Julián Gallardo, red and blue and halogen white, and Carlos' killer – half his head missing, his police-uniform stained – stepped out of the light.

2

My eyes opened. Maya's knuckles were rapping the car window.

'You said you'd be at Arrivals!' she said and swung open the door.

'And where did I park?' I swallowed the cobwebs in my mouth, pointed at the red sign glowing above the airport door. It was a foggy night. There weren't many cars.

'As in, *standing* at Arrivals.' She slung her bag into the backseat and sat in the front.

'Ah, no, that was a bridge too far.' I yawned and started the car. Coffee-cups and donut boxes rattled around my feet. But, as I was about to turn around, I saw a white face standing beside a jeep, a white face wearing wraparound sunglasses and a square beard.

'You going to drive or what?' Maya said.

'Huh?' I blinked. The face vanished. It could have been anything – frames from a dream, a flash of bad memory, whatever, I saw stuff that wasn't there all the time these days. 'Oh. Yeah.'

'You spaced out there,' Maya said.

'Occupational hazard.' I drove us away from the airport, turned us onto the highway from Montevideo back to Colonia.

'What occupation?' Maya said. 'You haven't been doing shit since you moved here.'

'I don't know, managing trauma, or whatever. Speaking of which: you ready to talk yet?'

'Not really, no.' She reached into the backseat, rummaged for a second, then pulled out a giant orange candle shaped like an elephant.

'We're good for candles,' I said, and then I saw the needle as thick as my finger that was stuck in the elephant's flank, and the note – '*GET OUT OF HERE, WHORE*' – that the needle was holding in place.

'Oh, right,' I said.

'This was in my hotel-room,' she said. 'In Poza Rica.'

You remember all this – Maya had been due to stay with us while she did the write-up of the investigation into what Carlos and I had uncovered in Veracruz, all about how the state government and oil companies had been using gang members and bad cops as death squads to drive indigenous people off their land, to silence activists, and to threaten journalists into silence. The governor and his people would launder their money by paying companies that didn't exist for public services that wouldn't happen.

After all that stuff had come to light, it had seemed a lot safer to dig around, and so that's what Maya had been doing. Yeah, well, there's safe, and there's Mexican safe.

Meaning Maya's editor had called you and I the night before, saying he'd paid to change her flight, and would be sending her down on the first plane that could get her to us.

'Any idea why?' I said. The roads broken white dividing line flicked towards me through the dark. My heartbeat was starting to quicken.

'Those shell companies.' Maya eased her seat back with a click. 'I went to their addresses – you know, all these fake places. Taxi-ranks. Old peoples' homes. Oxxos. Last one I went to was in an open-air car park. Guy was sitting there, this old guy, a few curls of hair left. And so I ask him, "Are you the CEO of this company?", and I hold up the piece of paper I print out from the Freedom of Information request, and he spits and says, "I look like one for you", which sounds like a fucking "Yes" to me, quite frankly, but whatever, I go back to the hotel, and the manager's at reception, and he waves me over, and he lifts this candle out from behind my desk, and this enormous valet comes up behind me with my bags. *Y ya.*' She did jazz-hands at me. 'So here I am.'

'Thought you didn't want to talk.'

'Nature finds a way,' she said, easing back against the seat.

'That's terrifying, though. Jesus.'

'Occupational hazard. How're you, anyway?'

'Oh, you know. Happy. Quietly so. But happy.'

Maya looked at me sidelong. I could never get anything past her.

'Is that code for "bored"?' she said.

'No comment.' I flipped the indicator. 'It's just new, you know?'

253

'I'm still hearing "bored".'

'"Bored" is good,' I said. '"Bored" means safe. I *wish* I was bored. But I'm still too scared.' The roadside lamps striped the inside of the car with white light.

'Yeah,' said Maya, staring out at the dark. 'I hear you.'

'Could do with all of that stuff being ten years ago already. Like a dog snapping at my heels.'

Maya didn't say anything.

I pointed at the elephant. The needle was stuck fast in a divot of wax. 'They let you fly with that thing?'

'Told them it was an art project.'

'Fair.'

The night was clear, quiet – no light pollution blotting at the glitter of the stars, no chug and thud of cumbia from the clubs, no kids trying to sell us knock-off Marlboro Red at the lights. It was basically the opposite of Mexico City around here. Sometimes I hated that.

'You hungry or anything?' I asked, as we slowed towards the Old Town. The orb lamps on the main square made me feel like I was back in Mexico City's half-wrecked Centro Histórico backstreets. The nick of woodsmoke on the air briefly became the tang of beer-suds, the just-fucked musk and rained-on leather of the clubs became mine and Carlos' sweat-run aftershave, but I shoved the memory away.

'Not really, no,' said Maya. 'Wouldn't say no to a cheeky cigarette though, yeah?'

'Get thee behind me, Satan.'

She nodded off not long after that. Shock'll do that to you. The sallow bones of a right whale glowed in a display sunk into the wall of the fortress, and I turned past it and slowed towards home. Maya woke at the snapping-bone noise of the brake.

'Wow,' she said when she saw the house. 'Nice place.'

'Ah yeah,' I said, and got out to carry her bags. Inside I got her settled in the spare room downstairs.

'Right, so,' I said, and gave her a hug. 'Sleep well.'

'If I can,' she said.

'I believe in you,' I said. 'You need anything, just scream.'

'Blood-curdling or standard?'

'Oh, standard will do.' I shut the door and climbed up the stairs.

3

'Those are getting really bad,' you said, at the sound of me coming into the room.

'What are?' I sat down on the edge of the bed and took off my shoes.

'Those nightmares of yours,' you said.

My hand stopped in mid-air. 'You mean I had another one?' I said. 'Huh. Can't even remember it.'

'You should see someone,' you said.

'What, like an affair?' I lay down. 'There'll be no polyamory in this house.'

'Like a *therapist*.' You swatted me with the back of your hand. 'You're still seeing him, aren't you?' You'd been good about the Carlos dreams at the start. But it's hard to stay patient with someone who's just not getting better, I suppose.

You checked the time on your phone, then flopped back down again. 'Oh, for God's sake.' You folded the pillow around your head with one arm. Your Peñarol jersey had ridden up, so I smoothed it down to cover your back, but you jerked away. 'Your fingers are freezing!'

'Alright, alright.' I swung my legs from the bed to pull on my track-pants.

Your alarm went off. You flailed, batted the mattress with your fist.

'Let me get that.' I reached under your pillow, found the phone, pressed *Snooze*, then zipped up my hoodie.

'How is she?' you asked.

'Yeah, OK. And excited to meet you. I've been bragging.'

'Liar.'

Bluish 5 a.m. light threw the shadows of firs against the blinds of your bedroom. The dodgy floorboard creaked as I laid my foot down.

'How did you wind up upside-down?' I rubbed your chest.

'Your bad dream. You yelped.' You wiggled a little, scratching yourself. 'Thought it was the alarm. So I sat up. But then I fell back asleep.' You yawned and stretched, kicking, then squeaked like those otters whose Instagrams you followed. 'And then I fell over. Now quiet.' You pulled my pillow over your head. 'Too early for speech.'

A plump cinnamon blur zipped past the glass, cheeping insistently, as I climbed down the ladder from the loft room.

'Alright, alright,' I said. 'I'm coming.'

After shoving nuts into the plastic feeder by the door, I went downstairs to light the stove. Maya was sitting at the kitchen table, her laptop open.

'What, no sleep?'

'Too wired.' Her chin rested on both her hands. 'There's coffee.'

'Nice one.' I heated water for your yerba maté and turned my phone on.

A missed call popped up from a Mexico City number and the breath went steam-hot in my nose.

'What?' Maya said.

She looked at me.

Like I said – there was nothing I could ever get past her. My knuckles rapped the table.

'Anyone after you?' I said. 'Like, specifically.'

'That I know of?' She shook her head.

'Nobody who'd, like, follow you here. For example.'

'Don't think so.'

'Alright.' I held up the phone. 'Like, I could be just being paranoid. But I got a wrong-number call, and, well. I don't know.' I blocked the number. 'Maybe it's nothing.'

Maya looked at me over the rim of her mug.

'Shit.'

I started doing my stretches – hand against the wall, leg raised, everything like that. 'It'd be worse if you weren't here.'

Maya bobbed her head from side to side.

'I mean, for me, maybe.'

The kettle boiled, and I stopped stretching to fill your Thermos and to tamp yerba into your favourite maté gourd. The rumble of the boiler and the slap of sud-thickened water were filtering down from upstairs.

'Don't think about it.' I lifted the Thermos and gourd. 'Just going to feed the kraken now.' I went upstairs.

★

'Maya OK?' you said from inside the shower when you heard me come through the door.

'Ah, yeah.'

I opened the door and held the straw through the gap so you could sip while you shampooed yourself.

'Maybe you should ask her how she's dealing with all the stuff she's got going on.' You turned away from me, into the spray.

'What stuff?'

'I don't know. The stories she does. They're a bit like yours.'

'Yeah. Maybe.'

The anger surged through me, then the shame. All you knew of the story was what everybody knew – that Carlos' killer was dead, and so was the owner of the company responsible for all the horror we'd uncovered, a man called Roberto Zúñiga. What you didn't know was that I'd been there on the night that Zúñiga had been shot, and that I'd been sent there by his killers as a diversion tactic.

The wrong number I'd seen on the screen of my phone flashed in my head, my chest went tight again, and I sat down on the toilet, huffing as much as I could of your menthol shampoo, your Carolina Herrera 212 face-wash, your pH-neutral soap, into my lungs.

'Is she seeing anyone?' you asked after a minute or so.

'Like dating?' I said, even though I knew where this was going.

'Andrew.'

'Right. I'll ask.' I left the gourd beside the sink and opened the door and leant in to give you a kiss on the back of your neck. There was no point saying anything else, and that's not because we were speaking Spanish: it'd be hard in any language, because there are things you can see, and there are things that happen to you, and there are things you can talk about, and they're really never the same set of things. 'Back in a bit.'

'OK,' you said. 'Love you too.'

Maya had gone back to her room when I got downstairs. Outside, I left my hood down so the drizzle could freshen me awake. The tang of rain on fallen pine-needles gave me a shiver. My breath smoked in the air. All of that was more real than the dreams, I tried to tell myself, but none of it was more real than the stuff that was still following Maya and I around.

The firs were a thin black cursive against the white fog. Red-bibbed *degollados* were hopping around the ruined fortress, and the sky was fishbelly-grey, with thunderheads massing in the east. The air stank, though, a dog-food odour of rotting sargassum weed. For weeks now, brown clumps of the stuff had been coming in with the tide, killing the beach-wedding industry. Some papers said that an algal bloom had fed the weed. Other papers said that the algae had only bloomed because the sea was up half a degree from this time a year ago.

'Guess you just warmed this place right up,' you had said one morning, kicking a clump of the stuff as we walked along the strand. 'My warm-hearted European.'

'That's not the stereotype at all,' I'd replied, but you just laughed. Today a small yellow digger was clearing a track through the heaps of seaweed that covered the place we'd been walking that day.

A chunk of wall loomed up to one side of me as I ran, the words *UNIVERSO PARALELO ENTRADA AQUÍ* beginning to fade from the whitewash. The black dog who lived on the beach sprang from his tussock of grass and jogged over to rub himself along my trailing hand.

'*Buenos días, güey,*' I said.

He warbled, tossed his head so hard that dirt and gravel flew from his moustache, then began to run alongside me. Drifts of mist cooled my shins and darkened the hairs on his legs. Razor-shells and pebbles crunched underfoot, and I hopped a sea-darkened plank of wood, dodged a vodka bottle sunk past its neck in sand. A gull squawked at me from a nest of toothbrushes, clothes-pegs, and old combs, her head blotched and her eyes reddened by whatever was in the sea that morning.

'So much for her,' I said to the dog. 'How're you getting on?'

He just panted.

'Yeah.' I was starting to pant as well. 'I feel you.'

The Mar del Plata was a grey shimmer that slowly ignited to white as I ran. When my watch beeped a count of ten thousand steps, I let myself drop onto the sand, my eyes shut, my legs shaking, my breath a raw scorch, too tired to be scared anymore. Moments like that, they're what I used to drink for, that emptied-out clarity, where all you are is what's happening around you – the salt nick of the air, the cool sand under your nape, the crash of the ocean loud and rhythmic and pouring into your ears.

The dog stood over me, his tail beating the strand.

'Mind these, won't you?' I stripped off my T-shirt and shorts and stepped out of my shoes.

The dog sneezed.

I launched myself into waves gone reddish with leaf-shred. Tapes of sargassum wrapped around my shins. Six waves out, the water was so cold that it felt like a scald. When I was done swimming, I let the tide drag me shorewards.

'Much appreciated,' I said to the dog as I retrieved my things.

He didn't pay much attention: that fat brown Labrador, the one who slept in your hotel's driveway, she'd showed up to sniff him, and he was trying to play it cool.

The café had opened. After getting a three-chili brownie and a flat white to go, I headed past the pier, and another flash hit me from the previous night's dream – a boat slowing towards the dock, a man with a scar down the middle of his face chucking a mooring rope, Carlos' corpse pulling the blanket from his face – and I had to close my eyes, lean my forehead against a wall, wait the pictures out.

A tinny whirr lowered in behind me, and I turned, saw the lens of a small white drone glinting back at me, the red dot of its recorder beady, red, insect-like.

For a second it was hard to tell whether the drone was really there or not, and I just stood there gawping in my shorts, with a coffee in my hand, while the drone yawed off towards the fortress.

A vein ticked in my temple. The coffee was lukewarm by the time my legs felt steady enough to walk home.

That's how it is, this reporting thing.

Sometimes you find out the truth.

Sometimes the truth finds out where you live.

Acknowledgements

Call Him Mine wouldn't have happened without Lourdes Pintado Gallardo, who helped me get the job that first brought me to Poza Rica. Without Jonathan Levinson, who insisted we go back to Veracruz as many times as it took until we had something like a story, this novel would have remained nothing more than a pitch in my Drafts folder. Without Fabio Barbosa, Érika Ramírez, Edgar Escamilla, and Nancy Flores Nández, Poza Rica would have looked to me like just another crumbling oil town. To all I owe a great debt.

Alfredo, Amy, Azam, Béne Caf, Cristy, the Three Daves, Diego, Donovan, Dudley, Duncan, Keith, Luises Orozco y Kuryaki, Lucía, Mara, Nathaniel, Rafa, Robin, and Steve: your fingerprints are all over this thing. Thank you.

My tutors and fellow students at UEA all left a helpful mark on the initial manuscript, but I need to single out Giles Foden for making this book what it could be. Still amazed by your help. Senica, Tom W., James, Sophie, Philly, Alan, Cara, Grace, Deepa, Joe, Mónica, Sumia, Timothy, Kathy, Kunzes, Laura, Harriet, Tommy K., Alake, Naomi – thank you all for getting me through that year in different ways. Also, I'm sorry for all the vape.

Sincere thanks to Sally and Oisín for helping me to turn a very baggy first draft into something I could be proud of; to Cathal, Chloe, Hannah, Karl, Kevin, and Roisín for helping me keep my head up when it was all going a bit pear-shaped; and to John the Shed and Tom M. for making sure I got here in the end.

Jools and Rose gave me a home away from home for far longer than any of us expected, and always with such grace and kindness. Thank you both, truly. The Autumn Meal is on me.

The other members of Legends Club and the Earthen Cat Tree have kept me fuelled with encouragement, careful notes, and reading / watching recommendations for absolutely ages. Only a policeman would mention you by name, but you know who you are.

For always being there with pep-talks and a protective eye, I'm grateful to Sam Copeland in a way that football banter can't fully express. Even so, if writing were the Premier League, he'd be Jürgen Klopp. Natasha and Max helped me out so much with early drafts of *Call Him Mine*, while Eliza's patience seems to know no bounds: thank you all so much.

For taking on the project, for making the book better than I believed it would be, and for making me a better writer, Federico Andornino has my endless thanks. Thank you to the whole Weidenfeld & Nicolson family and the wider Orion Publishing Group, for taking a punt on a story I never thought would see the light of day. I want to thank Jo for her sniper's eye in spotting all the typos and continuity errors also – knowing me, that wasn't easy.

I want to gratefully acknowledge the Arts Council of Ireland, whose support was crucial in completing this project, and particularly the assistance of Jennifer, Kate, and Ben.

My mother, my father, and my sister, Beck, have always been behind me with their unstinting support. My partner, Jany, believed in me long before I ever did. Everything we do and talk about makes me a better person as well as a better writer. She's the best driver, reader, and hype-woman that I've ever come across. To her I owe just about everything. My love and gratitude to this family of mine is boundless.